JONATHAN'S STORY

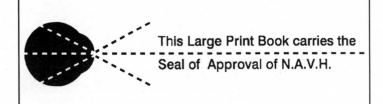

This Large Print Book carries the Seal of Approval of N.A.V.H.

Jonathan's Story

Julia London
with Alina Adams
conceived by David Kreizman

THORNDIKE PRESS

An imprint of Thomson Gale, a part of The Thomson Corporation

THOMSON

™

GALE

Detroit • New York • San Francisco • New Haven, Conn. • Waterville, Maine • London

LIBRARY OF CONGRESS CATALOGING-IN-PUBLICATION DATA

London, Julia.
    Guiding light. : Jonathan's story / by Julia London with Alina Adams ; conceived by David Kreizman.
        p. cm.
    ISBN-13: 978-1-4104-0447-3 (hardcover : alk. paper)
    ISBN-10: 1-4104-0447-1 (hardcover : alk. paper)
    I. Adams, Alina. II. Guiding light (Television program) III. Title. IV. Title: Jonathan's story.
PS3562.O78745G85 2008
813'.54—dc22   2007042583

Published in 2008 by arrangement with Pocket Books, a division of Simon & Schuster, Inc.

Printed in the United States of America on permanent paper
10 9 8 7 6 5 4 3 2 1

JONATHAN'S STORY

PROLOGUE

Reva Shayne felt the back of her car fishtail as she careered around a bend in the country road and cried out with fear. But she didn't dare take her foot off the gas and risk losing sight of her son. Instead, she gripped the wheel tighter and sped up, catching sight of the bumper of Jonathan's car just as it rounded another curve, still in pursuit of Alan Spaulding's limousine.

This was Alan's fault! Showing up at Tammy's funeral. What did he think would happen? What did he think Jonathan would do when Alan laughed at his grief, called it a performance? Reva should've taken Alan out right there, clubbed him with a prayer book or an angel statue, left *him* for dead. Because of Alan, Tammy was gone forever, and now Reva feared what Jonathan would do in retaliation.

She rounded another corner, banking the car wide and praying no one was coming toward her on the other side of the road. She quickly straightened her car out and resumed her reckless speed. Ahead of her, she could see a cloud of dust where Alan's and Jonathan's cars must have turned onto a gravel road.

As she raced ahead, she tried to banish the image of Jonathan's shattered expression when they'd wheeled Tammy's casket out of the church, the weight of his grief so evident in the slope of his shoulders. *"Focus,"* Reva admonished herself, blinking back tears.

She'd had a feeling Jonathan was going to do something crazy, in spite of his assurances that he wouldn't. Not while he had her grandbaby Sarah with him. But she'd heard it in his voice, seen it in his eyes. Something she hadn't seen there in a long time, not since Tammy's love had changed him. "We won't be safe," he'd said. "He won't stop until he has Sarah. He'll *kidnap* her." He never stopped looking at his daughter in Reva's arms as he spoke.

Reva knew Jonathan was right. Little Sarah, born to Jonathan and Alan's granddaughter Lizzie, was the heir to the Spaulding empire, and Alan had vowed to keep her in his family so she could be raised properly — as a Spaulding. That Sarah was

rightfully with her father made no difference to him — what Alan wanted, Alan got,
at any cost. Just look what he'd done to
Tammy. Good, sweet Tammy. How do you
get over something like that? How do you
survive when someone murders the love of
your life?

Maybe you survive by seeking comfort in
your infant daughter. And maybe you survive by seeking revenge. Reva knew Jonathan was planning something. She knew
because they were alike. Quick to anger and
slow to forgive. That was why she had come
back to the church.

It was a miracle she'd seen them at all —
Alan's sleek black limo cruising along the
outskirts of Springfield, Jonathan's green
sedan following closely behind. Reva had
had a feeling in the pit of her belly —
whatever Jonathan thought he was doing,
she had to stop him. She'd tried to catch up
to them, but had lost them in the many
turns of the road and had just caught up to
them again.

She whipped her car onto the gravel lane
and bounced along the rough road. She
drove between two barns and out through
barren fields. She could barely make out
the cars ahead of her through the dust, but
she saw the limousine make an abrupt left

in between two silos. She did not see Jonathan's car follow it.

She did not see Jonathan's car.

"No," she said, and gripped the wheel tighter. "No no no no . . ."

She reached a curve in the road and saw the signpost warning that the edge of the quarry lay straight ahead, and her heart sank. *"Jonathan!"* she screamed, and slammed on the brakes so hard that her car slid into a patch of evergreen trees. Reva threw open her car door and pushed through the tree branches.

She heard a loud scraping noise as she ran down an old walking path marked with the fresh tread of tires. She reached the edge of the quarry just in time to hear the sickening crash of metal and glass against rock and saw the car explode upon impact at the bottom. Her mind could not comprehend it — her *son* was in that car! So was his baby, Sarah, a tiny little being with so much life ahead of her!

As the flames roared and rose higher, it seemed to Reva that the world was suddenly spinning the wrong way. She opened her mouth to cry for help, but what came out was a scream, a bloodcurdling scream of her son's name. *"Jonathan! Jonathan! Jonathan!"*

Another explosion sent a fireball into the air, and Reva screamed again.

Out of nowhere Alan appeared at her side — Alan Spaulding, the monster who had caused this tragedy. Horrified, he watched as the flames engulfed the car that had carried his beloved Sarah, his heir, his future, his salvation.

It seemed impossible, unreal to Reva, as if she were watching a bad movie. No amount of screaming would make it stop; the car just kept burning and burning, the flames growing higher and more ferocious, burning with them all her hopes for a son who had known more pain in his life than a body ought to, burning all her dreams for her granddaughter.

They were gone. So were all of her hopes and dreams for them. The son she'd fought so hard to tame, the son who finally came to believe he was loved. Jonathan and Sarah, gone just like that — as long as it had taken that car to sail from the top of the cliff to the bottom of the quarry.

It was all gone.

1

Aubrey Cross liked to do her shopping when most everyone else in the dusty town of Tourmaline, California, was sitting down to dinner in front of the TV. The fewer people she ran into who knew her or her family, the better, and in Tourmaline, it was impossible to go anywhere without someone knowing her because of her dad. That was because he was Ezekiel "Zeke" Cross — the county sheriff, which he'd been as far back as Aubrey could remember — who made this godforsaken town his home.

Everyone who knew Zeke loved Zeke — everyone except Aubrey. She couldn't stand him. One might go so far as to say she hated Zeke. And hating Zeke made her the town's pariah.

Okay, maybe not the town's *pariah* — she did have one friend. Sort of. Not the kind of friend she'd go to lunch with and then go shopping with, because Aubrey wasn't much of a shopper, and they'd only recently become friendly at work. But Noelle Fischer was someone Aubrey could talk to, and she had the feeling that Noelle was really on her side.

Aubrey didn't get that feeling from most people in Tourmaline, and while she wasn't exactly a pariah, she sure felt that way sometimes.

She just didn't fit in with the sleepy pace of this town. Her mom used to talk about how different the town had been when she was a kid, when they were still mining tourmaline here and the economy was thriving. But the tourmaline had been mined up before Aubrey was born, and most people who wanted to make a good living had moved to San Diego or Phoenix. To Aubrey's way of thinking, that left the old people, the deadbeats, and those with no ambition in life — the very sort of people who were easily influenced by a bully like her father.

He *was* a bully, maybe even worse, even if she was the only person who knew it.

Just this afternoon, they'd had another verbal brawl. He wanted her to move back home. When she'd come back for Mom's funeral three months ago — and ended up staying for reasons that had seemed noble at the time, but now seemed insane — he didn't like that she hadn't come home to be with him. Zeke said her living in the small apartment she rented when he had a big house right in the middle of town left her open to talk.

But Aubrey knew it was because he couldn't control her as easily if she wasn't under his thumb.

"I'm only going to be in town another month, if even that," she'd said warily when he'd started in on her again today. She'd watched him walking around her little apartment, his hands on his gun belt, that ever-present sneer on his lips as he looked at the few things of Mom's she'd managed to salvage before he threw all her mother's belongings away.

Most women thought Zeke Cross was handsome — tall, dark-haired, with a nice smile when he decided to summon it — but Aubrey thought he was the ugliest man on earth. She could hardly bear to look at him when she said, "I'm going back to San Diego so I can start school with the fall session."

"And what are you going to live on, your good looks and charm?" he asked snidely. "You don't have any money, and I'm sure as hell not giving you any. I'm done throw-

15

ing money down black holes, especially now that your mother is gone."

She winced at the stab of pain caused by the reminder of her mother's death. As for the money, she couldn't care less. It had been three years since Aubrey had lived at home. Three years since she'd earned enough money to move to San Diego and start college. In those three years, she'd never forgotten how abusive her father was, but the pain of it had faded. Now, she was sorely reminded of how debilitating his nastiness could be to one's psyche, and he was just getting warmed up.

By the time he'd left her apartment, she'd been reduced to the size of a garden gnome.

She was still feeling unsettled when she pulled into the lot of the local supermarket and parked. She pulled a black corduroy newsboy cap down over her eyes, which did nothing to keep people from recognizing her, but made her feel as if she couldn't see them. She pushed her short, black hair behind her ears, straightened her black T-shirt advertising the band Radiohound, which she wore over a pair of low-rise, tight-fitting jeans, topped with a killer metal belt she'd picked up in San Diego, and got out of her car.

She checked herself in the reflection of

the car window — she liked her style, which her friend Franny at college said was a cross between urban hip-hop and California tree hugger. Frankly, Franny — a performance artist — had introduced Aubrey to style, all of it different and expressive and so much better than what seemed to be the standard uniform for women in Tourmaline — capris and a white shirt.

Aubrey lifted the long strap of the small cloth satchel she used as a purse over her head, so that it hung diagonally across her body, and quickly looked around the parking lot. There were hardly any cars, which was a good thing. She eyed the supermarket as if it were a mined war zone. *Get in, get out,* she told herself, and began marching in that direction, her arms swinging in her haste to get the few things she needed.

She was hit with a blast of arctic-cold air that carried the tune "Tie a Yellow Ribbon" as the glass doors opened automatically and she walked in. The place smelled like Pine-Sol, and big yellow cones marked where the floor had been mopped. Aubrey picked up a red basket, stepped around the CAUTION sign, and quickly ducked into aisle one before she ran into Bev Mackey.

Bev manned the checkout lanes on the evening shift. She was here every night with her knitting, and she loved to share the minutiae of her day with the few denizens of Tourmaline who ventured inside before the doors shut at eleven. Aubrey knew this because she had been captured more than once by Bev's chatter. By the time Aubrey exited the store, she'd know what Bev had had for breakfast, if Old Man Carney had made his daily sojourn through the store with the aid of his walker or if he'd used the motorized cart, and Bev's feelings on the rising cost of lettuce.

Safe from Bev for the time being, Aubrey strolled down the cereal aisle and picked up a box of Lucky Charms. Not exactly the healthiest cereal on the shelf for a vegan, but some things never changed. She rounded the corner and worked her way up the condiments aisle, debating for a few minutes over the pickles, then deciding against them.

At the end of the aisle, near the videos and greeting cards and auto supplies, Aubrey found a display of organic whole-wheat couscous. She thought that would be a good balance for the Lucky Charms. She picked up a box, turned it slightly to read the nutritional content, and noticed a baby in a cart on the greeting-card aisle. She was cute — probably not even a year old, a chubby, little, dark-haired, blue-eyed princess in a romper with ducks marching across the bib. She was kicking her little legs and chewing on a ring of plastic keys.

Aubrey smiled and began to read the box while the baby gurgled. A moment later, she heard the plastic keys fall to the floor and glanced over her shoulder. The baby was staring at Aubrey, her bottom lip trembling. It was only a matter of moments before that little mouth would open and a wail would come forth.

Aubrey put down the box of couscous and peeked out from her aisle — no one was around. The baby put a fist in her mouth and kicked harder. The little butterball was not happy. So Aubrey retrieved the plastic keys, but as she rose up in front of the baby, she thought she'd better not give them to her because they had been lying on the floor. Apparently, that was the worst thing Aubrey could have done, for when the baby put out her hands for the ring, and Aubrey didn't give it to her, she let out a howl that rattled the rafters.

Still, no one came.

The baby's face mottled red; she cried great gasping sobs. "Don't cry, sweet cheeks," Aubrey cooed, running her hand over the girl's dark curls. But the baby cried harder. Aubrey put down her basket and lifted the baby out of the car seat; she had hardly settled the baby on her shoulder when a man was suddenly rushing toward her from the end of the greeting-card aisle. He was tall, at least half a foot taller than Aubrey's respectable five feet six inches, and had long, shoulder-length dark brown hair. He was wearing a dirty T-shirt that he must have been wearing to roll around on the floor of a garage, and it hugged a broad chest and muscular arms. He was carrying two cans of motor oil in one large hand, and he looked furious.

"Put her down!" he shouted at Aubrey.

Aubrey gasped and unthinkingly took a step backward; the man threw the oil cans into his cart and lunged for her, snatching the baby from her arms. The baby cried harder as he hugged her securely to his chest with one arm. He backed away from Aubrey, his gaze so hot and livid that she could almost feel its burn. "Get the hell away from my baby!"

He spoke to her as if she were a pervert, and that snapped Aubrey out of it. "Hey!" she said, shaking a little from the intensity of his anger. "I'm not the one who left a baby unattended!"

"I didn't," he said far too loudly. "I could

see her the whole time."

"She was *crying* —"

"Yeah, babies do that. They cry."

"I was just trying to help!" Aubrey exclaimed angrily.

"By taking her?" he demanded as he carefully caressed the baby's back.

"*Take* her?" Aubrey exclaimed. "Dude, you are off your rocker. Didn't you hear her crying? I was trying to help!"

"Yeah, well, try and help someone else."

"No problem," she said hotly. "But maybe you shouldn't go waltzing off, leaving your kid unattended, because next time, you really might lose her to some weirdo."

"Why? Why would you say that?" he asked, his eyes narrowing suspiciously.

The guy was hot, but he was obviously crazy. "*Why?* Think about it, genius," Aubrey said, and grabbed her basket. With a glower for him, she marched away, purposefully turning into the canned-goods aisle where she was out of his sight. She leaned her back against the shelves to try to collect herself. Her heart was pounding erratically; she was having trouble catching her breath. The baby had stopped crying, apparently — but then again, Aubrey couldn't hear anything but the pounding of her own heart. What confused her, what kept snatching her

21

breath from her lungs, was that she didn't know if she was still trembling because of the mad-dog way he'd looked at her while he was yelling at her, or because he was so damn *hot.*

They didn't make guys like that in Tourmaline. They didn't make guys like that *anywhere.* If he wasn't so Looney Tunes, Aubrey would believe he'd just walked out of an ad for one of those men's health magazines. One other teeny-tiny thing had caught her eye — he was wearing a Radiohound T-shirt, just like her. Except his was grimy.

With a shake of her head and a sigh, Aubrey pressed her hand over her heart for a moment, then pushed away from the shelves and went on with her shopping.

She didn't see Mad Dog again. She didn't hear his baby crying, either. When she checked out with her cereal and peanut butter and milk, Bev was her usual chatty self. "Hi, Aubrey! Back so soon? Oh my goodness, you're *already* out of Lucky Charms? It was only Tuesday you bought some, right?"

"Did I?" Aubrey asked.

"Well, you better stock up. The county fair rolls into town next week, and those people can go through a lot of food! Are you going to the fair?"

"I don't know," Aubrey said with a shrug. She was hardly listening, just nodding and smiling a little when she thought she ought to.

"I am. I can't *wait!* I am taking three nights off and taking my grandkids every night. My sister plays in the polka band, did I ever tell you? The trombone. My mother always said that the trombone was a waste of good money, but Betty proved her wrong, didn't she? I am so glad they have peanut butter back on the shelves, aren't you? But this jar's a little too big for just one person, isn't it?" Bev asked, holding up the jar of peanut butter.

"Ah . . ."

"Oh! I saw Keith Stanley in here last night." Bev wiggled her eyebrows which had, by the look of them, recently been dyed to match her dark red powder-puff hair. "Guess what?"

Aubrey did not take the bait.

Not that Bev cared. "He's not seeing anyone," she quickly added in a singsong voice.

Okay, that was it. This was going down in the official annals as one of the most annoying days of Aubrey's life. First the confrontation with Zeke, then the crazy

Mad Dog guy with that incredibly cute baby, and now Bev, the cashier at the supermarket, who was trying to hook her up with an old boyfriend Aubrey had dumped four years ago. "Good for him," Aubrey muttered as she dug in her bag for her wallet.

"Oh, come on, Aubrey! Aren't you just a little curious?" Bev asked brightly.

"No. I'm not." She handed Bev the money for her groceries.

Bev's smile faded a little. "I'm just offering a bit of friendly news," she said with a sniff.

"That's not exactly news. Sounds more like gossip to me." Aubrey tried to smile, but it was obvious her words hadn't come out as she'd intended. She didn't have the gift of gab that so many women had. So Aubrey did what she normally did when she couldn't seem to get her meaning across — she walked away.

She was brooding as she carried her bag to her car and hardly noticed the three guys leaning against the back of a pickup directly across from where she'd parked until she was almost upon them. They were having a few beers on the tailgate. Aubrey recognized the one in the middle. He was called Spider for reasons she didn't want to know. He'd made a big splash playing football his senior year in high school, but when he'd graduated last year, he'd stayed in Tourmaline, where, according to Aubrey's friend Noelle, he made trouble almost daily.

Exactly the sort of guy Zeke ought to lock up, but preferred to keep in his pocket.

"Hey!" Spider called out to Aubrey as she fumbled in her purse for her keys. "Nice hat!"

Aubrey ignored him as she grasped her keys.

"Hey! I'm talking to you!" he shouted.

Aubrey juggled the bag of groceries and the keys as she struggled to get the key in the lock of her trunk. She had it in when she heard Spider right behind her. "What's the matter, freak? Are you deaf? I *said,* I am talking to you!"

Aubrey closed her eyes and sighed. There was no avoiding it — she was going to have to deal with Spider. She carefully put the bag of groceries on top of the trunk. She could hear them snickering at her back, knew this was going to be difficult. Then she removed her purse, put it next to the groceries, and turned to face them.

They were standing in the middle of the lane. Spider laughed as his gaze raked over her. "What in the *hell?*" he said, and tapped one of his pals in the chest. "Look at this chick! She's a freakin' doper by the look of it!"

As if she derived her fashion sense from Tourmaline. "Spider, what do you want?" Aubrey demanded. "I'm not bothering you. I just want to get my groceries and go home."

"Is that the way they dress in San Diego?" Spider asked before taking a swig of beer. "They wear those stupid hats in San Diego?"

"We have to wear them to cover our horns," Aubrey said as one of the guys casually walked up to her trunk and began to rummage through her groceries. "Stop that!" Aubrey said to him. "Those are my groceries!"

The guy shrugged and withdrew her box of Lucky Charms, ripped the top open, and thrust his hand into the box.

"Over here, freak," Spider said, drawing her attention back to him. "Let me get this straight." He swayed a little and crossed his arms over his chest, the beer bottle dangling between two fingers. "Are you telling me there are other freakazoids in San Diego who wear those stupid hats?"

Aubrey's pulse began to pound with anger. She despised bullies. Spider was a punk kid who hadn't seen even a smidgen of the world, had no idea what sorts of hats were out there in the big, vast universe. Who was he to try to intimidate her? She tried to make light of it. "Spider . . . you're wearing a cheap Polo knockoff. That really doesn't give you a lot of room to criticize my hat."

The three guys all looked at one another and then suddenly howled with delight. One of them tossed the jar of peanut butter from her bag to the other one as Spider took a menacing step forward.

"You better watch it, freak," Spider said. "You think you're too good for us in Tourmaline now that you've lived in San Diego? Well, guess what? You're Tourmaline, through and through, just like us, so you better watch your mouth."

Aubrey's mouth was moving before she could think clearly. "Or what?" she asked, squaring off with him.

That was all the invitation Spider needed.

2

The car was juiced up with the oil and cool-
ant he'd just bought, but Jonathan found
the radiator leak that had plagued him since
leaving Arizona. He guessed the radiator
would need about a day's worth of work to
keep it from leaking.

In the parking lot of the supermarket,
Jonathan slammed his hand against the
hood and muttered a few choice opinions
about the 1987 fastback Mustang he'd
bought a few months ago. It was his third
car in seven months — the trick was to keep
the junker running until he could trade it
for the next piece of crap. It was a pain-in-
the-ass way to live, but he had no choice —
he could never trust that Alan Spaulding
wasn't one step behind him, one step from
taking Sarah from him.

Jonathan figured he'd find some place
near town to camp. He ducked his head
inside the driver's open window and

checked on Sarah. She was safely settled in her car seat in the back. They were used to traveling this way — they'd established a rhythm of always being on the move, of always looking for the place they would finally stop and settle down. While he drove, Sarah did whatever babies did until she got tired or hungry or wet.

"We've got to make another stop, baby," he said irritably.

Sarah's response was to toss the filthy little stuffed kitten she clutched in her sleep every night to the floorboard, then lean over the arm of her car seat to look for it. Tammy had given Sarah that kitten. Jonathan believed with all his heart that Sarah was attached to that kitty because she remembered Tammy had given it to her and missed Tammy almost as much as he did. *Almost.* No one could hurt as wide and as deep as he did. It felt like a chasm had grown in him, one full of the pain of missing her . . . every lousy day.

He sighed, straightened up, resting his arms on the hood of the Mustang, and gazed out beyond the parking lot, to the brown and green hills that bordered the town.

They'd traveled down a stretch of California roadway that ran through nothing but industrial plants and truck stops, where someone was always wondering about a man alone with a baby and asking nosy questions — like, Where was his wife? Sometimes he wanted to answer, to grab the nosy jerk by the throat and scream the answer into his face. *She's dead! Tammy's dead and cold and buried in a box because Alan Spaulding made her that way. He hired someone to hit me with a car and she jumped in the way and . . .* But he'd swallow down the pain and the rage. He'd smile politely, squeeze Sarah tightly, and they'd move on down the road.

But then they'd come to Tourmaline, California, population 9,346, according to the sign on the edge of town. He sort of liked the look of the town. There were a lot of empty stores and boarded-up houses on the outskirts, he'd noticed when he and Sarah had slid into town — it looked as if it had been a lot bigger at some point. But what was left of it was clean and inviting and looked like a place a man could settle down and raise a kid.

He and Sarah had driven around a little and had pulled into a church parking lot to let the engine cool down while Jonathan changed and fed Sarah. They'd sat on a stone bench beneath an elm tree, Sarah with a bottle, Jonathan just enjoying the clean air and looking at the houses up and down the wide, tree-lined street. The houses were typical Craftsman homes with big green yards and tree swings and little-kid tricycles cluttering the sidewalks. The houses and lawns were surrounded by colorful chrysanthemums and shaded with towering gum and magnolia trees. The town was picturesque, set against the hills as it was.

"See that?" he'd said to Sarah, pointing to a playscape in one yard. "Lots of other munchkins around. You'd be happy here."

Sarah had gurgled at that.

The street reminded Jonathan — the way so many things seemed to do — of Tammy. Once, when the leaves had begun to turn in Springfield, and the air was crisp and smelling of chimney smoke, she had talked him into walking down one of the old streets of Springfield. They had strolled arm in arm, gazing up at the old Victorian houses with the lights blazing in the windows. Tammy, looking as beautiful as ever with her big blue eyes and silky blond hair, paused on the sidewalk to admire each house, her expression full of wonder and happiness. He had admired her as he always did. He'd never thought he would fall in love with a woman like her who was so pure and full of joy —

31

everything he'd thought he hated in the world.

"Guess who lives there?" she'd ask at every house, and would then invent an idyllic family, a scene right out of a Norman Rockwell painting, smiling with that big, infectious grin of hers. But all Jonathan saw were cheerful facades that hid the ugliness inside, just as in the house where he'd grown up.

"I think a *big* family lives here," Tammy said when they were in front of a big, two-story Victorian with a wraparound porch. "See that window, way up at the top?"

Jonathan looked up.

"That's the boy's room. He's probably up there right now, making a science project with a plunger and some glue and something explosive." She laughed, her blue eyes glimmering in the light of the streetlamp. "And see the window just beneath it? That's the girl's room. She's arranging the outfits for her Barbie dolls to wear tomorrow and matching up the shoes and purses."

She glanced at Jonathan, who was frowning a little. "What?" she asked, nudging him playfully. When Jonathan didn't respond, she pointed to the big picture window on the ground floor. "And you know who is in there?"

"Yeah," he said. "The old man is knocking around his boy for being stupid."

Tammy's face fell — he realized, too late, that he'd ruined her game. But before he could take it back, before he could laugh it off or apologize or snap at her to stop dreaming, she abruptly turned and took his face in her hands and smiled up at him. "In *my* fantasy, it's a happy house. The husband and wife love each other and their children very much and they find joy in the house. Not pain, Jonathan. They've put all that behind them. In my fantasy, they don't have to hurt anymore — they are full of joy." She'd kissed him, a tender, sweet kiss, and he'd fought hard not to let her see his knees tremble.

When they had moved on to the next house, Jonathan tried hard to play along. He couldn't help it — he always wanted to be where Tammy was. He'd managed to invent a dog to go with her imaginary family.

He'd always wanted a dog when he was a kid.

But the memory made him feel angry and restless now. He slapped the roof of the Mustang. It was time to go — dreaming of what might have been was pointless.

He'd found the market easy enough, and

with the exception of that pretty little nut job who'd tried to take Sarah, Jonathan was getting a good vibe from this town. As he wiped his dirty hands on his T-shirt, he heard howling laughter.

He looked over the top of his car and spotted the nut job; she was surrounded by three men who were much larger than her. He knew something wasn't right — he could feel it.

He ducked into the car, found Sarah's pacifier, and stuck it in her mouth. "Be a good girl," he said. "I'll be right back." He stood up again, looked across the lot, and winced — that little nut job had her hands on her waist, her legs braced apart. Jonathan had had enough experience with women to know all the signs of feminine ire. She was about to go off on one of those guys. Now how smart was that? One woman against three men.

He started in that direction, pausing once to make sure he could see Sarah. As he neared them, he heard the tall guy with the goofy haircut call her a freak, then was surprised when the dude suddenly knocked the hat from her head with enough force that he could have knocked her flat on her butt. It was a chickenshit thing to do, and Jonathan quickened his step, picking up the pace when he realized she was going to strike back.

He managed to get in between her and the jerks who were bullying her just as she launched herself at the tallest one. Jonathan caught her almost in midair and took three steps back, holding her aloft.

"What are you doing?" she cried. "Put me down!"

He put her on her feet. Her copper-brown eyes were filled with fury, and she shoved hard against him. Jonathan hardly even moved when she did, which made her eyes sparkle with fury that much more.

"Calm down, Wonder Woman," he said. "Think. You can't take those three on."

The three idiots behind him laughed.

"You don't know anything! You don't know what I can do!" she cried.

She was a spitfire, intent on going after them. With one hand, Jonathan caught her again and held her in place.

"Just get out of the way! I can handle my own problems!"

"Awesome job so far." He let her go, was about to tell her to get in her car and drive away while he was there, but one of the jerks behind him said, "Don't waste your time on a freak."

Jonathan's hackles rose instantly. He reacted by suddenly spinning around and swinging his arm, making contact with the tall guy's jaw. The tall guy went sprawling onto the asphalt and landed with a thud.

"Hey!" one of his pals said, and swung at Jonathan with what he thought was a jar of peanut butter. But Jonathan was too quick for him — he ducked and clipped him right in the gut. That guy went sprawling, too, almost landing on his head. Jonathan straightened up and looked at the third guy, who made no effort. He hurried to help the tall one to his feet.

"You shouldn't have done that, pal," the tall guy said, pausing to spit blood from his mouth. "You're going to pay for it."

Jonathan simply gestured for them to come at him.

"She's a freak," the tall guy said, pointing at Aubrey. "And *you're* a friggin' dead man."

Jonathan laughed. As if these guys could hurt him any worse than he'd already known. "Do it," he challenged, throwing his arms wide. But the guy was backing up and away from Jonathan. So were his friends.

"Come on, Spider, let it go," one of them said, clapping the tall guy on his shoulder. "Let's get out of here."

Spider glared at Jonathan, but he allowed his friends to drag him to the truck. He pointed once more, said something Jonathan couldn't make out as his pals shoved him into the cab. A moment later, the engine revved up and the truck lurched forward, its wheels churning over the yellow concrete block that was supposed to stop it. Once they'd cleared that, the driver hit the gas; the wheels burned against the pavement and the bed of the truck fishtailed as they exited the parking lot and screamed down the street.

Jonathan glanced at his car — he could see Sarah in the backseat. She'd fallen asleep, judging by the angle of her head. He looked at the girl. She didn't seem quite as dangerous as he'd believed in the store. She seemed . . . well, she seemed way too feminine to be taking on three big guys. She was slender, wearing jeans that hugged her curves like a glove. And she was staring at him with those big copper eyes, her mouth slack, like she was seeing some strange exhibit at the zoo.

"What?" he asked self-consciously.

"You just . . . you just *saved* me," she said disbelievingly.

"Nah." He dipped down to retrieve the box of Lucky Charms. "I got rid of a couple of cowards."

"That's what I mean, you saved me —"

"No," he quickly interjected. He didn't like the sound of that — he didn't *save* people. He handed her what was now an empty box of cereal. Brightly colored charms littered the pavement. But she took the box, wrapped her arms possessively around it while she stared up at him.

"Quit looking at me like that."

"I'm sorry."

"You cool?" He couldn't look at those glimmering brown eyes, so he gestured toward her car, wanting to be on his way.

"Mind if I ask your name?"

"It doesn't matter," he said gruffly.

"Yes, it does. What am I going to tell my friend? That I was rescued by a guy named Mad Dog?"

"Mad dog?" he said, raking his hair back from his forehead.

She gave him a soft, lopsided smile. "You were sort of rabid in the store."

"You snatched my kid."

"I wasn't snatching her," she said, but that soft smile didn't waver and had his full, male attention. "So do you have a name or don't you?" she asked again.

He debated telling her anything at all. "J.B.," he said reluctantly.

"J.B.? That's it? Just J.B.?"

He threw up a hand to keep her from asking more. "Just . . . J.B."

"I'm Aubrey." She quickly wiped her hand on her jeans, then extended it to him. He looked at her hand, then at her. "Thank you, J.B. Thanks for saving me from those three goons."

Jonathan shoved his hands into his pockets and glanced anxiously at his car. "Soon as I'm gone, you call the cops."

"Ah — no thanks," she said curtly, and squatted down to pick up her hat.

That was interesting. "They ought to know those guys are harassing you."

"No way. I can handle them myself."

He chuckled. "You weren't even close to handling them."

"How do you know what I was close to? You jumped in before I could do anything." She stuffed the empty box of cereal into the brown paper grocery bag a little too emphatically.

"You were going to kick him in the shins and run? Let me tell you something — a wise man once told me not to pick a fight I couldn't finish. You'd do well to do the same."

"Really? Well, thanks for the advice!" she said with sarcasm. "But you can save it." She popped open the trunk of her car. "Didn't you leave a baby unattended somewhere?"

Jonathan turned his back on her, striding across the parking lot. He checked on Sarah and took the pacifier that was hanging off her bottom lip, then opened the driver's door. Just before he got in, he glanced across the top of his car.

Brown Eyes was still standing there, holding her torn grocery bag with the empty cereal box, the hat pulled low over her eyes, watching him. She looked oddly vulnerable, standing there like that. She was cute. Real cute. And she had a lot of spunk — misguided spunk, but spunk all the same — which he grudgingly admired. He almost smiled as he got into the driver's seat and turned the key. It wasn't every day a person got to see a woman with more nerve than weight go up against three guys. So she had a tendency to wig out — but she also liked Radiohound, judging by her T-shirt, so she couldn't be all bad.

Wait, wait, wait . . . what was he thinking? *"Damn!"* he said hotly, banging his fist against the wheel, waking Sarah. She cried out with surprise and continued to cry.

With a sigh, Jonathan stopped the car, got out, and got in the backseat. He took her out of her car seat and held her on his shoulder while she cried, humming softly, stroking her back. "It's okay, Munchkin. It's okay." As Sarah began to calm down, he leaned his head back and closed his eyes, visualizing his beautiful wife smiling at him as she threw her arms around him and kissed him. "Sorry, Tammy. It's just . . . I've been on the road a long time."

That was the end of his wandering thoughts. He had to think about where he and Sarah were going to settle down. He smiled down at his baby. "I know I said this might be it, Munchkin." He glanced out the window just as the red, older-model Jetta with the Greenpeace bumper sticker Aubrey was driving pulled out of the parking lot. "But maybe I spoke too soon."

Sarah wasn't listening. Her eyelids were heavy, and Jonathan put her in the car seat. He stroked the soft, dark curls on her head a moment, then resumed his seat behind the wheel. As he pulled out of the supermarket parking lot, he looked up at the sky — it was turning pink. He had less than an hour to find a place to pitch a tent before he lost all light.

It was always something. He pointed the car west.

3

Sarah did not sleep. She began to whine, and on the outskirts of Tourmaline, where the road hugged the hills and made little winding turns, Jonathan searched for a sign that would point him toward the freeway as Sarah's whining from the backseat grew more insistent. He glanced in his rearview; one arm was sticking out of the car seat, and her head was turned. He glanced to his left in the direction her arm pointed and saw the perfect place to bed down.

Jonathan drove to the first place he could turn around and headed back, slowing down as he approached it.

It was a white clapboard house built on a small rise. It had dark green shutters and a weather vane shaped like a rooster on the roof; the yard was fenced in by a chain-link, through which someone had strung outdoor patio lights. A big oak tree was in the front yard, and from its lowest branch hung a tire that swung lazily over green grass.

But the most appealing thing about the house was the small FOR RENT sign stuck in the yard. It looked like it had been there awhile — the red background paint was faded and the sign was sitting at an angle, as if it had been roughed up by the Santa Ana winds.

"What do you think, kid? Should we have a look around?" he asked.

Sarah began making *ba ba ba* noises from the backseat.

Jonathan pulled into the gravel drive and drove the thirty yards up to the house. In the waning light of day, the house looked idyllic, like something off a postcard. Jonathan got out, ducked into the backseat, and fetched Sarah from her car seat. She wasn't walking yet, but she liked to stand on her toes, so he put her up against the fence. Her little hands curled around the chain links and she pressed her face against the fence and began to babble like he'd never heard her babble before.

With a laugh, he squatted down next to her. "You like it?"

Sarah didn't look at him — she kept babbling and clinging to that fence.

He liked it here. It was peaceful, serene. They were on some old and seldom used county road. There wasn't a sound but the evening breeze rustling the leaves of the trees. Jonathan pried Sarah's hands from the fence, hoisted her up to sit on his shoulders, and, holding her in place, walked around the house. It was definitely empty, and better yet, there didn't seem to be anyone around for miles. It almost felt as if he and Sarah were the only two people in the world.

"Seems as good a place as any to pitch a tent."

Sarah answered with another babble.

Jonathan fetched a quilt from the car and laid it on the grass. He put Sarah there with her favorite toys while he dragged out the tent and the sleeping bags, just as he did every night.

He pitched the tent around the corner of the house — not as visible from the road — and out from beneath the canopy of trees. They liked sleeping under the stars. He spread one sleeping bag on the pallet he'd made, then the other one on top. Sarah was getting bigger now — she needed her own bed, he knew. But for the time being, this would have to do.

Outside the tent, he dug out a blue plastic pail, a camping stove, a can of beans and franks for him, and a jar of strained chicken and noodles for Sarah. With some bottled water, he mixed her formula and gave that to her while he fired up the little camping stove to cook his gourmet meal.

While his meal heated, he fed Sarah, using the time-honored technique of the airplane-in-the-hangar. She laughed and tried to grab the spoon each time. In the end, he gave in. Sarah banged the spoon on the quilt while he heated water on the stove.

Fortunately, the water was still on at the house — he filled the pail about a quarter deep from the spigot, then a small pan, which he heated on the stove. When it was warm, he added it to the pail of water. The result was a bath for his daughter. "At least you're getting a bath tonight, kid," he said as he sat her in the bucket. "You're just going to have to put up with your old man until I can find a shower."

If Sarah had any objection, she hid it by squealing with delight and splashing in the water. Jonathan had to hand it to his kid — she hadn't had the easiest ten months, but she was a trouper. She was a good baby, rarely cried, and seemed to take their nomadic lifestyle in stride. Yet Jonathan would give anything to find a place he could call home. Some place where he felt like he could stop running and settle down, where they were safe from Alan's long reach.

After he'd bathed Sarah, he put a sleeper on her by the light of a gas lamp. It was a warm summer night, so the two of them lay on their backs on the quilt, looking up at the heavens above them. Well, Jonathan looked. Sarah was talking to her kitty, which she flung at Jonathan from time to time. "Look up there, Munchkin," he said, giving her a gentle squeeze. "See the big, bright star? That's Tammy. She's looking down on us. Someday we'll be up there, and we'll find her, and then we'll all ride raindrops together. Doesn't that sound like something Tammy would say? Riding raindrops?"

Sarah threw her kitty against his chest. He smiled at his daughter. "I miss her, too." He gave her the kitty, which she promptly stuck in her mouth. Jonathan turned his gaze to the sky again. He kept his hand on Sarah's leg, because when he looked up at the stars like this, he felt so small, so tiny in the vast world, that he feared he would lose Sarah. She needed him to look out for her, to hang on to her.

She needed him.

After twenty-three years of his feeling so alone, it was strange that someone so small and helpless would need him as much as Sarah did. She not only needed him, she

46

needed him to give her a home, and a bed, and medical-care facilities, and other kids to play with . . . all the security Jonathan had never had.

He'd tried his best not to be a father. He had nightmares about the kind of parent he might turn out to be. Would he become like his own stepfather, a man who'd sooner smack him in the mouth than hug him? And who was Jonathan to raise a little girl, to teach her right from wrong, to teach her that she'd always be loved, always be protected? Those were lessons he was still learning himself, lessons Tammy had taught him every day until her last. He'd loved her deeply but nearly lost her when a one-night stand with Lizzie Spaulding produced a baby. He'd never wanted to hurt Tammy.

Yet he wouldn't trade any of it now, because he had Sarah. And he would move mountains, if that's what it took, to give her the peace and security he'd never had. He was determined that Sarah would have a better life than he'd had. She would know she was loved, she would know where she belonged. Sarah needed him and he . . .

He needed to stop running.

He had no idea what time it was when they crawled into the tent and bedded down under the sleeping bag. Sarah slept wedged between him and a body pillow, so she wouldn't roll away. Jonathan was still in the clothes he'd worn all day. He lay on his back with one arm slung over his eyes, his nose wrinkling at the smell of motor oil on his clothing. The sound of Sarah's breathing, the soft whisper of her baby's breath, was soothing to him. It was usually enough to put him to sleep, but not tonight.

Tonight, his head was filled with the events of the day, his worries about the car, his desperation to find a place to raise Sarah . . . and Tammy, of course, always Tammy.

He thought of all the plans he and Tammy had once made for being a family with Sarah. Jonathan had focused on the tangible things — a house, lots of toys, maybe a cute dog to round out the picture. Tammy was the one who'd had to remind him that there was more to life than stuff. She'd asked him once, "What do you want for Sarah?"

And when he'd started on his long list of things they could buy, she interrupted, "No. I mean, what sort of person do you want her to be? A superathlete? A beauty queen? Run for president? Go to college?"

"Definitely college." Jonathan hadn't really thought of it before that moment, but, sure, he wanted his kid to go to college.

"What else would I want?"

"How about a Nobel Prize winner? Someone really smart who makes the world a better place."

"Yeah," Jonathan said, nodding. "I'd like that."

"Know what *I* want for her?" Tammy asked, putting aside the bottle and lifting the baby up and balancing her on her little legs on her lap.

"What?"

"I want her to know what it feels like to be loved. Totally and wholly and completely." She looked over Sarah's head at Jonathan. "Like me."

Jonathan laughed. "That would be great . . . but he's gonna have to get past me first."

Tammy laughed and rolled her eyes. "I think Sarah is going to have you wrapped so tightly around her little finger that all she'll have to do is smile, and you will grant her every wish."

Jonathan sat up abruptly and caught the back of Tammy's head in his hand and kissed her forehead. "I can be pretty tough when I want to be."

"Oh, really?"

"Really."

Tammy leaned to her right as she put

Sarah on her shoulder to burp her and nodded toward a box full of toys in the corner.
"You've been really tough with the toys,
huh?"

"She's entitled to a few toys." Jonathan
laughed as he caressed Sarah's back.

"She's two months old!"

"And she can already point," he said with
a grin.

"Let's see how tough you are now."
Tammy held Sarah up to him. "She needs a
change." She wrinkled her nose, then
laughed, the sound of it so bright and warm.

Remembering it now sent a shiver down
Jonathan's spine. He'd loved Tammy's
sunny laugh. He had a voice mail on his cell
phone that Tammy had left the day they got
married. She said, "Jonathan Randall, where
are you?" And she laughed, her voice full of
joy and lightness and the excitement of
throwing together a quick wedding.

For weeks after she died, he'd listened to
that message. He hadn't listened to it in a
long time, though. It was too painful.

That was the thing about remembering
Tammy. Sometimes, it just hurt too bad.

Jonathan eventually slept. When he woke,
the sun was shining and his stomach was
growling. He stretched and scratched his

chest, then sat up, propping himself on one arm and looking down where Sarah was sleeping.

His heart stopped — Sarah wasn't there. She wasn't in her spot, she wasn't there where she'd been only a couple of hours ago. *She wasn't there.*

Jonathan came up in a fury, digging through the bedroll, hoping that Sarah had just worked her way to the bottom in her sleep. But she wasn't there. *"Sarah!"* he yelled, kicking the bedroll aside and clambering out of the tent.

She was nowhere in sight.

Jonathan's heart began to pound painfully against the vise of panic that was closing around it. He'd never felt such fear in his life; he could hardly draw a breath. Myriad scenarios ran through his head as he ran around to the back of the tent. *"Sarah!"*

She'd been abducted or dragged off by wolves or worse —

The terror choked him. *"Sarah!"* he bellowed, and ran blindly toward the front of the house. As he neared the front, he heard her. She was babbling excitedly. He had only seen her do that with his mother, Reva. Someone had her. He rounded the corner — and came to a dead halt.

He couldn't believe his eyes. Sarah was in

the front yard, and she was . . . she was *walking*. She'd obviously pulled herself up against the trunk of the tree, and now she was wobbling toward the FOR RENT sign that was stuck in the yard.

Jonathan couldn't move. He was frozen by the sight — she'd never walked before. Night after night he would lead her around the campsite, holding her little hands carefully in his as he guided her to take a step. But the moment he let go, she would fall to her bottom and crawl.

Yet here she was, taking her first steps.

He sank down to his haunches, just watching her, his fist against his mouth, swallowing back tears that were suddenly clouding his vision — tears of happiness that his baby was taking her first step. Tears of sorrow that Reva wasn't here to see it. He liked to think Tammy could see it because he felt she was always watching over them from above.

Sarah made it four steps before falling, but the girl had some grit — she crawled to a tree stump and pulled herself up again, then did that wobbly walk to the FOR RENT sign. When she reached it, she gurgled happily and began to babble as she hit her palm against it. But she struck it too hard and toppled backward, onto her bottom. She lifted her hands to the sign and began to wail.

Jonathan went to her, picked her up, and hugged her close. "I am so proud of you, baby," he said, kissing her face several times. "Daddy is proud of you."

But Sarah was not interested in his praise. She twisted in his arms, her arms outstretched toward the FOR RENT sign. Her cries became louder.

"Okay," he said, turning her around in his arms, but that did not appease her in the least. "All *right,* Sarah." He put her down on her feet. She took two wobbly steps and pressed up against the sign again, her cries fading into a constant stream of babble. It was almost as if she were talking to the sign.

When Sarah pressed her palm against it again, something tripped in Jonathan. A light went on inside him; he suddenly realized that Sarah had taken her first steps at this house, to that sign, because she was trying to tell him something. Yeah, okay, she was a baby, but she was trying to tell him that *this* was where they were supposed to be. He settled a hand on top of his head, looked at the house, then at Sarah. Then at the house again.

"You're right, Munchkin," he said. "It's

perfect." And it was — it was close enough to town that Sarah could have friends, but far enough away from people that he didn't have to worry about anyone getting too nosy. Close enough to San Diego if Sarah needed medical treatment. And the house was small — just right for the two of them.

The realization that he'd found the place after months of being on the run, he'd finally found it, elated him. Jonathan grabbed Sarah and swung her high over his head. She gurgled with delight.

"We found it, baby!" he said happily. "This is where we are going to live!" He swung her down, then up again, and Sarah squealed with laughter. "You'll have your own room and Barbies and birthday parties and whatever else little girls like." That gave him pause, and he lowered her again, held her straight out. "You're going to have to help me figure all that out, because I don't really know what little girls like." He laughed, held her against his chest again. Then the doubts crept in. Did he really have a right to feel so happy, so excited? Nothing had ever gone right for him for long. He had to slow down and keep his eyes open.

Sarah grabbed for his nose.

He took her hand, let her grasp his finger, then retrieved his cell phone from the car and dialed the number on the FOR RENT sign.

"Jancowitz and Hardin Realty," a woman with a pleasant voice answered.

"Yeah, hi," Jonathan said, bending his head slightly, as Sarah was trying to take his phone, "I'm calling about a rental property . . ."

A quarter of an hour later, having convinced the woman that three months' rent up front in cash was worth a bit of sketchiness about his background — which was helped along by the fact they had not been able to sell or rent the place in over a year — Jonathan clicked off the phone and smiled at Sarah, who, having found her sea legs, was toddling in slightly longer stretches. Each time she went bottom down, he would stand her back up, and away she would go. "The lady said we pay the deposit and rent, and the place is ours, Munchkin."

Sarah did not seem impressed. She was far more interested in the blade of grass she had uprooted.

"Sarah, do you understand? We did it! We found us a home!" He grabbed her up like a football, then pulled up the FOR RENT sign and jogged up the steps to the wooden porch. "Wanna see your room?" he asked.

The door was locked. But Jonathan felt a weird sort of tug on him, an urgency to be inside the house. He put Sarah down a safe distance away, then using the sign's metal pole, he broke through a window, reached through, and unlocked the door. "I'll fix that later," he said with a wink for his baby as he scooped her up.

As they walked inside, a sense of joy spread through him — the place was perfect. There was a brick fireplace and bookcases that lined either side of it. The wide oak-planked floors looked original. The ceilings were high, at least twelve feet, marked with scrolled crown molding. There was plenty of natural light — windows lined the front of the house, and a pair of them rose up next to the bookcases.

Jonathan moved on, into the kitchen. It was a farmhouse-style kitchen — big and roomy. A good-size table could fit in here, and Jonathan could picture Sarah at that table with her finger paints or crayons while he stumbled around trying to prepare one of those well-balanced meals.

He walked through a door leading from the kitchen into a hallway. Here, there were four doors. At the end of the hall, near the front of the house, was the master bedroom. It had a bay window and a window seat, and an adjoining bath. It connected to a smaller room that Jonathan supposed was a sitting room, but would for now be a nursery. There were two more bedrooms, each with tall windows and a view of the California hills and trees. A bathroom with black-and-white tile and black fixtures was nestled between the two bedrooms.

"Yeah," he said again as he wandered through the house with Sarah on his hip. "This is it, baby. This is where we are going to put down roots." He returned to the living room, where he'd discarded the FOR RENT sign. He put Sarah down and picked up the sign. "Check it out, Munchkin — our first piece of furniture!" He jammed it down, wedging the pole in between two floorboards. He threw his arms wide and grinned at his baby. "We're home, kid!"

4

In Springfield that morning, Reva Shayne picked up the mail on her way out to do a little shopping. She quickly flipped through the mail before stuffing it in her purse — bills, junk mail, pizza flyers. The usual. But the last item was an envelope with nothing but her name and address written on it.

There was no return address, nothing but a postage cancellation mark that was almost illegible — Reva couldn't make out anything but *Az.* But she recognized the handwriting. Her pulse began to race as she tore the envelope open — he'd taped it shut, made sure the contents would not be lost. She pulled out a newspaper clipping.

FAMILY FUN DAYS: TWO PLAY FOR THE PRICE OF ONE!
Come Join Us Saturday! Butterfield Golf Course, Wellton, AZ
Two play 9 holes for the price of one.

Games and rides for the kiddies.
Bar-b-que and potluck dinner, BYOB

That was it, a newspaper clipping. There was no note, nothing to indicate why he'd sent it to her. Reva took a deep breath, willing herself to remain calm.

It was from Jonathan, his subtle way of telling her that he'd had to leave Wellton, for reasons Reva would never know. This was their code — he would send her an unsigned flyer or coupon from a local business wherever he and Sarah landed so that she would know where they were and that they were safe. The same thing happened when Jonathan had to leave town — he sent another coupon so she would know he'd gone.

How many nights had Reva lain awake, unable to sleep, worrying about him and Sarah? Wondering where they were, or why they'd left whatever town he'd managed to find? Just when she thought he had finally found a place to stay, she'd get another coupon or clipping that would tell her he'd moved on.

Reva hoped Jonathan would find a place to settle down, and soon. Life on the road was no place for a baby, especially after Sarah had been so sick. They needed a place to land, to put down roots. Jonathan had never had that, and Reva would give the world for him to have that now.

She closed her eyes with a sigh and thought of Jonathan in happier times, with Tammy. She remembered once, at a benefit gala to raise money for cancer research — she'd bought her entire family tickets — she'd caught sight of Jonathan and Tammy dancing. She remembered being surprised — she'd never thought Jonathan was the dancing type, and judging how the two of them went around in a tight little circle, she was right.

Reva smiled at the memory.

It wasn't the dancing that had moved her. It was the way they had looked at each other. They were off in a corner, but they might as well have been on a desert island. To those two, there was no one else in the room. They had gazed at each other with that sort of young love that makes you feel like you can leap tall buildings — Tammy smiling and talking to him, Jonathan his usual stoic self, responding with one word or a nod, but looking down at her with that expression of wonderment, as if he couldn't believe he held her in his arms.

Reva had watched them until the music ended, a smile on her face. She remembered what that was like, to dance with someone you loved more than life. She remembered feeling as if she and the love of her own life, Joshua, were the only two people in the world. How there was a whole wide world out there to explore, and how exciting it was to have that special someone with whom to explore it.

If only Jonathan could find someone to explore the world with him now.

If only he had a home and a woman he could love with all his heart, who would love him just as much in return. God knew how much Reva wanted that for him, especially after his having tasted that sort of love with Tammy. But their happiness had been cut tragically short with Tammy's death.

Unfortunately, judging by the slips of paper that Reva had received over the last several months, he was not getting any closer to finding the right place. "Will you ever find peace?" she whispered.

With a mournful sigh, she stuffed the clipping into her purse and drove to Main Street.

After she'd parked, she walked into the outdoor common area and had just walked up to the CO^2 coffee stand when a man called her name.

Reva closed her eyes and sighed heavenward before turning around. It was Alan Spaulding — tall, handsome, regal in bearing, and absolutely rotten to the bone, to Reva's way of thinking. He was the bane of Springfield, the one blight on what was otherwise a lovely city. "Not now, Alan."

"And a cheerful hello to you, too, Reva."

"I'm here for coffee, you can hold the arsenic."

"A latte for the lady," Alan said to the kid behind the stand as he reached for his wallet.

"Hey! No thank you," Reva said sharply.

"Make it two," Alan said, and tossed a ten onto the counter.

Exasperated, Reva glared at him. "Is this the part where I'm supposed to be overwhelmed by the milk of human kindness bubbling through your veins?"

"Please try to contain your theatrics," he said, picking up the coffees the kid placed on the counter. He handed one to Reva.

She took it reluctantly. The man inspired rage in her like no one else could — the sort of rage that had her struggling to keep from throwing the coffee in his face. There was enough history between them — including his trying to have Jonathan killed and killing Tammy instead, and then forcing Jonathan to flee with Sarah — to justify doing that. Reva could scarcely contain her disdain for Alan.

"A few moments of your time, that's all I ask," Alan added, as if reading her thoughts.

"The clock is ticking," Reva snapped. "Go."

Alan didn't say anything. He looked down into his coffee. When he looked up, she could see the pain in his eyes. "It's been seven months since the day I lost Sarah."

His words sent her reeling — she spent most days trying hard *not* to think of that day. "Don't you mean the day we all lost Sarah? The day I watched my son and granddaughter die?"

"If only your son hadn't been so stupid and reckless —"

"What is this, Alan? Having trouble dealing with your guilt over killing your own flesh and blood?" Reva breathed, and thrust the coffee cup into Alan's chest, forcing him to take it. "My son and granddaughter are dead because of you!" She whirled around, moving away from him.

"Reva!" Alan called after her. "If your son had been a decent —"

"Go to hell, Alan!" Reva shot back over her shoulder, and stalked into the nearest shop. She paused just inside, her hand clutching her purse, her heart pounding.

"Hello!" the shopkeeper called out.

"Hello," Reva said, and whirled around to a rack of clothes, where she tried to catch her breath while she pretended to be looking at the shirts.

A few years ago, Jonathan had entered her house for the first time. She'd found him there, waiting to confront her. He'd been so angry, so hurt, lashing out at her, wanting to take his pain out on her for having been abandoned all those years ago. "I've always wanted to hurt you more than you hurt me," he'd said.

Reva had tried to explain to him how it had happened, how she'd believed she was giving him a better life. "It broke my heart to give you away. But I did what was best for you."

Jonathan would have none of it, and she could hardly blame him. What she'd thought was best for him had turned out to be the worst for him. He'd been abused and neglected and then cast aside like trash. And that afternoon he'd come into her house, she'd tried to make amends, but Jonathan had raged at her. "I don't *want* to be fixed!" he'd shouted at her.

Oh, but he had wanted it. She could almost feel her son's pain that day, as if his heart were connected to hers.

Oddly enough, she felt that connection now. Through nothing but a slip of paper, she could feel his heart, and she would do whatever it took to keep him safe from Alan. Whatever it took — even if it meant never seeing her son or granddaughter again.

"Are you looking for something in particular?" the saleswoman asked Reva.

She was looking for an answer, a solution, a light to guide her son. But they didn't sell those things here. She smiled at the woman. "I'm always looking," she said, and moved on to the shoes.

5

The first stop Jonathan made after availing himself of the shower in the house was the Realtor's office, where he paid the deposit and three months' rent and smiled at the lady as he gave her his standard explanation: widowed and looking for a place to start fresh. One look at Sarah, and most women bought it.

With the key to his house in his pocket, Jonathan's next stop was a small department store on the town square. He strolled in with Sarah securely in his arms and a grin on his face.

A woman with short brown hair and wearing a sleeveless red jacket with a nametag on it stepped out from behind the counter.

"Good morning, sir. May I help you?" she asked, eyeing Sarah curiously.

Sarah twisted in his arms to look over his shoulder, *bababa*-ing in his ear.

"Yes, you can," he said cheerfully. "We've

come to get this munchkin her first crib."

The clerk looked at Sarah, then at him. "You mean . . . a bigger crib? Surely she's in a crib."

The smile on Jonathan's face faltered. "Ah . . . she sleeps with me."

"Oh." The clerk, whose nametag read Debra, arched a brow in a manner that suggested she did not approve. "We have some nice models over here." She gestured to the back of the store.

Jonathan hesitantly followed her, holding tight to Sarah, who was squirming in his arms.

"Here we are." Debra pointed to at least a dozen cribs that were lined up in a row like incubators, not any two alike.

The sight of them dismayed Jonathan. Which one should he buy?

As if she were reading his thoughts, Debra asked, "Do you know what you'd like in a crib?"

"Ah . . ." He laughed nervously. "One that she can sleep in."

Debra gave him a thin smile. "I mean, do you prefer a canopy? A traditional crib? Or perhaps you are in the market for a convertible?"

Jonathan tried to smile. "She'd look good in a convertible, don't you think?" he joked.

Debra did not smile, but turned to the nearest crib. "This is a fine midrange convertible. It includes teething rails, an adjustable mattress, and a pull-and-play arch —"

"A what?" Jonathan asked as he wrestled a restless Sarah with two hands.

"A pull-and-play arch," she said, looking at Sarah. "You know, like an activity gym?" At Jonathan's blank look, she frowned a little. "It has a variety of colorful, noisemaking toys to stimulate cognitive development."

Jonathan blinked.

Debra cocked her head to one side. "Perhaps you'd like to come back with your wife."

Her condescension was grating on him. "Just give me the basic crib and ring me up," he said curtly. "I don't have time to come back."

"Of course," Debra said, and marched away from him, toward the back of the building. "Mark!" she shouted. A young man appeared almost instantly and eagerly hurried toward Debra. He was no more than sixteen, if that, Jonathan guessed. And he had Down syndrome.

"I need you to find this model of crib in the back," Debra said, jotting down the information on a Post-it note. "Do you

68

understand? A baby bed," she said sternly. Mark nodded. "Find it and bring the box to the front." She handed the Post-it to Mark. He studied it earnestly. "And, Mark . . . get the *right* box. The gentleman does not have time for mistakes."

Jonathan was really disliking this woman. "It's cool, Mark," he said with a look for Debra. "No hurry."

Mark looked at Debra for confirmation. "Go on," she said, her voice softer.

"Yes, ma'am," Mark said, and disappeared into the back.

Debra turned back to Jonathan. "Are you sure you wouldn't like to look at some other items? We just got in some developmental gyms. It's important for your child's development."

"Thanks, but I think she's developing just fine without all that Baby Einstein stuff," Jonathan said as Sarah tried to climb over his shoulder. "Right now, all I need is a crib. That's it."

Debra pursed her lips together and walked to the counter. As she rang up his purchase, Mark reappeared, wrestling a large box on a rolling dolly. He banged into a shelving unit on his way to the front, and Debra sighed irritably.

Jonathan could feel his irritation rising.

He drew a long, steadying breath — an exercise he'd been practicing to keep himself from flying off the handle. Fights tended to draw attention. Attention drew suspicion, and he couldn't afford suspicions. He stuffed his wallet into his back pocket before Sarah could grab it and throw it.

Throwing was her favorite activity these days, after walking.

He wondered if that was developmentally correct, or if Debra was judging his kid. Sarah didn't have developmental gyms, and for all Jonathan knew, she ought to be walking and talking and performing stunts by now.

Sarah must have sensed he was thinking about her because she gave him a wide smile and laughed.

"Your baby is cute," Mark said.

Jonathan smiled at him.

"Is it a boy or a girl?" he asked cheerfully, in spite of Sarah's sundress.

"A girl."

"What's her name?"

"Mark," Debra said sternly. "Take the crib out to his car."

"Oh. Okay." Mark leaned over the counter to tickle Sarah's belly. "Hi, baby," he said in a singsong voice. "Hi, baby."

"Mark!"

"Lady, he's just saying hello," Jonathan said sternly. "Give the kid a break."

She frowned as she handed him a receipt.

But Mark was already awkwardly maneuvering the dolly with the crib out the door. Jonathan stuffed the receipt into his pocket and followed Mark out, but Sarah was squirming and wanted to walk. He put her down on her feet; she grasped his finger and began her laborious trek to the glass doors at the front of the store.

"Come back and see us," Debra said.

Not on your life, Jonathan thought, and kept on.

By the time they got outside, Mark had the back of a Suburban open.

"Hey, sport — over here," Jonathan said, pointing to his Mustang.

"Oh!" Mark shut the back door of the Suburban and rolled the dolly over to the Mustang.

Jonathan met him there and told him to hold on while he strapped Sarah into her seat. She did not want to go in her seat, she wanted to keep walking and began to cry. "Hold on, baby," Jonathan said. "We're getting your bed, remember?"

Her cries turned to screams when Jonathan left her and walked around to the back of the car to pop the trunk.

"Wow," Mark said. "You've got a lot of stuff!"

"Yep," Jonathan said, and picked up the box, shoved it in as deep as he could get it on top of the clothes and baby supplies he had stuffed in the trunk.

"Are you moving?" Mark asked.

Jonathan grinned at him. "Moving in. Got a place right outside of town." He glanced up; Sarah was still screaming.

"Is your baby all right?" Mark asked.

"She's fine, but she's hungry. Is there some place around here we could get something to eat?"

Mark thought a moment as Jonathan tied the crib down in his trunk. "Oh, I know!" he said, his face lighting up. "Dot's Diner!"

Jonathan couldn't help but smile. "You know where it is?"

"Yeah!" Mark turned fully around and happily pointed down Main Street. "I think it's down there. It's by the gas station. There's a gas station down there, but you can't see it, and the diner is next to it."

"Great. Thanks, sport." Sarah's screams had turned to hiccups. She was tired, she was hungry, and she was probably wet. Jonathan pulled out his wallet and extracted a ten. He held it out to Mark.

Mark's eyes widened. "What's that for?"

"It's a tip. All good delivery guys get a tip."

"But I'm not a delivery guy."

"You delivered this box to my car, didn't you?"

Mark had to think about it a moment, but he suddenly smiled and took the ten, grinning down at it.

Jonathan clapped him on the shoulder. "That's for you, pal. Not Debra. She doesn't need to know you got a tip for doing a good job, because it's all yours. So put that in your pocket and don't tell her, okay?"

"Okay."

"We'll see you later. I've got to go feed this little girl."

As he pulled away from the curb, Mark stood on the sidewalk waving to Sarah. "Bye, baby! Bye!"

Sarah held up her hand and opened and closed her fingers, waving back.

6

The day-care center where Aubrey worked was a zoo. Three more kids than usual had shown up today, all of them toddlers. For one little boy, it was his first time away from his mother, and he was clingy — particularly to Aubrey.

"I don't know what it is about you," Nancy Fischer, the owner, said. "But babies love you. Joan always said as much."

Joan, Aubrey's mother, had been Nancy Fischer's partner in this day-care center. They'd opened it a year before her mother had been diagnosed with breast cancer. Within three years, she was dead, and with her death came all the issues of transferring ownership of the day care to Nancy. At least that had been one area where Aubrey could trust Zeke not to interfere. He'd hated the day-care center from its inception, hated that Mom had ever gotten involved, and hated Nancy Fischer in general.

Nancy was a jovial woman partial to high-pocketed mom jeans, Keds, and patriotic T-shirts. She had a heart as big as the sky when it came to kids, which automatically made her Not Zeke's Type. And as the day care had yet to turn a substantial profit, he'd been willing to let it go.

It helped that Mr. Fischer was a prominent dentist in town. Zeke rarely made waves in public. He liked to project that good-old-boy, friend-to-all, enemy-to-none persona. He reserved his true nature for Mom and Aubrey.

"I can't believe how much this place has grown in the last few months," Nancy sighed as she gathered boxes of crayons and brightly colored papers so the kids could draw pictures. "Joan would have been so happy. She always insisted that we advertise in the local papers, and I guess she was right again. Oh, how she would have loved to hear me say that," Nancy said with a laugh.

Aubrey smiled. "I know. She said up until the very end, 'I'm not going to be an invalid, Aubrey. I am not going to let this disease rob me of a single hour without fighting for it.' That was Mom for you. She was always so determined."

Except in leaving Zeke.

"Well, she was a lot smarter than me. But

75

that's not saying much, is it?" Nancy asked with a wink, and continued to stack the papers and boxes of crayons. "The advertising worked like a charm," she added wistfully.

It had worked so well that Nancy had been overwhelmed when Mom died. She had begged Aubrey to stay and help and had even offered a decent salary if she'd just stay through the summer until Nancy could get her daughter Noelle — whom Aubrey had gone to school with — trained and ready to help her. Nancy needed someone who could pick up the day-to-day operations while she handled more of the business end. Not to mention the legal hassles that had been presented to the co-ownership as a result of Mom's death.

Aubrey hadn't wanted to stay, God knew she hadn't wanted to stay. She'd wanted to go back to San Diego and away from Zeke as soon as her mother was buried. But this place had meant so much to Mom — she and Nancy had dreamed of it for years before they'd actually put it together. And when they'd opened it, Mom felt as if she was finally making something of herself, after years of being put down by Zeke.

That was what had decided Aubrey in the end. It was her mother's chance to stand up to Zeke, to be her own person, and Aubrey couldn't let it falter now. Besides, she could definitely use the money.

So she'd agreed to stay until the fall semester, which was still more than a month away. She'd gotten her own apartment in order to keep Zeke at arm's length. How bad would it be to live in the same small town with her father, really? But she hadn't imagined — would never have imagined — what she'd learned about her father. Now she knew just how brutal and depraved he really was.

She'd discovered it one unusually rainy afternoon about a month or so ago, when she'd driven up to a little town in the hills where she could get some organic produce — something the merchants of Tourmaline hadn't yet seen fit to carry — and she'd taken what she thought was a shortcut through the hills and had ended up lost, driving aimlessly for a time until she found a road she knew.

On her way back to Tourmaline, on County Road 78, she'd spotted her father's big patrol pickup truck on the side of the road by a wooded area, and Keith Stanley's big, black king-cab truck parked just behind it. Aubrey had thought that was really odd — what could they be doing up in the hills, in the middle of nowhere? So she'd pulled up beside the trucks — to this day, she wasn't entirely sure why she did — and got out of her car. But when she did, she heard the unmistakable sound of a gunshot echoing between the hills. And then a second one.

A shudder of nausea had shot through her, and Aubrey had quickly climbed into her car and driven away, taking great gulps of air to keep from vomiting. Her visceral reaction had been bizarre, but she'd had a strong intuitive feeling that the two men had no business shooting in the woods. Her dad was not a hunter. And even if he were, it wasn't hunting season.

A few days later she'd heard from Bev that Roger Martinez had gone missing. "Drove off with a truckload of farm equipment from the farm-supply store," she'd confided in Aubrey.

"How do you know it was him?" Aubrey had asked, mildly curious.

"Your daddy told me. He said Roger Martinez had been stealing food from an honest man's plate, but now he'd been run off and wouldn't be a problem anymore. That's why he's sheriff of this town," Bev had said with an adamant nod as she rang up Aubrey's groceries. "Your father's a good man and a better sheriff."

But Aubrey knew differently. She'd scarcely made it out of the supermarket, running to the corner of the building before she was sick. She knew what had happened, deep in her gut she knew what her father had done. He and Keith had killed Roger Martinez.

She was so certain of it that days of agony and doubt had passed until Aubrey had found the courage to mention to Zeke one day, when she ran into him at the diner, that she'd seen his truck up on 78 that rainy afternoon.

Zeke had become so angry that she could tell he was restraining himself from hitting her, even though they were standing on the sidewalk in front of Dot's. "You don't know what you're talking about. But don't you *ever* mention that to me or anyone else again, do you understand me?" he'd said low. "Or you will be very sorry, Aubrey."

Just the memory of the look of venom in his eyes made her shudder. There was no telling what he was capable of, particularly now that Aubrey believed he dispensed his own brand of justice.

Aubrey was grateful when little Trevor shook her from the upsetting memory by banging on her leg.

"See?" Nancy said, smiling down at the towheaded child. "They love you. Joan was right — you're a natural for this sort of work. You'll make a great pediatric nurse."

Aubrey didn't know if Trevor loved her as much as he loved the dozen or so wire-thin silver bracelets with tiny rhinestones she was wearing. They sparkled under fluorescent light, and he liked pushing them around her wrist. And whether or not she'd ever make it to becoming a pediatric nurse . . . at the moment, she'd be happy just to finish college with a degree in early childhood development.

She squatted down next to Trevor and held out her wrist. "You want to push them some more?"

He nodded and began methodically twisting them around in a circle.

She did like kids, though. They were so pure, so full of life and joy and eagerness to see all the things their little worlds had to offer them. Best of all, none of them judged her. Not one of them looked at her hair or her clothes or the small tattoo on her ankle and judged her. Yeah, she liked kids. A lot. Which was why, she supposed, she'd been so alarmed by that beautiful baby girl sitting alone in that cart yesterday at the supermarket. She liked kids and didn't like to see them abused or neglected or put in any sort of danger.

She watched the bracelets going round and round on her wrist, but she was seeing J.B. and his long, dark hair, the fierce protectiveness in his eyes when he had taken his daughter from Aubrey's arms. She thought of him standing up to those three thugs in the parking lot. He'd been absolutely fearless. And he'd done it for her.

A strange little shiver coursed down her spine. No one had ever stood up for her. Even her own mother — God love her, she'd tried, but her mother had been so easily cowed by Zeke. Aubrey shook her head to clear her thoughts of a guy she'd probably never see again, and with a sigh, she stood up. "Come on, Trevor," she said, putting out her hand. "Let's go color."

She'd just gotten Trevor set up with paper and crayons when Noelle breezed in, carrying paper bags from the supermarket. "It's hot as blazes out there," she said as she put the sacks down on a bench. She put her hands on the small of her back and leaned backward. Noelle was a smaller version of her mother — a little chunky, in mom jeans and a red-white-and-blue-striped polo shirt.

Noelle and Aubrey had not been particularly friendly in high school — Aubrey hadn't had any friends really, for fear of their finding out the truth about Zeke. But Noelle had always seemed nice to Aubrey, and in the three months Aubrey had been home, she had really come to appreciate Noelle.

"Did you get the pizza?" Nancy asked.

Noelle groaned and bent backward. "I knew I was forgetting something!"

"Oh, honey, I'm starving!" Nancy complained as one little girl held up two hands covered in Play-Doh.

"I'll go out again," Noelle said, but her son launched himself at her leg. "Mommy, come see!" he said excitedly.

Aubrey picked up her purse. "Noelle, you stay here. I'll run over to the diner and get us something. They're usually pretty quick."

"Oh, great," Noelle sighed. "I don't think I can eat another club sandwich."

"I don't know if I can, either," Nancy sighed, but Aubrey knew better. Nancy was not one to turn down a sandwich.

Noelle looked at Aubrey. "Are you sure?" she asked with a wince as she tried to pry her son's hands from her leg. "I'm really sorry."

"It's no problem," Aubrey said. "I'll be back before we put them down for naps. The usual for everyone?"

At Noelle and Nancy's twin nods, Aubrey went out, grateful for the fresh air and the chance to be alone.

7

Aubrey walked the two blocks to Dot's Diner. She passed a couple of middle-aged women who disapprovingly eyed the cowboy boots she wore with a flouncy, red, knee-length skirt and her favorite heavy-metal T-shirt. Aubrey ignored them. Franny would be proud of her outfit.

But when Aubrey stepped into the diner, it seemed as if all heads swiveled in her direction, and she felt the wave of disapproval. Nothing ever changed in Tourmaline. Everyone marched to the same drummer, and God forbid anyone find his or her own beat. To make matters worse, the place was hopping today — people were standing at the counter waiting for the booths to turn over. Aubrey pushed her dark hair behind her ears before lifting her chin and walking up to the counter.

Tommy Lynch, the gangly teenage boy who worked the lunch shift every day, wiped his hands on his dirty apron and flipped open his order pad. "The usual?" he asked her.

Were she, Nancy, and Noelle that predictable? "I don't know, Tommy, maybe something a little different today," she said breezily, and picked up the menu and began to peruse the items as if she didn't already have them memorized. *Meat loaf and mashed potatoes, chicken fried steak, beef tenders . . .*

This was really the only place in town to get a decent meal, and to her way of thinking, "decent" was stretching it. There wasn't a single item on the menu that wasn't dripping in saturated fats and cholesterol. It was not exactly a vegan-friendly kind of town. She closed the menu and smiled sheepishly at him. "The usual."

He wrote it down, stuffed the pencil behind his ear, ripped the sheet from the pad, and whirled around. "Two clubs and a rabbit plate to go!" he shouted, and stuck the order into the little carousel in front of the cook.

"Aubrey?"

She started at the sound of her name. She knew instantly who it was. She had managed to avoid him since she'd seen his truck parked next to Zeke's that horrible afternoon a little more than a month ago. But she'd known she couldn't avoid him forever and turned slowly. She tried to smile. "Oh, hey . . . hi, Keith."

She'd dated Keith Stanley on and off for a couple of years toward the end of high school and after she'd graduated. She'd been biding her time in Tourmaline, saving the money she earned clerking at the pharmacy until she had enough to move to San Diego. He was handsome and nice to her, but she'd always thought there was something a little off about him. He had a mean streak. He had made her feel ice-cold one afternoon when he had made cruel jokes about a disabled guy.

Keith looked pretty much the same now as he had then. Tall, sandy blond hair, and blue eyes. The hard edges of his youth had gone soft in the last few years, but he still looked good.

Noelle had told her he was working as a tractor salesman at the farm-supply place. "I always thought you two would marry," she'd said. "He was crazy about you, wasn't he?"

If Zeke had had his way, they would have been married. Zeke loved Keith, and the feeling was mutual. And it was true Keith was crazy about her. It mystified her — he could have any girl in Tourmaline he wanted, but he was fixated on her. Aubrey had never been crazy about him. He'd been someone to hang out with, and truthfully, when she was with Keith, Zeke let up on her a little. He'd been a refuge for her — but never more than that.

Even now, he was looking at her with an odd mix of yearning and disgust.

Aubrey nervously pushed her hair behind her ears. "So . . . how are you?"

"I'm good, I'm good," he said, nodding as he took in her short hair, her torn T-shirt, and her cowboy boots. "I'm still selling farm equipment at the farm supply out on Highway 78 . . . but I guess you knew that."

"Right," she said, nodding. As if she would ever forget it. It wasn't every day someone was murdered for stealing farm equipment.

"Doing pretty well," he said with sniff. "I just bought a house."

"Wow. That's great." She couldn't help but wonder how she'd dated him as long as she had. He was wearing a white, button-down shirt that said JOHN DEERE above the pocket, khaki pants, and lace-up shoes. He really wasn't her type. He never had been.

"How are *you?*" he asked. "Are you doing okay since your mom passed away?"

"Oh," she said, feeling that small curl of pain in her gut at the mention of her mother. "Yeah, thanks." She managed a small smile. "I'm doing okay."

He nodded. His gaze raked over her again, and he suddenly glanced over his shoulder and leaned in close to her. "Aubrey . . . why do you dress like that?" he whispered. "You're such a pretty girl. You don't need to wear stuff like that to draw attention to yourself."

They were as different as soy nut butter and duck sausage. Aubrey stepped back. "I dress this way because I like it. Why do you dress like that?"

He smiled. "Okay, that didn't come out like I intended." He held up a hand. "Never tell a woman you don't like what she's wearing," he added with a laugh. "It's just . . ." He glanced down at her boots. "It's just a little strange."

"Okay, well, listen, it was —"

"Do you get out much?" he asked, cutting her off.

"Like out of the asylum? Not really," Aubrey said as she took another step backward. The truth was that she didn't — there weren't exactly a lot of cultural events to attend in Tourmaline. Frankly, there wasn't anything to do but drink at the local bar. "I mean," she said, putting a hand to her nape, "I go back and forth between San Diego a lot." It was a lie. She would go to San Diego if she could afford the gas. "I don't stay in Tourmaline very much."

Keith looked confused. "Really? Because I see your car outside the Avalon apartment complex most days."

How long did it take to throw some vegetables in a box, for heaven's sake? She glanced anxiously at the kid behind the counter. He gave her a thumbs-up. "Are you sure it's my car?" she asked, feigning confusion. "Because I'm not here very much."

He shrugged a little and moved closer. "It doesn't matter. I was just thinking maybe you and I could get together for a beer down at Benji's some night," he said, referring to a local pub. "Maybe we could catch up."

"Here's the rabbit plate. Clubs are coming," the teenager said, shoving a styrofoam container at her.

She owed the kid one. "Oh, hey! Thanks!" She made a show of digging in her purse for the money, which she handed to the kid.

The teenager handed her the change and a plastic bag. "I'll be right back with the clubs."

Aubrey carefully put the vegetable plate in

the plastic bag, hoping vainly that Keith would magically disappear along with his invitation.

Of course he didn't. He was still standing there, waiting for her answer. "How about Friday?" he suggested.

"Friday," Aubrey repeated. She slowly shook her head. "You know, Keith . . . I don't think so. I don't think it's a good idea."

"Why not? We used to get on pretty good, didn't we?" He caressed her arm with his finger.

Aubrey pulled her arm away from him. "That was a long time ago —"

"Maybe so, but we had some fun." He shifted forward so he could touch her again.

"We didn't have that much fun," she blurted, moving away from him again. "I was just . . . I was just killing time."

Keith actually looked disconcerted, and Aubrey regretted her words. She hadn't meant to say it quite that way. She never meant things to come out the way they did. Her mother used to say she was "forthright." Aubrey thought she was completely lacking the tact gene.

"Wow," Keith said with a snort. "I guess I know where I stand."

"Keith —"

"So it was great seeing you, Aubrey." He stepped back, away from her. "Glad to see you're doing okay." With that, he turned and pushed into the crowd, disappearing from her sight.

"Here are the clubs," the teenager said, shoving two more styrofoam containers at her.

"Thanks," Aubrey muttered, and quickly slipped them in the bag. She glanced at the crowd again, then turned abruptly toward the door — and almost collided with J.B.

He caught the bag she almost dropped. His baby was strapped to his back, her dark head peeking out over his shoulder.

"It's *you*," she said unthinkingly.

"Yeah, me." He handed her the bag.

"Thanks." She glanced at his daughter; the baby grinned and reached her hand out to Aubrey.

The corner of J.B.'s mouth tipped up in something of a smile . . . or maybe it was a smirk, Aubrey wasn't certain. Whatever it was, it gave her a quiver deep inside, and suddenly the only thing she knew in all certainty was that it was very warm in the diner. She shifted a little awkwardly to her right, meaning to step around him and get out of there, onto the street where she could get some air. "Thanks," she said again, gesturing to the bag, and made a move to pass him.

"That was kind of cold," he said.

Aubrey blinked. "Huh?"

He glanced at her sidelong. "The way you brushed off that guy."

He'd *heard* her? She lifted her hand and anxiously rubbed the side of her neck. "That . . . that was none of your business!"

"Hey," he said with a shrug, "can't help it if you choose a public place to cut a guy off at the knees."

His baby reached her hand out again, her fingers grasping at air in the direction of Aubrey's bracelets.

"I didn't cut him off —" She shook her head — she hardly needed to explain herself to him. "You shouldn't be listening in on other people's conversations."

"You don't want people hearing you put a hole in some guy's balloon, don't do it in public."

"You honestly have no idea what you're talking about," she snapped. The baby began to cry and tried hard to reach Aubrey's bracelets. "And once again — your baby needs your attention."

"She needs food. That's why we're at a diner."

"She's crying because she wants my bracelets." Aubrey held out her arm to the baby. The baby grabbed them.

"Lady, you don't know a thing about my kid."

The man was insufferable. "You're right. But I know she wants my bracelets, and I know she stopped crying when I put them up where she could touch them. Babies are attracted to sparkly things."

"Wow. Call CBS and get a reporter down here," he said as he shrugged out of the baby carrier. "Woman discovers the big secret to babies! They like shiny things." He swiped his hand above her head like a banner before lifting Sarah out of the carrier. "Babies also cry when they're hungry. Maybe you can make that chapter two of your bestselling *Guide to Babies* book."

"I wasn't trying —"

"I know your type. You see a guy with a baby and think that gives you and every other woman on earth permission to tell me everything I'm doing wrong. Like I'm such an idiot I can't figure out my own daughter."

His admonition stung her. She glowered at him. "You know what? For a guy who apparently knows *everything,* you sure are prickly all the time."

"I don't like people in my business."

"I am *so* not in your business," Aubrey

shot back.

"Great. Now that we've cleared that up, maybe you can let us pass so I can feed my little girl."

She stepped aside and made a grand sweeping gesture toward the diner.

"Thank you," he said, and walked past.

Aubrey watched him . . . she couldn't help but watch him. In his faded jeans and black T-shirt, he cut quite a . . . *masculine* figure. She whirled around, pushed through the glass door, and fairly burst out onto the sidewalk, knocking her bag into the door at the same time and splitting the flimsy plastic sack. The three styrofoam containers fell to the ground.

"Dammit!" she muttered under her breath. The two club sandwiches emerged unscathed, of course, but her veggie plate was one sodden mess. She used the styrofoam box to quickly clean it up.

In a booth by the window, Jonathan dumped some Cheerios on the table and held Sarah in his lap, and while she carefully picked them up between her forefinger and thumb and stuffed them into her mouth, Jonathan watched Aubrey pick up the food she'd dropped and toss it in a trash can. He couldn't help but smile. She was kind of

94

goofy. Cute. But goofy.

When she'd cleaned the mess up — including kicking something that looked like broccoli under the mailbox when she thought no one was looking — she took off down the street, her full red skirt swirling around her knees. Jonathan leaned as far to his left as he could, watching her shapely legs in those cool boots and her hips sway as she marched away.

When he couldn't see her any longer, he sat up, the image of her hips still in his mind's eye.

But when he looked at Sarah again, he frowned. "There's a lot of stuff I don't know, Munchkin," he said, stroking her cheek with the back of his index finger, "but I'm going to learn it." He cupped the side of her head and kissed her face. "I'm going to be a respectable citizen and raise you up right." He wasn't quite sure how to go about it, but he'd figure it out, or die trying.

"Oh, what a cutie," the waitress said as she appeared at the table. She smiled at Jonathan. "I'm Randi. What can I get for you, sweetie?"

"Hi, Randi," he said with a wink. "I'll take a burger and fries, and for this one" — he put his hand on top of Sarah's head — "a banana, cut into little pieces, if you can manage that."

"Sure, sweetie. We can do that." She gave him a quick once-over, then sauntered away.

Jonathan looked out the window again, and without warning the image of a copper-eyed woman in a red skirt and cowboy boots marching down the street popped into his mind. He felt a strange twist of guilt and self-consciously sank down into the booth while Sarah continued to eat her Cheerios and tried to reach the salt and pepper shakers. He smoothed the back of her hair and closed his eyes for a moment.

Sorry, Tammy.

8

Before Jonathan could become a respectable citizen, he had to get his house in order. For the next couple of days, he searched around Tourmaline for suitable furniture and household supplies — a bed, a dresser, a rocking chair and couch for the living room. He bought a set of Pyrex dishes from the supermarket — he had four plates, four bowls, and four cups and saucers. He added to those four settings of stainless steel cutlery and three plastic-coated baby spoons.

At a flea market he found a few serviceable lamps and his prized find — a kitchen table. When Sarah was a little bigger, she'd have a place to finger paint. In the meantime, he bought a secondhand high chair, and the first night in their house, he sat her in it and dished up her favorite meal — squash, green beans, and chicken in a jar.

For the first time since Sarah was born,

he felt like a real parent sitting there feeding her. For the first time since Tammy had died, he felt like he was really the only person who should have this beautiful, precious baby girl. No one else but him. Not Lizzie, Sarah's crazy mother, and damn sure not Lizzie's grandfather, Alan Spaulding.

And for the first time since he'd faked his and Sarah's deaths, Jonathan felt confident that he'd found a place where Alan could not find him. He felt contentment, a sense that he and Sarah could belong here in this little town. Her childhood would be so different from his. Sarah would know she was loved every moment of every day; she would never have cause to doubt it. She would never believe she was loved and then have the rug yanked out from under her feet.

She wouldn't grow up as he had — Jonathan would make sure of it.

When he unloaded the furniture from the little trailer he'd rented and Sarah was down for a nap in her brand-new crib, Jonathan yanked the FOR RENT sign up from where he'd jammed it into the floor and leaned it against the wall, behind a drape so Sarah wouldn't see it and think it was a toy. He walked around in a circle near the hearth, looking at the floor. He finally knelt down on one knee and, using a hammer, pried up one of the floorboards that looked loose.

Just beneath the old floor was a base for the piers and beams that held up the house. It was the perfect spot to hide something. He went out to the car, and for the next quarter of an hour he worked to remove the backseat bench. When he'd done that, he reached into the little cubbyhole where he'd stashed the briefcase that contained what was left of his life.

Everything was in that briefcase — every scrap of paper, every napkin, every official document that defined Jonathan Randall, every picture of Tammy, of Sarah. It was funny, he thought, as he sorted through the contents, that even though he'd been on the run for so many months now, always moving, always looking — his life had actually stood still. It was all in this briefcase, waiting for him to settle down and resume his life, to put the past behind him and begin a new life with Sarah.

He took the briefcase into the house, wrapped an old shirt around it, then forced it down into the hole he'd created. Then, he replaced the floorboard, tapping it carefully into place so it didn't look as if it had been messed with.

His next task was his car. Whoever had owned a classic like this old Mustang and had not kept it up ought to have been shot. As it was, Jonathan spent the better part of a day repairing the radiator and cleaning the condenser. But by the end of the day, he had it purring . . . at least enough to get back and forth to town for a while.

That left him with one last task — find a job. There was no avoiding it — respectable fathers had jobs, and besides, he was running low on money.

The very thought of getting a job made him nervous. He was already on edge — he'd put Sarah down in her very own crib for the second night in a row, and for the second night in a row, he had stood on the other side of the wall, his fingernails digging into his palms as he listened to her wail herself to sleep. She wasn't used to sleeping alone. She wasn't used to sleeping in a crib.

He sat in the rocking chair he'd bought for the living room, one leg jumping with nervous energy, chewing on a fingernail as he contemplated his next move. There were so many things to consider — what to do with Sarah when he went to work, for one. He couldn't stand the thought of leaving her with perfect strangers. What if he was wrong about this place? What if Alan could find him here and found Sarah when he wasn't around? Forget Alan — what about all the nuts out there? How would he protect her from all of them?

But he really didn't have a choice — he needed to work. And he couldn't keep Sarah strapped to his back all her life. If he was going to do this, if he was going to make this work, he had to have a job.

"A job, Munchkin," Jonathan told Sarah the next morning as he bathed her in the kitchen sink. "Daddy has to find a job, which means you're going to have to stay with someone."

She splashed her hands in the water.

"I'm not kidding," he said cheerfully, poking her in the belly and making her laugh. "Your daddy is going to get a real job, and we're going to have a real good life."

Sarah was more interested in the water and the two yellow ducks that were floating around her than his job, but that was just as well, Jonathan thought. She would know soon enough that change was coming.

He finished her bath, dried her off, and dressed her. "First things first," he said as he pulled her socks onto her fat little feet. "We have to find out who's hiring."

Bad bad ba ba," she answered, reaching for her toes.

He smiled down at her. She changed every day. He wished Reva could see her. Reva loved Sarah — when Jonathan had left Springfield, she could hardly let go of her. She'd pinned her mother's cameo on Sarah's jacket as a charm — Sarah had been named for Reva's mother — and she had made Jonathan promise to take care of her.

"But who will take care of you?" she asked tearfully when Jonathan had met her privately at the bar he'd owned to say his good-byes. Reva was the only one who knew that he'd faked his and Sarah's deaths — he'd put Sarah in a gym bag, and at the last minute he'd jumped out of the car with her, landing in the undergrowth of the woods and watching the car go off the cliff.

Only Reva would understand why he'd done it. Alan Spaulding had pinned his entire future on Sarah's tiny shoulders, and he would stop at nothing until he had her. Reva understood how ruthless Alan was, and that Jonathan had to do what he was doing for Sarah's sake. But it was heartbreaking to say good-bye.

He wished Reva could see Sarah now. He didn't wish the same for Tammy, however — he had a feeling Tammy was on some fluffy, white cloud, watching over them every day.

"Ready?" he asked Sarah when he had her dressed.

Holding a foot in each hand, she rolled onto her back and babbled to him. Jonathan took that as an affirmative sign. She was as ready as he was to settle down and start a new life.

Aubrey's day was off to a spectacularly bad start, thanks to Zeke's unannounced and very early visit to her apartment. She was hardly even up, much less dressed, and was still trying to decide what to wear when he banged on her apartment door and shouted, "Open up! Sheriff!"

He always thought that was funny. He didn't care how many friends or neighbors he startled with it. Aubrey opened the door only a crack — she had no intention of letting him in, but Zeke shoved against the door and strolled inside.

He didn't even look at her — he just looked around her apartment, snorting at the picture she had of her and her mother on a shelf. He was notably absent from the photo. "Aubrey Lynne, don't you take out the trash?" he remarked as he looked around at the walls, painted a vibrant green to improve Aubrey's chi, and the crystals hanging in the window. "It smells funny in here." He batted a mobile she'd hung from her ceiling — the elegant swirl of hand-molded copper, a kinetic sculpture, spun positive energy into her house. With a father like Zeke, she really wanted to summon as much positive energy from the universe as she could so she'd become a better person.

Zeke shook his head and turned his gaze to her, examining her from the top of her head to the tip of her toes. "What the hell, Aubrey? Don't you have any more pride than that?"

She glanced down — she was wearing a short cotton robe. "It's a robe. I was getting dressed."

"Go put some clothes on."

Aubrey didn't bother pointing out that she was in *her* apartment alone, an apartment *she* paid for, and could therefore walk around wearing nothing but a sombrero if she liked — there was no point in arguing anything with Zeke. So she brushed past him and walked into her bedroom. She emerged a few minutes later in a pair of low-rise jeans that had holes in the knees and a white cotton blouse.

Zeke rolled his eyes. "Half-naked was better than *that.*"

She folded her arms defensively across her middle. "Is there a reason you came by this morning?" she asked coolly.

"I don't need a reason to see my own

daughter, do I?" He turned away from her before she could respond. "Is this the way you live on your own? There's junk everywhere!"

Aubrey felt a familiar coiling deep inside her, as if all her organs were curling up so taut that the slightest touch would cause an implosion — or make her violently sick.

"What do you want?" she asked again through gritted teeth.

"I'll tell you what I want. I know you can't come down off your high horse to show your own father any respect, but I expect you to at least show some respect to the people of this town! *That's* what I want. You will not make a fool of me, Aubrey Cross — do you understand me?"

He confused her — she could not imagine what he was talking about. "I don't understand," she said simply.

"Oh my Lord," he said with a cold smile. "You're dumb as a post, aren't you?"

The coiling inside her tightened; she could taste bile in the back of her throat.

"You still don't know what I am talking about, do you? Well, let me spell it out for you. I ran into Keith and he told me what happened and how you treated him."

"Nothing happened," she muttered.

"Oh, no? Maybe you're like your mother

and you don't understand that humiliating a good man in public is a little more than nothing."

"I didn't humiliate him," she said weakly, even as a voice inside her screamed there was no point in arguing with her father. It would only make the situation worse. But Aubrey couldn't stop herself — a small part of her could never stop fighting. It was just a tiny little voice that used to talk back to Zeke even after he'd hit her. The same little voice had grown to a roar when she was a teenager, leading to more abuse. And it was the weary little voice in her now that could never shut up, could never just let it go.

Predictably, Zeke's expression darkened. He braced his legs apart, rested his hands on his belt, and leaned forward with a glare. "*Excuse* me?"

"You heard me. I didn't humiliate him." She hugged herself tightly. "I just explained that I wasn't interested in renewing my relationship with him."

"I just don't understand that. I mean . . . do you honestly think you can do *better?*" he asked, incredulous. "Do you think you're that hot? Well, let me tell you something, father to daughter — you *can't* do better. You're damn lucky Keith has any interest in you at all."

Aubrey gasped. She hated Zeke. She despised him, reviled him. What cruel twist of fate had made him the creature responsible for her existence? They couldn't possibly be more different. So different, in fact, that for years, when Zeke would accuse her mother of running around on him, of having conceived Aubrey out of wedlock, Aubrey had secretly fantasized it was true. She fantasized Zeke wasn't her real father, that her mother had had a true love affair, and she was the result of it. That somewhere out there was a man who was kind and who would love Aubrey if he only knew she existed.

Unfortunately, Aubrey's mother would always destroy her fantasy by assuring her that Zeke was her father, and that his accusations of her infidelity were just his insecurities talking.

He didn't seem very insecure now. Whatever part of Aubrey was Zeke, she wanted to cut out of her body and burn. "I may be undesirable," she said. "But at least I'm not a murderer."

Zeke suddenly lunged across the small space of the living room and shoved her up against the wall, his hand on her throat as he pushed her head back so that she had to look at him. "You better watch your mouth, missy," he spat as she clawed at his hand around her throat. "You think you're too good for *me?* Don't you *ever* forget that I made you and I can unmake you. Show your father some damn respect and stop talking nonsense." He let go of her.

Aubrey grabbed her throat with both hands and began to cough violently. Zeke stepped back and adjusted his gun belt, watching her with a look of revulsion. "Next time you see Keith, you smile real nice." His gaze swept over her. "And for chrissakes, don't dress like such a slut."

With that, he opened the door and walked out as Aubrey tried to catch her breath. He paused just outside and looked up at the sky, as if they'd just had a friendly cup of coffee. He didn't look back, but continued walking to his car.

Aubrey waited until he was in his car before she slammed the door shut and went to the bathroom. She tilted her head back and looked at her neck. It was red from his handling of her, but she doubted it would bruise. Nevertheless, a bandanna would be a good idea for work today. Here she was again, hiding the truth about her father.

9

Jonathan's foray into gainful employment was not particularly successful. He started with the local newspaper. It was a week old, but he scanned the want ads for something he could do. Fry cook, janitor, and part-time paralegal was the extent of the employment listed.

He decided he would have to visit the local employment agency. It was not something he wanted to do — it felt a little as if he were exposing himself. But he reasoned that he'd have to present himself to someone somewhere if he wanted a job, and with Sarah in his arms, he made himself visit the office.

He should have known when he walked in the door and found no one waiting that it was going to be a dead end.

The girl behind the counter — a short, blond girl who cooed at Sarah — printed off a list of job openings in the area. She handed it to Jonathan. "Just take a seat, review the list, and let me know which ones you'd like to pursue, and we'll get started."

He maneuvered himself into a small schoolroom desk with Sarah on his lap.

"You want to put her on the floor?" the girl asked. "It's okay. No one's around."

He didn't like the idea of Sarah rolling around on this floor — who knew what sort of germs were there? Considering some of the places he had eaten and slept in his life, he couldn't believe he'd turned into the kind of guy who worried about germs. "Nah," he said, glancing sidelong at the girl. "She's fine."

Sarah wasn't fine. Sarah wanted down and he had to fight her to keep her from squirming out of his grip.

He began to peruse the list. *Fireman.* He had to smile at that one — he was much better at starting fires than dousing them. *Teacher's assistant.* Oh, yeah, he'd be a regular Mr. Rogers with a bunch of kids, wouldn't he? *Hairstylist.* An Edward Scissorhands he was not.

He turned the page, and his smile faded as he read over the list of available positions. *Nighttime dockworker. Nurse's aide. Summer camp counselor.*

A bad feeling sprouted in his gut. There

was nothing on the list he was suited to do, but then again, what did he expect? His work experience wasn't exactly great. His last gig had been running a bar, and he didn't see any openings for a bartender on this list.

He got up, walked to the counter with a fussy Sarah under his arm, and pushed the sheet of paper across to the girl.

The girl, who looked like she was maybe seventeen and had a better job than he'd be able to get with no background he could share, and no experience, took the list and looked at it.

She glanced up at him, clearly confused. "You didn't circle anything."

He pressed his lips together and shifted Sarah's weight onto his hip.

The girl looked at Sarah, then at him. "Do you need me to explain the jobs to you?"

"I can read," he snapped.

"Yes, of course you can," she said quickly, and her expression changed to something that looked like pity. "Are you sure you don't want to pursue any of them? We have some employers who will consider a wide variety of backgrounds."

"It's not my background," he said gruffly. "Those aren't jobs for a man."

"What about fireman —"

"I'm not a fireman," he said sternly.

She looked at him warily. "What about dockworker? That sounds like a manly job."

Jonathan bristled. "You don't get it — I've got a kid. I can't leave her at night."

"Well . . . maybe your wife can —"

"Look," he said, cutting her off. "These aren't the kind of jobs I'm after. I'll find something on my own." He wheeled around.

"But, mister, wait! I have more!" she called after him.

Jonathan ignored her. He paused only to swipe up the diaper bag and strode out of the office, kicking the glass door open with his foot and barreling through it. A woman who was on her way into the office reared back and gaped at him.

"What are you looking at?" he demanded as he strode by.

He put Sarah in her car seat, got behind the wheel, and sped out of the parking lot. He squealed to a stop at the light and banged his fist against the steering wheel. Sarah began to cry.

"Don't worry, baby," he said, looking at her in the rearview mirror. "I'm going to find a job." He put the car in drive, turned onto the main road through town, keeping his eye out for help-wanted signs in the windows as Sarah wailed behind him.

After combing the streets of Tourmaline, he spotted two help-wanted signs. One was at a day-care center. The only thing he took from that sign was the phone number for future reference.

The other help-wanted sign was in a feed-store on the edge of town, adjacent to a farm-equipment business. That looked promising. But when Jonathan inquired, the lady took one look at Sarah and said they'd hired someone.

Jonathan glanced at his baby, who was rubbing her fists into her eyes from weariness, then at the woman. "Ah . . . I'm the one looking for a job," he joked. "She's independently wealthy."

The woman didn't laugh. She stuck her pencil in her hair and shook her head. "It ain't the baby. We already hired someone."

Jonathan had to bite his lip to keep from telling her off. He could see she thought it was weird that he had a baby with him.

Dejected, he grabbed the latest edition of the newspaper from the news box outside the store and took his *Tourmaline Today* to a small municipal park he'd seen in town. He put Sarah in a baby swing, sat next to her on a kiddie swing, and with one hand pushed her while he went through the want ads.

What he found was pretty much the same thing he'd seen in the dated paper he'd already perused . . . but one new listing gave him a glimmer of hope: construction worker. He'd spent a little bit of time working for the construction firm owned by his stepfather Josh Lewis.

He gave a gurgling Sarah a gentle push as he dug his cell phone out of his pocket and dialed the number.

"Grace Construction," a woman chirped into the phone.

"I'm calling about the ad in the paper for a construction worker," Jonathan said. "I'm new in town and I have some construction experience."

"*New* in town?" The woman laughed. "Sorry, but there aren't a lot of people moving to Tourmaline. So what sort of experience do you have?"

"Commercial buildings," he said, forgetting to push Sarah a moment. "Large-scale projects."

"Anything we'd know?" she asked cheerfully.

"Ah . . . probably not," he said, not wanting to reveal anything if it wasn't necessary. "Hospitals, office complexes. That sort of thing."

"All right. The owner isn't in right now,

but he will be in the office tomorrow. Could you come in around two to meet him?"

"Yes," Jonathan said, just as Sarah began to cry. He winced, caressed the top of her head. *Not now, baby.* "You're down on Main Street, right?"

"Just past the Chevrolet dealer," she said as Sarah drew a large breath for what Jonathan knew would be a wail. "Who shall I say is coming in?" she asked.

Sarah wailed. Jonathan frantically pushed her in the swing, which only exacerbated her cries. "J.B."

"J. B. . . . ?"

"J. B. Winslow," he said quickly, thinking of Tammy's last name.

"Okay, J.B. We'll see you tomorrow!" she said brightly, and with a cheery good-bye she hung up.

Jonathan instantly fished Sarah out of the baby swing. "I know someone who could use a nap," he said, putting her on his shoulder, caressing her back. "Let's get you home."

As he picked up their things, he decided he liked the sound of that. *Home.* Hopefully, tomorrow he'd have a job and it would really be home.

Later, when a fussy Sarah would not take

her nap, Jonathan realized he was going to have to arrange for someone to look after her when he went to the interview tomorrow. He couldn't risk having a ten-month-old melt down while he was trying to convince some guy that he could work, and work hard.

He fished the number for the day-care place out of his pocket and stared hard at it. He hadn't left Sarah alone with anyone since they'd fled Springfield, and the thought of doing it now made him a little queasy. How could he know she'd be safe? First of all, kids carried all kinds of germs, and with her weak immune system, he worried. Sarah had been diagnosed with infant anemia a few months ago, necessitating a bone-marrow transplant. She was okay now, and according to her last checkup, normal on all fronts. But he'd never forget how sick she'd been, with all the tubes sticking in her. Even though she had a clean bill of health, he was scared of risking any kind of infection.

Moreover, kids were snatched off the street all the time, and if, on the slimmest chance, Alan were to track them here, he could grab Sarah if Jonathan wasn't there to protect her.

Jonathan's apprehension led him to pace

the living room, thinking. There really was no other option. He could hover over Sarah the rest of his life, or he could take a chance that his instincts were right, that she was healthy and this was the place they were supposed to be, and let go of some of that fear. He sometimes thought about what it was like before he was a father, before he was much of anything. Things were easier when he was alone, when he had nothing. He smiled at Sarah. Harder, too.

He flipped open his cell phone to make the call. Then closed it again. Then just as quickly flipped it open and dialed before he lost his resolve. It rang twice before a woman answered, "Bright Horizons Day Care. Noelle speaking."

In the background, Jonathan could hear little kids singing.

"Hello . . . I, ah . . . I've just moved to town and I have a ten-month-old daughter. You would really help me out if I could leave her with you tomorrow while I go on a job interview."

"Tomorrow? Oh, I'm sorry, sir, but we don't have any room tomorrow. We've got a couple of extra kids this week, and we don't have the staff to add any more."

"No room?" He pinched the bridge of his nose. "Are you sure?" he asked, a little

117

frantic. "She's no trouble at all. She's a good baby, a real good baby —"

"Oh, I'm sure she is. But we don't have the staff, sir. We're looking for people now."

"But . . . but I have to have someone watch her so I can go to a job interview," he said, more to himself than to her.

There was silence on the other end for a moment. "Where do you live?"

"On Highway 78," he said hopefully. "Just a few miles out of town."

"Oh, that's perfect. I can give you Mrs. Young's number. She lives out that way and she babysits for practically everyone in town. Maybe she can watch your baby. And if you get the job, you can bring your daughter to us on Monday. How's that?"

"Mrs. Young?" he said hesitantly. "Who's Mrs. Young?"

"Everyone in Tourmaline knows Mrs. Young. She's the best — she's a grandmother to half this town. Your daughter will be in excellent hands."

"Okay." He cocked the phone between his ear and his shoulder to write the number down. What choice did he have? He had to get a job. "Thanks. Thanks for your help."

"You're welcome, Mr. . . . ?"

"Mr. . . . Mr. Winslow," he said, and clicked off.

He bit his lip as he thought about having someone in this house. He didn't like the idea at all . . . but he was fairly confident she wouldn't be able to find his briefcase, and really, with Sarah trying to walk, she required almost constant attention. So he dialed the number.

Mrs. Young was kind on the phone. She was thrilled to hear he'd rented the old Haney place. "That fine house has sat vacant for far too long!" she declared.

When Jonathan explained his dilemma, she said, "You poor thing. Of course I can help you! What time would you like me to be there?"

By the end of the conversation, Jonathan was feeling much better about having Mrs. Young in his house. He asked her to come early — he wanted to make sure Sarah was comfortable with the sitter.

Having hurdled his first fear, he tiptoed to Sarah's room and peeked around the corner, relieved to see she was finally napping. One sock was hanging through the crib's spindles, and she had somehow managed to turn herself perpendicular to the side of the crib. She was sound asleep on her back, her arms flung wide, one chubby leg bent at the knee.

She looked angelic, and Jonathan felt that

deep-seated ache of missing Tammy he often felt when he looked at Sarah. He could imagine Tammy standing here beside him, holding his hand and watching that beautiful baby sleep, just as they'd done before she died.

"She's beautiful," Tammy had whispered. "She looks just like her dad," she'd added, squeezing his hand.

"I hope she doesn't turn out like her dad," Jonathan had muttered.

"Do you want her to turn out like Lizzie?" Tammy had joked, and Jonathan had groaned.

"I hope she turns out like you," Tammy said softly. "I hope she has passion for the things she believes in, like you."

Jonathan hadn't known what to say to that.

Tammy had smiled up at him again. "You think I'm kidding," she'd said with a playful nudge. "But it's true. No one has more passion for what he believes than you, Jonathan. I admire you for it."

It had startled him. He couldn't remember a time anyone had admired him for anything.

There was another memory he had, one that he could not erase — Tammy on her deathbed, making him promise he would take care of Sarah and keep her safe.

He was taking care of his baby the best he knew how. But sometimes it felt hollow, as if one of his arms or legs were missing. But Tammy wasn't here, and he had things he needed to do. He quietly pulled the door shut.

In town, Noelle put the phone down and shook her head. "I can't understand why anyone would willingly *move* to Tourmaline."

Aubrey stopped her sweeping and looked at the phone. "Who?"

"Oh, who knows." Noelle flicked her wrist at the phone. "So!" she said, brightening a little as she glanced around the room and found that they were alone. It was the end of the day and it looked it — dropped snacks littered the floor, chairs at the little kiddie tables were overturned, and someone had glued glitter to the chalkboard. "I hear Keith is after you again."

"What?" Aubrey cried.

"Keep your voice down," Noelle whispered. "Mom said not to bother you with it and would kill me if she heard me now."

"Nancy is outside with the last kids waiting to be picked up," Aubrey said. "What have you heard?"

"Okay, I'll tell you," Noelle said excitedly. "Remember Renee Brown from high school?"

Who could possibly forget Renee Brown? She had everything — money, boobs, and long blond hair. She *was* everything — Homecoming Queen, Most Popular — if Tourmaline High had an award to give, Renee was usually the recipient. Not that Aubrey had ever cared much — she'd spent her entire high school experience wishing she were somewhere else. "Yes, yes, you know I do," Aubrey said impatiently.

"Well, she and Dave broke up. You know that, right? He got some job in L.A., told Renee he didn't want her to come, that he wanted to see who else was out there, and upped and left Tourmaline. So now, Renee is on the prowl."

Aubrey could honestly say she didn't care about Renee and Dave's relationship. *"And?"*

"And, everyone knows she has a thing for Keith now."

"She *does?*" Aubrey said incredulously. "In high school, she didn't even know his name. He wasn't handsome enough or cool enough for her."

"Well, *yeah,*" Noelle said, as if that were obvious. "But that was then. You know how things change, and they sure did for Renee.

She's had a thing for Keith for a long time now."

"That's great, Noelle. I hope they are both very happy." Aubrey turned back to her sweeping.

"Aubrey, I know you don't have it for Keith anymore. But last night, a bunch of people were at Benji's, and someone mentioned to Keith that Renee was interested, as if he didn't know — he'd have to be *blind* not to know," Noelle said with a roll of her eyes. "But anyway, he told this person that he wasn't interested in Renee because *you* were back in town."

"Oh my God," Aubrey sighed.

"What?" Noelle cried, punching her playfully in the arm. "He's *cute*. And he's making good money."

He could never make enough money to tempt her. And he wasn't that cute. "Noelle, come on . . . he's not my type," Aubrey reminded her, gesturing to her clothes.

"Honey, he'd *be* your type with a little encouragement."

"No," Aubrey said, and defiantly began her sweeping. "I'm leaving Tourmaline as soon as I can —"

"You can take college extension classes at the annex, you know. It's only ten miles from here."

"But I don't want to. I have a *life* in San Diego."

"Okay, well, you're obviously going to be here for a few weeks. Why not have a little fun?"

There was no way Aubrey could possibly explain why she could never have fun here. Even her mother had never confided in Nancy about what went on in their house, Aubrey was certain of it. If she had, she was sure Nancy would have mentioned it. Actually, she was fairly certain Nancy would have done something about it.

"Because it *wouldn't* be fun," Aubrey said with a glower for Noelle.

"Well, okay . . . do you have a boyfriend in San Diego?"

"Noelle!" Aubrey complained. "I don't *need* a boyfriend. I have school, and I will have a job, and stop looking at me like that!"

"Like what?" Noelle asked, trying to look completely innocent.

"The bottom line is that I don't really *like* Keith. I don't want to date him — I don't care how much money he has or how cute you think he is. He and I aren't on the same wavelength."

Noelle sighed. Then shrugged. "Suit yourself . . . but I think you are making a big mistake. Keith is a great guy. And

Tourmaline isn't so bad when there are two of you."

"Noelle . . . ," Aubrey started. But she closed her mouth, pressed her lips together. Years of living with Zeke had taught her that anything she said would come back to haunt her. She liked Noelle — they'd formed a friendship they had not enjoyed growing up — but she couldn't confide in Noelle. If Aubrey could find it in her to be attracted to Keith somehow — which she knew she couldn't do — there would never be just two of them. There would be three, one casting a long shadow that would douse the light from her life. Not to mention living with the horror of what she suspected Zeke and Keith had done.

So she forced a smile and lifted her shoulders. "What can I say?"

Noelle groaned and resumed lifting the chairs and putting them on the table.

10

"Oh, she's *adorable,*" Mrs. Young said when she bent over Sarah's rolling walker and ran her hand over her dark curls the next day. "She certainly resembles you, doesn't she?"

Jonathan smiled proudly. "Some people see it, yeah."

"What's her name?"

"Tammy," he said, having reasoned it was safer not to use her real name. Alan would not be looking for Tammy Winslow, he'd be looking for Sarah Randall.

"Well, Tammy, darling, you're a sweetheart," Mrs. Young cooed.

Apparently pleased, Sarah bounced up and down in her seat.

"She'll be no trouble at all," Mrs. Young said to Jonathan. "She's an angel."

There was something familiar about Mrs. Young, something Jonathan couldn't quite name, but liked. She was round and soft the way a grandmother ought to be, had short gray hair that was brushed back, and wore a shirt that buttoned up the front and had two pockets. She'd come with a sack of children's books, some knitting, and a big metal lunch box, the kind that men carried to construction sites.

"I'm only going to be gone maybe an hour. Two, tops," he said, and picked up the piece of paper on which he'd written a variety of instructions. "I've got a list here of some, you know, stuff that she likes and doesn't like."

"All right," Mrs. Young said. Beside her, Sarah jumped up and down in her seat, babbling at the elderly woman.

"Her favorite food is oatmeal with applesauce. And she really likes bananas with apples and pears." He pointed to the containers of baby food he had lined up on the kitchen table. He wanted to make sure Mrs. Young had a variety to choose from. "But she doesn't like peas." He pointed to five containers on the top of the refrigerator, placed there so Sarah wouldn't even have to see them. He'd tried to introduce her to peas two days ago — she'd made a face, pushed the spoon away, and refused to eat them.

Mrs. Young chuckled. "Okay. No peas."

"And her bottle is here." He held it up. It

was already full — he'd mixed it. "There are two more in the fridge. She won't eat that much. But I just thought, you know, if I was hit by a bus or something —"

"I doubt you will be hit by a bus, Mr. Winslow. We don't have bus service in Tourmaline."

"Right."

Sarah had found his keys — she was banging them loudly on the tray of her rolling walker. He swooped down, took them gently from her so she wouldn't cry, and substituted a set of plastic teething keys, which she promptly put in her mouth.

Mrs. Young smiled, and the corners around her eyes crinkled in a way that reminded Jonathan of Reva. He felt instantly and surprisingly comfortable with this woman. "This cat's her favorite." He picked it up, showing it to Mrs. Young. Sarah instantly held out her hands for it. *"Keee,"* she said.

Jonathan nervously continued, showing Mrs. Young the paper. "There's my phone number, right there. If she doesn't want to eat or if she cries, you call me. Right away."

"Mr. Winslow," Mrs. Young said, reaching for Sarah, "you worry too much." Sarah went willingly; she seemed interested in Mrs. Young and put her hand on her nose.

"Tammy will be just fine." Mrs. Young lifted the baby's hand from her nose and kissed her palm. Sarah laughed. "I've had four babies of my own, six grandbabies, and I'd guess I've sat with dozens of babies over the years. We'll get along just fine . . . won't we, Tam-tam?"

Sarah stared at Mrs. Young.

"Yeah, well . . . Tammy's not used to strangers."

Mrs. Young smiled at him. "I know what it's like to be new in town. I'm still new here myself." At Jonathan's confused look, she laughed. "Granted, we came to town thirty years ago, but some old-timers at church still call us the new family, because not many people have come to Tourmaline since the mines shut down. All I am saying is that I know what it's like to be new in town. You don't know anyone, and you don't know who you can trust with your precious child."

"No offense," he said with a sheepish smile.

"None taken. But don't worry a moment longer, young man. I know what I am doing. And if something were to happen to this precious angel, I would know who to call."

Still . . . he cupped the back of Sarah's

head. She was fixated on the small cross that hung around Mrs. Young's neck.

"What does bring you to Tourmaline?" Mrs. Young asked cheerfully as she held the cross out for Sarah to take in her hand.

"It seemed like a cool place to settle down."

"Well, you couldn't have chosen a better place in America, in my opinion. I love Tourmaline. The people here are so friendly, and the schools are good. The people in this town have solid values."

"Yeah," Jonathan said, looking anxiously at Sarah. "That's exactly what I want for my baby."

Mrs. Young smiled again and looked at Sarah. "Where is little Tammy's mother? Will she be joining you?"

A knot of tension twisted in Jonathan's chest. This was precisely the kind of question he wanted to avoid. "She's . . . we're not together anymore."

Mrs. Young looked at him expectantly, clearly wanting more information.

But that was all she would ever get from him. Jonathan picked up his keys.

Sarah was bending over Mrs. Young's arms, her attention now on a red truck on the living room floor. "Good luck, Mr. Winslow. I am sure you will do fine."

Jonathan couldn't take his eyes off Sarah, in the arms of a woman he'd known for all of fifteen minutes. Fear began to build in him, and he muttered, *"No,"* to himself, hardly realizing he'd said a thing. "No," he said again, and stepped forward, taking Sarah from Mrs. Young's arms and holding her tightly to him.

Sarah didn't want to be held — she wanted the toy — and began to fuss in his arms.

But Jonathan couldn't let her go. He would kill himself if anything happened to her. He didn't know this woman! What if she was incompetent? What if Alan had gotten to her somehow? He wouldn't put anything past that man.

"Mr. Winslow —"

He turned his back to her and buried his face in Sarah's neck, inhaling the sweet scent of her skin, feeling the smoothness of it against his rough cheek. How could he possibly leave her with a stranger? How could he walk out the door and away from the most important thing in his life? He couldn't. He couldn't possibly.

"Mr. Winslow," Mrs. Young said again, her voice soft. She touched his shoulder. "Now you know that you can't provide for your baby like a father ought to do if you don't work. She'll be fine. You run on ahead now. The sooner you go, the sooner you can come back. You just call me every fifteen minutes if you have to, but you go on and do what you need to do."

Again, something in the woman's mannerisms reminded him of Reva — the slightest hint of a Southern accent, maybe, or the inflection in her voice. Whatever it was, it put him somewhat at ease. And she was right — if he was going to provide Sarah any kind of life, he had to get a job.

He kissed Sarah. "I'll be home soon. You won't even notice I've been gone."

Mrs. Young stepped in and took Sarah from his arms, setting her down on her feet. Sarah didn't seem to care that he was leaving — she rocked back and forth on her feet for a moment, then took a few, tentative steps before going down on her bottom. She didn't miss a beat — she began to crawl toward the red truck.

"Go on now, Mr. Winslow," Mrs. Young urged him.

Jonathan reluctantly did as she bid him. At the door, he took his jacket from a wall hook and shrugged into it, his eyes on Sarah. "You saw where I left the food, right? Bottles, too?"

"Indeed I did," Mrs. Young said, walking

behind him as he stepped out the door. "You don't want to be late," she added pleasantly but firmly. "We'll be here when you get back."

Jonathan had a glimpse of Sarah on the floor with the red truck as Mrs. Young pushed the door almost shut. "Good luck, Mr. Winslow!" she said cheerily through the crack, and closed the door.

Jonathan stood rooted to his spot, listening for Sarah's cries, which he was certain would follow. But several moments passed, and he heard nothing but Mrs. Young's pleasant voice.

He made himself step off the porch, made himself get in the car and start it up. He could feel a panic rising in him as he turned onto the highway, but he pressed the gas pedal to the floor and sped out of the gravel drive.

Five-year-old Lindsey Peters started running a fever that morning. When Nancy called her father, Steve Peters, who worked at Grace Construction, he refused to leave work to come and get her. Marsha Peters, Lindsey's mother, was stranded at home — she'd taken her car to the shop and didn't have a ride to come and get Lindsey.

Nancy, Noelle, and Aubrey jointly decided

that it was better if one of them took Lindsey home before she infected the entire group of kids.

"I can't go," Noelle said. "My gas tank is sitting on empty and I can't buy gas until we get paid."

"Well, I can't go," Nancy said. "The state inspector is coming by today."

Both women looked at Aubrey.

"Okay," she said with a sigh. "I'll go."

"Hey, it's not that big of a deal," Noelle said cheerfully. "You know Marsha and Steve, right?"

"Sure, I know them," Aubrey said, picking up her purse. Marsha was Tourmaline's answer to society. She liked to throw big parties around their pool. Aubrey could count on one hand the number of times she had actually spoken to Marsha. Steve Peters was another matter. He was a member of the Chamber of Commerce and considered himself something of a ladies' man. She was forever bumping into him around town, and he was forever making suggestive remarks to her.

But that wasn't the worst of it. Three days a week, Aubrey volunteered her time at a YMCA late-afternoon program designed for special-needs kids. It was the only program in the community for them — most of them had Down syndrome, but there were some with autism, too. The program was run by a social worker and three volunteers, and the goal was to teach the kids socialization skills with the hope that one day, they could function in society.

It so happened that the Peterses' oldest son, Mark, had Down syndrome. Aubrey had run into Marsha one day and suggested they think about putting Mark in the program.

An expression had come over Marsha's face that was half-incredulous, half-fearful. *"No,"* she'd said instantly, shaking her head. "We can't do that! Mark is sixteen. He's too old —"

"But he's not," Aubrey had quickly interjected. "There are actually four teens in the program."

"Aubrey, I appreciate what you are trying to do, but that's not going to work for us," Marsha said firmly. And she'd hurried off before Aubrey could convince her.

She'd even made a couple of subsequent phone calls to Marsha, hoping to tell her a little more about the program, but they'd ended abruptly. The last call had ended with Marsha trying to remain calm as Steve bellowed in the background he wasn't putting his son in a room with a bunch of retards and telling Marsha to hang up the damn phone.

"Oh, hey, Aubrey, can you pick up a check while you're over there?" Nancy said, taking Lindsey's lunch box down from the shelf. "The Peterses are two months behind again."

"Nancy, no — don't make me!" Aubrey protested. "You know how I hate the business end of the work!"

"I'm not particularly fond of it either," Nancy said cheerfully. "But it's the sixth account in arrears this month." She smiled at Aubrey. "Joan was so much better at this than me."

Aubrey groaned. She really missed her mother and knew Nancy did, too. "Fine," Aubrey said with a sigh of resignation. She turned around and looked for Lindsey. The little girl was sitting at a table with her head down. "Poor kid." Aubrey took the lunch box from Nancy and walked over to Lindsey. "Hey, kiddo," Aubrey said, squatting down next to her. "You want to go home?"

Lindsey nodded her head.

"Then come on." Aubrey hoisted the girl up into her arms. Lindsey wrapped her legs around Aubrey and laid her head on her shoulder.

"I'll see you guys later," Aubrey said, and carried Lindsey to her car.

11

Steve Peters — the new owner of Grace Construction whose father had retired last year to make room for Steve, according to Cheryl, the office secretary — kept Jonathan waiting a half hour.

He finally sauntered in, a thirtysomething guy wearing steel-toed work boots, a denim jacket, and jeans that were covered in dust.

"Any messages, Cheryl?" Peters asked as he glanced at Jonathan from the corner of his eye.

"Four. And your wife called. She said they need a check at the day care."

"Somebody always wants something, don't they?" He sighed and quickly shuffled through the pink slips of messages she had given him.

"You've got an appointment," Cheryl added, nodding toward Jonathan.

"Yeah, I know." Peters turned his head and looked at Jonathan.

Jonathan stood up.

Peters turned to face him fully then, slowly sizing him up, from the top of his head and the hair he'd pulled back in a ponytail, the three-day growth of beard, and on down to the tips of his boots.

Jonathan extended his hand. "J. B. Winslow."

Peters looked at his hand a moment, then reluctantly took it, shook it quickly, and let go. "What's J.B. stand for?"

Jonathan shrugged. "Been so long, I've forgotten."

"Really?" Peters said, eyeing him closely. "It's been so long you forgot your *name?*"

"I've always been J.B."

Peters did not smile. He motioned toward an adjoining office, the door of which was propped open with project books. "Come on in." He turned around, walking ahead of Jonathan, stepping around rolls of blueprints, over skill saws and various sizes of PVC pipe that had been cut from one thing or another.

The office was just as cluttered as the reception area — tile squares were stacked against one wall, and on the opposite wall, a huge eraser board had some drawings of an electrical system hastily scribbled.

"Have a seat," Peters said, and walked

around behind the desk, sat in a creaky old leather chair, and propped one boot against the edge of the desk. "So . . . J.B. who can't remember his name, you're looking for a job."

"That's right."

"Got any experience in construction?"

"I worked for my stepfather back East. He built hospitals and commercial buildings."

"And you worked on those projects?" Peters asked, looking at Jonathan's arms.

Jonathan nodded.

"Anyone who can verify that you did?"

"You mean a reference?"

Peters chuckled derisively. "Yeah, J.B. A reference."

Jonathan knew this was coming and had prepared for this. "Unfortunately, no." He forced a sad smile. "My stepfather . . . my stepfather was killed on a job —"

"Work-related?"

What the hell did he mean, work-related? "He wasn't murdered, if that's what you mean," Jonathan joked. "A crane hit him."

"A crane."

"Yep. A crane swung around and smacked him in the head."

Peters's eyes narrowed.

"Killed him instantly. It was a real mess," Jonathan said with a grimace.

"Tragic." Peters clasped his hands behind the back of his head.

"Yep. Tragic. The company went belly-up after that — we lost contracts and couldn't make payroll. So my mom, she disbanded the company."

"Wow."

Jonathan clasped his hands tightly together. "There's no one around who can vouch for me."

Peters nodded, then abruptly sat up and propped his elbows on the edge of the desk. "I don't know, J. B. Winslow," he said, squinting at him. "I find it's kind of hard to hire a guy when I can't check him out. You know what I mean?"

"I know what I am doing."

"I don't think I can use you."

Jonathan thought quickly. Peters was looking at him like he was a piece of trash, and he didn't like it. "Look," he said, his smile fading. "I *need* this job. You need someone who can work. Just give me a chance."

"Come on, dude," Peters said with a laugh. "Why should I?"

"I have a baby girl. I need to work, man," Jonathan said sternly.

Peters shrugged and leaned back again. "Sounds like a personal problem." He flashed a cocky smile. "I mean, sure, every

141

man's got to do what he needs to do for his family. But that doesn't mean I have to hire some shady new guy in town with no references who can't remember his own name. I'd be crazy to do something like that."

Jonathan leaned forward and pinned him with a look. "You need good workers. And I'm a good, hard worker."

"Too bad there's no one to vouch for that."

Jonathan was about to tell him what he could do with his job when a woman's voice interrupted them. "*I* can vouch for him."

He knew instantly who it was. He jerked around and saw Aubrey standing in the doorway. She looked at him uncertainly.

"Well, well, if it isn't Aubrey Cross," Peters said. "Look at you, sweetheart. You look like you're in a punk rock band."

She looked at Peters and her posture changed. She stood up straighter and gave him a seductive smile. She moved into the room, her hips swinging in a sultry, feminine way that definitely got Jonathan's attention — and Peters's, too, by the look of it. She was wearing some tight camouflage pants, a pair of heeled boots, and a cropped V-neck T-shirt pulled over another T-shirt that hugged her body closely and was short enough that Jonathan could see the bare skin of her abdomen.

The woman had some outstanding curves.

And Peters was devouring her with his gaze, his eyes cruising her breasts and her hips. Frankly, up until this moment, Jonathan had not realized just how hot Aubrey was. Until now, she had seemed more moppet than seductress. But she was looking at Peters in a way that made Jonathan feel a little warm under the collar.

"So you can vouch for this guy, huh?" Peters scoffed.

"Yeah." Aubrey stuffed her hands in her back pockets. "I know him."

"What's his name?"

She laughed. "J.B."

Peters's gaze flicked between Jonathan and Aubrey. "J.B. what?"

Aubrey's smile deepened. "Come on, Steve. You know you need the help." She put one hand against his desk and leaned over it. "J.B. does good work. You're a fool if you let him go."

"You've seen his work," Steve said disbelievingly as he checked out Aubrey's cleavage.

"You'd be doing me and my friend a favor."

Steve grinned wolfishly and cocked his head to get a look at her rear end. "What sort of favor, sweetheart?"

"Not *that* kind of favor, Steve. You're married, remember? You know what I mean," she said silkily. "And besides, the sheriff would really like to see that recreation center you're building finished as soon as possible."

Peters shifted his gaze to her eyes. Neither of them spoke, but Jonathan could almost feel the current running between them.

Peters suddenly looked at Jonathan. "Well, J.B., it looks like you got yourself a job — with a probationary period of three months. The first time you screw up, or we find out something we don't like about you, you're outta there." Peters stood up, leaned over the side of the desk, and picked up a beat-up hard hat. He tossed it to Jonathan, who caught it with one hand. "Come in here at eight sharp Monday morning and fill out the paperwork, then Cheryl will direct you to the job site."

"Thanks," Jonathan said, grinning. He stole a quick look at Aubrey, then nodded at Peters. "You won't regret it."

"Yeah, well, I'll be the judge of that." Peters pointed to the door. "Cheryl can give you the wage scale on your way out."

Jonathan looked at Aubrey again, but she averted her gaze as he walked out.

When he'd left, Steve looked at Aubrey and smirked. "Is that your boyfriend or something?"

"No, but he's a good guy."

"Looks like a thug to me. If one thing goes missing from that job site, I'm going to come looking for you, sweetheart."

"He's not going to steal," Aubrey said, annoyed. "Just give the guy a chance, Steve."

"Are you deaf? I gave him the job! Anyway, forget that punk for now — you got your favor. Now maybe you can do me one," he said with a leer.

"I'm already doing you a favor," she said coolly, and thrust the day care bill at him. "I am keeping Lindsey in day care. But you need to pay up."

His expression turned dark, but he opened a desk drawer and pulled out a ledger, which he slapped down on the desk. "Why are you always so cold?"

"I'm not cold. I am just asking that you pay for the services we've provided your daughter for the last two months. It's not a free babysitting service, you know."

"Always had that air of superiority, that look about you that says you think you're better than everyone else in Tourmaline," he said angrily, ignoring her.

Why did people keep *saying* that? She'd

never done anything but try to keep her distance, and that had nothing to do with a feeling of superiority, but everything to do with the secret she carried, and more important, with self-preservation. When she was younger, she'd been petrified of earning Zeke's wrath, and it never took much to bring it out.

Steve yanked the check free of the ledger and thrust it at her. "Here's your money, Aubrey."

She looked at the check. "Thank you," she said, and folded it in half. "I'll leave you to do whatever it is you do." She stuck the check in her back pocket.

"You know what, Aubrey?" Steve snapped. "You'd do really well to smile once in a while. You know, try and strike up a friendly conversation with folks. You'd get along a lot better in this town if you did."

It was ridiculous, but his admonishment stung a little. She didn't think she was so awful, but he made her sound like a cold monster. "Don't worry," she said bitterly, "I'm not planning to be in this town a moment longer than I have to."

"Good," he said behind her as she walked out.

Good, she thought as she pushed the door open and strode out into the bright California sunshine. Frankly, she couldn't *wait* to get out of Tourmaline. She couldn't wait to get away from narrow-minded little men like Steve Peters and Zeke Cross.

She marched across the parking lot, anxious to get out of there. She didn't see J.B. until she all but walked straight into him as she rounded a van that was sticking too far out in the lane. J.B. was leaning back against the hood of his car, his arms folded.

"Oh!" she exclaimed when she saw him. "I . . . I didn't see you there."

"Hey," he said, looking at her as if he was trying to make out who or what she was.

"What?" she asked, eyeing him curiously.

"Question for you — what the hell was *that?*" he asked, gesturing to the office.

Great. Couldn't anyone ever say *thank you* anymore?

12

Copper eyes flashed with a woman's ire; Aubrey punched her fists to her hips and glared at him. "I'm so sorry," she said with mock airiness. "I thought you *needed* my help. My mistake."

And she began to walk.

"Wait," Jonathan said, and quickly fell in behind her. "How did you know I was here? Are you following me?"

"*Following* you?" she echoed incredulously. "Oh my God. Believe it or not, J.B., I happened to be over here for something that had nothing to do with *you.*"

"Okay," he said, trying to be patient. "Then why?"

She stopped so suddenly he almost collided with her back and turned to look at him as if she thought he were insane. "Why *what?*"

"Why did you help me?" he demanded. "What's in it for you?"

Something in her gaze sparked, and for a moment Jonathan thought she was going to launch herself at him. She didn't launch, but she did suddenly shove him with two hands planted firmly in his chest. "What is the matter with you?" she cried. "Are you always so paranoid? Can't a person just help out once in a while? Does there have to be a *reason* or a payoff?"

"Yes," he answered honestly. Aubrey gaped at him. With a sigh, Jonathan dragged his fingers through his hair as he tried to work it out. He couldn't imagine why she would have helped him like that if she didn't want something in return. But she looked so furious with him at the moment that he considered the possibility that maybe he'd missed the mark. "I'm not used to people taking up for me."

"Clearly," Aubrey said pertly. "Look, I thought you needed my help. So I helped. That's it. No conspiracy, no ulterior motive. I was behaving like a human being. Is that so hard to understand?"

"He was about to tell me to get lost," Jonathan reluctantly acknowledged.

Aubrey snorted and glanced at the office. "Yeah, well, Steve has some very definite ideas about what people should be like. Okay? Are you satisfied? Am I allowed to leave now?" She didn't wait for an answer — she turned around.

"Hey." Jonathan unthinkingly touched her arm. He might as well have touched her with a cattle prod — she jumped about that high. "Hey, hey, calm down. I'm just trying to talk to you."

"I think we've talked enough. I've got to go." She pointed her key fob at a red Jetta and punched a button. The car responded with a flash of taillight and a chirp. Aubrey walked to the driver's door and reached for the handle.

But Jonathan wasn't ready to let her go. Something down in the pit of him didn't want her to go, felt a need to thank her. "Aubrey . . . will you *wait* a minute?" he insisted, and this time, caught her arm, making her turn around to face him.

Aubrey shook him off. "I thought you wanted the job and I was trying to help. I know you don't like me to help, you've made that perfectly clear, but I was thinking of your baby. You need that job for her."

Jonathan had never had such a hard time thanking someone in his life, and he couldn't help but smile at her fiery determination not to be thanked. "I know I need the job — I'm trying to thank you for helping me *get* the job. Like I said, I'm not used to people trying to help me out, and I can't figure out why you would."

"Wow," she said, squinting at him. "You really must be jaded. Okay, listen, it was the least I could do." Her voice was softer. "I wanted to help you after you helped me in the parking lot the other day. I mean . . . not that I really *needed* your help — I could have handled it — but it was nice of you to come to my aid. Very noble."

He kept quiet, but there was no way this little pip-squeak could have handled that business in the supermarket parking lot. What was she, maybe five feet six? Small frame . . . and lips and eyes that could make a man's mouth water. No, she definitely could not have handled it.

"No problem," he said, his gaze on her mouth.

Aubrey gave him a curious look and self-consciously pushed her hair behind her ear. "Anyway . . . I was just returning the favor."

"And I was just saying thanks. We're even."

She seemed to accept that and gave him an appraising look. "So . . . are you planning on staying in Tourmaline?"

He shrugged noncommittally out of habit, not wanting to give away anything.

Her eyes narrowed and she seemed suddenly irritated. "You know what, J.B.? You can do me a favor."

"What's that?"

"You can take your pretty little girl and get the hell out of Tourmaline. This is no place for a baby — or you, for that matter."

"What?" He laughed. "What are you talking about? This seems like a great town."

"No." Aubrey shook her head. "It's *not* a great little town. It may look that way on the surface, but trust me, there's nothing great about it. You'll be doing yourself a huge favor if you get out now."

Jonathan's smile faded. He tried to read her, to figure out where this was coming from. Mrs. Young had extolled the virtues of Tourmaline. Even Steve Peters hadn't turned Jonathan completely off it — he figured Peters had a right to be suspicious of a man with no background.

Aubrey's fingers began to flutter against her key chain. She was nervous, he realized, but he didn't know if he made her nervous, or if it was something else.

"What's going on —"

"Nothing!"

She spoke far too adamantly for it to be nothing. "My kid likes it here," he said, wondering why he was explaining himself to her.

"Oh, great. Just great," Aubrey said petulantly, and reached for her car door, yanking it open.

"What is wrong with you?" Jonathan asked as she slipped into the driver's seat. "It's really none of your business what I do."

"I know, it's none of my business." She glared out the front window a moment. "I would just hate to see anything happen to that little girl."

Jonathan felt a surge of panic. He put his hand on her arm to keep her from closing the door. "What? What do you know about my daughter?"

"I told you, Tourmaline is no place to raise a kid. That's my advice — you can take it or leave it." She grabbed the door handle and pulled it shut, forcing Jonathan to remove his hand before she shut the car door on him. And just like that, she was gone, her little car going much too fast as she turned onto the main road that ran in front of the construction offices.

Jonathan absently chewed a nail as he watched her turn right and speed toward town. She was a mystery, that one. One minute he was thinking she was pretty as hell, and the next he was thinking she was a nut job.

He shrugged and turned back to his car. Something was bothering her, he told himself. An old boyfriend, a nowhere job. Maybe it was just boredom — there wasn't much happening in Tourmaline by the look of it, and maybe that was what she meant. But a little town without a lot going on appealed to him. It seemed the perfect place for Sarah. And he was confident that Alan would never think to look here.

And maybe, just maybe, she really was a little nut job. Sarah's biological mother, Lizzie Spaulding, was pretty and had turned out to be certifiably insane — maybe this woman was, too. He tossed the hard hat he'd left on the top of his car into the backseat and drove out of the parking lot, his thoughts now on Sarah. He was anxious to get back and see how she'd fared with Mrs. Young.

As for Aubrey Cross? By the time he turned onto the highway leading to his house, he'd forgotten everything about her except the way her eyes shimmered when she was mad.

Jonathan wasn't the only one thinking about eyes. Aubrey was thinking of his, too, and how they peered so intently at her, boring through the facade she had learned to put up years ago. It made her feel exposed and vulnerable and furious.

And okay, she couldn't help it, but it made her feel hot and bothered inside, made her feel as if she were *churning* from just a touch. That made her crazy. She did not want to be so wildly attracted to him — the guy was absolutely nuts, bordering on some paranoid personality disorder if he wasn't already there. So what was it about him that made her so crazy?

Okay, yes, he was hot, she decided as she pulled into the parking lot of Bright Horizons Day Care — about as gorgeous as any man she'd ever seen. He was built like a sculpture — big and muscular and with hands so large that they could span her rib cage, were he ever to touch her there, which he so would not do.

He was mysterious, too. Seriously, what was a young single man with an infant daughter doing in Tourmaline? Her curiosity was killing her, and on top of that, it made her feel as if she related to him on some level. He seemed like an outsider, just like her.

"Okay, *enough,*" Aubrey muttered. She was not going to start fantasizing about some hot guy who could, for all she knew, be completely psycho. So what if he was going to stay in Tourmaline with that cute, cute little girl? It was stupid, but, hey, it was his life. *She,* on the other hand, was *not* going to stay in Tourmaline, and the sooner she got out of here, the better. Maybe she'd have a chat with Nancy this afternoon to talk about how things were going. Maybe she could leave work today with a firm date of when she would be departing Tourmaline once and for all.

Aubrey turned off her car and was gathering her things when she heard a car door shut. She glanced in her rearview mirror and saw a portion of a big, black pickup truck behind her. When she opened the door and got out, she suppressed a groan. Keith Stanley was sauntering toward her, a smile on his face.

"I saw you pulling up, and I decided to say hello."

"Hello, Keith." She glanced at the door of the day care and the brightly colored animals that had been painted along the front of the building. "I can't really talk — we're a little shorthanded."

"I won't keep you." He propped an arm on top of her car, effectively blocking her in between him and the open car door. He smiled down at her, shaking his head with bemusement as he took in her camouflage pants. "Looks like you're going hunting or something."

When Aubrey glowered at him, he quickly changed tack. "I was driving down Elm Street on my way back to the office and I saw you talking to that new guy."

That caught Aubrey off guard. "What? *Who?*" she asked dumbly, knowing full well who.

"That hippie-looking guy I've seen around town a couple of times now. You were talking to him outside of Grace Construction."

Her hackles rose instantly. "Are you *spying* on me?" she snapped.

Keith looked up from his perusal of her body, his smile gone. "Just wondered if you had something going on with him."

Aubrey was so stunned, she didn't know what to say. She didn't know where to *begin.* "Okay, Keith —"

"I was just wondering if that's why you're not interested in seeing me, because you're seeing someone else," he continued with a bit of an edge to his tone. "But then I wondered how you could be seeing him so quickly — he's only been around a couple of days as far as I can tell."

"Are you serious?" She clutched her satchel to her like a shield. "Are you seriously prying into my business? Like you have some *right* to pry into my business?"

He didn't move, didn't so much as blink,

but stood there waiting for her to answer.

Aubrey bristled. "I can't believe this. It's none of your concern who I see or don't see, Keith. We dated a few times *four years* ago. That's it. You have no right to ask me anything or *assume* anything. And for the record, I am not *seeing* him. I was just talking to him. As far as I know, that's not yet a crime in Tourmaline."

"I'm just asking, Aubrey. That's not a crime, either. Can't a guy ask a simple question?"

"There are never any simple questions in Tourmaline, and you know it," she said angrily. "I really have to get back to work. Will you let me by?"

He looked at her once more, his gaze piercing hers, then slowly backed up and dropped his arm.

Aubrey quickly shut the car door and walked away without another word. When she entered the day care, she shut the door firmly behind her.

"Are you all right?" Noelle asked as Aubrey stood with her back to the door.

Aubrey shook her head to clear it. "I'm fine!" she said with false cheer. "And what's even better, I got the Peterses' check." She hurried to the office before Noelle could question her further.

In his truck, Keith sat and watched the door to the day care for a long moment. He finally took his cell phone off the hands-free device and punched in a number.

"Hello?"

"Sheriff, Keith Stanley."

"Hello there, Keith! Good to hear from you. You doing all right?"

"Fine, fine," Keith said congenially. "I just remembered I owed you a beer on that bet we made on the SC and UCLA game last week. Thought maybe you'd like to grab it sometime next week."

"I haven't forgotten," the sheriff said with a snort. "I wondered when you were going to pay up. Did you see that game? My deputy had to peel me from the ceiling," he said with a chuckle.

"I saw the game. And I am a man who pays his debts. So when are you free?" Keith asked, and arranged to meet Sheriff Cross for a little man-to-man chat.

13

Sarah lit up with a smile when Jonathan came through the door and instantly started babbling as she held her chubby arms out to him.

He scooped her up from the blanket Mrs. Young had put down, where she was playing with her musical and light-flashing piano. Mrs. Young appeared from the kitchen, wiping her hands on a dish towel, and smiled warmly. "There, you see? She's just fine."

"Oh, no," Jonathan said, grinning at her, "the munchkin's not fine. She's perfect." He kissed the baby's face a dozen times and put her down. Sarah took a couple of steps before going down and crawling for a toy.

"Did you have any trouble?" he asked anxiously.

"Not at all. She's an angel," Mrs. Young said with a beaming smile.

"Did she eat?"

"Every bit I put in front of her."

"What about a nap?"

"She had her nap and she's been up a half hour. She was *fine,* Mr. Winslow. She was as good a baby as any I have ever kept." Mrs. Young folded the dish towel neatly and handed it to Jonathan. "How did your job search go?"

"Good. Got a job with Grace Construction. I start Monday."

"Oh, that's wonderful news!" She seemed, Jonathan thought, genuinely pleased for him. "That's a solid outfit. My husband was good friends with Mr. Peters. Poor man had a heart attack and retired last year and now his son Steve has taken it over. I've always heard good things about the company."

That was good to know, Jonathan thought. Maybe his initial meeting with Steve Peters wasn't the best indicator of how the job would go. He fished a few bills out of his wallet and handed them to Mrs. Young, who took them graciously and put them in her purse.

"Now you call me anytime you need a sitter, you hear me? I will be more than happy to sit with that angel." She picked up her tote with all her things. "Are you going to need me to sit on Monday? I have an appointment with the beauty shop at two in the afternoon, so we'll have to make accommodations —"

"That's okay," Jonathan said, but lost his train of thought as he noticed a stack of folded clothing on the kitchen table. He hadn't left the clothes there. He'd left them on the floor of his closet.

Mrs. Young followed his gaze. "Oh, I did a little laundry for you. I figure you had enough on your hands."

Jonathan shot her a suspicious gaze. "You did my *laundry?*"

She laughed. "I just straightened up a little while Tammy was sleeping. I've never met a man yet who was worth a darn at laundry, so I thought I'd lend a hand."

He could feel his blood start to rush. He had to restrain himself from turning to see if she'd discovered his hiding place beneath the floorboards. That was probably ridiculous — how could she find it? And if Mrs. Young had seen anything, if she *knew* anything, she was playing it awfully cool.

Nevertheless, he'd feel better once he checked it out.

She dug for her keys in her bag and then, having found them, hoisted the bag over her shoulder. "What do you plan to do with Tammy on Monday?" she asked pleasantly.

Jonathan watched her closely for any sign

that she knew something, any glimmer in her eye. "I'm taking her to day care. Bright Horizons."

"Oh!" Mrs. Young said happily. "Nancy Fischer runs that day care, and she is the best. You couldn't possibly do better than her day care in *any* town, I promise you that. You be sure and tell her I said hello," she said as she opened the door.

"Will do," he said, following her out on the porch, his hand clenching and unclenching, anxious to check his hiding place.

Mrs. Young paused on the porch and inhaled deeply. "Good clean air." She smiled up at Jonathan. "You won't get that in a big city or anywhere around Los Angeles. You've chosen the right spot, Mr. Winslow. I predict you and Tammy will be very happy here."

He watched her walk out to her car. She turned and waved, called up a cheery reminder for him to call her anytime, then drove off in her large, old tank of a Buick.

When he could no longer see her car, he hurried back inside. Ignoring Sarah's cries for his attention, he grabbed the FOR RENT sign from behind the drapes where he'd left it, and using the tip of the signpost, he pried up the loose floorboard. The briefcase was still inside, still wrapped in the shirt. He pulled it up, pushed the shirt open, spun the combination lock, and yanked open the top.

It looked the same, untouched. He released the breath he hadn't even realized he was holding. Sarah was crying harder, crawling toward him, her knees dark from dirt on the wood floor. "Coming!" He closed the briefcase and locked it, then put it down beneath the floor again as Sarah reached the FOR RENT sign and began to bang on it. He replaced the floorboard, took the sign from Sarah, and slid it under the couch and out of her reach. She wailed, but he scooped her up and kissed her cheek. "Munchkin, don't you ever let Mrs. Young under the floorboard. If she goes near it, you start howling, you hear me?" He kissed her again. "Come on, let's take a little walk." Mrs. Young was right about one thing — the air here was as clear as he imagined it was in heaven.

He spent the weekend puttering around his new house, trying to make it feel as homey as Reva's house felt to him. He only ventured into town twice: once to grab a bite at the diner with Sarah, and the second time to stock up on groceries before the work-week. At the diner, Randi, the same waitress he'd had before, waited on him and gave Sarah a little stuffed penguin. She loved that penguin and alternately chewed it and banged it on the table. From Randi he learned a fair would be starting next week. "People come from miles around," she said. "It's a great place to take the family."

Jonathan thought he had to be the luckiest guy on the planet. A great little town with a fair was almost something out of a book. He was surprised by how much he liked it.

But he was brought down to earth at the supermarket. He had the uncomfortable feeling that more than one person was looking at him a little too closely, a little too disapprovingly.

That ate at him, made him wonder who was right about Tourmaline — Mrs. Young? Or Aubrey? He pondered what Aubrey had said, to get out now, and how adamantly she'd said it.

As he went through the weekend, it continued to eat at him. He felt a little at sea, uncertain of his own judgments. He wondered what Mrs. Young would say to Aubrey's declaration that all that was good about this town was just a facade for darker things going on.

But what could that possibly be? This

place seemed too wholesome for anything nefarious to be happening. Jonathan still couldn't be certain it was anything more than Aubrey's personal baggage that gave her such a pessimistic view. Nevertheless, it bothered him.

On the eve of his first day at work, Sarah was unusually fussy. Jonathan worried about her — her health had been good lately, but at one time she had not been so healthy, and every bit of fever, every bit of unusual fussiness, filled him with a sense of helpless panic.

She was not running a fever — he checked it with a thermometer — but she cried when he put her down and clung to him when he held her. And she kept looking over his shoulder as if she expected someone to come walking through the door at any moment.

Jonathan knew his kid, and he knew something was not quite right with her. He paced as he held her, trying to calm her down. He rocked her in the rocking chair he'd bought in Tourmaline, but she just tried to crawl off his lap. She squirmed in her high chair and kept trying to look out the door.

"What?" he asked her more than once. "No fever, no wet diaper, no teeth coming in," he said as he ran his palm over her head. "What's wrong with you?"

Sarah's response was to raise her chubby arms to him. He was at a loss what to do. She was a good baby, but this was one of those times when he really missed Reva. His mother was wild and unorthodox in many respects, but she was a good grandmother, and she always seemed to know what was wrong with Sarah.

"Come on, kid," he said as he tried to divert her with an alphabet toy that lit up and sang a song about each letter, "what is it?" She pushed the toy away and wailed desperately.

Even a bath — one of Sarah's favorite activities — didn't soothe her. Jonathan felt helpless and ignorant. He silently berated himself for ever having believed he could be a father. Frustrated with his inability to soothe his daughter, Jonathan finally put her down in her crib and stood on the other side of the door, his back to the wall, his face twisted in agony as he listened to her scream herself to sleep.

She did, at last, drift into sleep, but Jonathan didn't. He'd slipped into an old and bad habit of second-guessing himself. What if Sarah was getting sick again? He was stuck in a little town with no one to help him, and the closest hospital was in San Diego.

He slept fitfully. Every sound Sarah made woke him, and several times he sat up, listening. But she was just cooing in her sleep.

At some point in the night, however, he heard Sarah calling out to him, *"Da, da, da, da . . ."* It was her name for him, the thing she said when he held her and she put her hand on his nose and mouth. *"Da da da da . . ."*

He bolted upright, straining to hear. Just when he thought he'd dreamed it, Sarah began to jabber and laugh, as if she were talking to someone. He pushed his legs over the edge of the bed, listening. She continued to jabber away, even squealing with delighted laughter at one point. Curious, he stood up and leaned to his left. He could see the room was illuminated by moonlight.

He padded across the floor; as he moved closer, he could see Sarah standing in her crib. She held on to the rail with one hand, and she pounded the palm of her other hand against it, or held on and rocked back and forth with excitement as she continued to babble. It struck him as extremely odd, and frankly, it scared the hell out of him. Sarah was good about sleeping through the night — he'd never seen her do this. Moreover, looking at Sarah from an angle as he was, he could swear she was talking *to* someone. "Sarah!" he said sharply, and lurched toward the door, catching himself on the jamb.

Sarah laughed with pleasure when she saw him and pounded the railing harder as she shifted her gaze to something near the closet.

Jonathan followed her gaze — and felt his breath leave his lungs.

Tammy.

14

He thought he was dreaming, that Tammy had come to him in a dream. He could even smell her perfume. But as he moved across Sarah's small room to her, he stepped on a toy and realized this was no dream. That was really Tammy standing there in a milky white haze, smiling at him.

His heart skipped. He raised his hand, palm up. "Tammy?" he whispered. "How are you here? Where did you come from?"

She didn't speak, but turned and glanced at him over her shoulder as she disappeared into shadows.

Jonathan hesitated — Sarah was still babbling, still rocking back and forth as she gripped the railing, cooing happily after Tammy. But the lure of Tammy was too great — Jonathan strode after her, to the spot where she'd disappeared. As he neared it, something happened.

Inexplicably, he was standing on Main

Street in Springfield. Tammy was there, too, beside him, wearing jeans, a red sweater with sparkly things on it over a white T-shirt, and a red coat. She smiled up at him, her eyes full of gaiety. "You followed me."

He couldn't find his voice or make himself move. He was paralyzed by her eyes, as big as blue china saucers, and so startlingly real.

"Good. I wasn't sure if you'd be able to come back here. I wasn't sure if *I'd* be able to come back here." She laughed. "If people thought it was weird for us to be together before, what would they think now?"

Everything ceased to exist for Jonathan; everything moved in slow motion as his heart ground to a painful halt. He was rooted in the common of Main Street, surrounded by so many people he knew from Springfield. He didn't understand how it was possible, how Tammy could be there, too, walking into the middle of the common, then turning around to him, her arm extended. "Aren't you going to say anything to me? It's been a while," she said.

"It feels like forever," whispered Jonathan. Then he caught himself. "What are you doing? What is this?"

"I put a lot of work into you, Jonathan Randall. Loving you wasn't always easy, but it was always worth it. And just because I left doesn't mean you get to go back to who you were. It doesn't mean you get to close up shop."

Jonathan wanted to rub his eyes, but he was afraid that if he closed them for an instant, closed them even to blink, she'd be gone again. *Make it real,* he told himself. *Act as if it's real.* He moved up beside Tammy. "My life without you in it, it's . . ." He faltered, but tried to explain. "Sarah helps, but it's dark. The light you brought to it . . ."

Tammy finished his thought: "It's still there, Jonathan. That doesn't go away."

She turned away from him and suddenly leaped up on a bench. "Hey, Springfield! Listen up! I am Tammy Winslow and I have something to announce!" she shouted, just as she had one cold fall morning when she was alive. She'd thrilled him then, announcing her love for him to the entire city. "I love Jonathan Randall! Deal with it! I am in *love* with Jonathan Randall!" she shouted again, then fell back laughing.

Jonathan lunged to catch her, felt her weight in his arms, but they were falling, landing on a bed covered in rose petals.

He was stunned by it for a moment and slowly stood up, looking around. The scent of roses filled the air. Champagne chilled next to a wedding cake, and dozens of candles illuminated a room. Jonathan recognized it as where he and Tammy had made love on their wedding night.

Tammy wasn't in his arms or on the bed, but standing a few feet away from him, wearing the strapless, beaded wedding gown she'd worn to marry him.

Just as she had that day, she took his breath away — he could not imagine a more beautiful sight. "You look like a princess," he said reverently.

"I felt like a princess that day," she said, and twirled around, catching the long veil in her hand with a soft laugh. "That day seemed like the end of a long journey, didn't it?"

"No," Jonathan said, shaking his head. "The beginning."

"We'd been through so much," Tammy said, as if he hadn't spoken. "Fighting not to be in love, then hiding it until finally . . ." She moved closer to him. "*Finally* . . . marrying you was the best day of my life."

Jonathan choked as a rush of emotion filled him. "Come back, Tammy. For good. You're here. You don't have to leave," he said, reaching for her.

Tammy smiled at him with a wicked look in her eye and twirled around again. Her tiara twinkled in the candlelight, the wedding ring sparkling on her finger. "I can't come back, Jonathan. I'm only a memory."

"You're real. To me you're real."

"Nope," she said with a smile. "Just a memory. Close your eyes and remember."

"If I close my eyes, you'd better still be here when I open them," he demanded.

"Close your eyes," she whispered.

Jonathan refused until it seemed as if her long veil surrounded them both, surrounded him, making it difficult for him to see her. . . .

How could he bear to remember what had happened in this room? It had been the most magical night of his life. He had carried her across the threshold, had deposited her on the bed, and knelt down beside her.

And now, Jonathan went down on one knee. He felt like he was moving in a dream, but her hand was in his, her fingers long and delicate, folded over his, as he kissed her wedding band.

When he reached for her, touched her body — he knew it was Tammy, he knew her body as well as his own. He knew how her slender waist flared into her hips, how her breasts filled his hands, how his hand spanned her rib cage.

He felt all that in his hands, and the row of tiny buttons on the back of her gown. As he had done their wedding night, his fingers flew down the buttons, opening her gown, baring her soft skin, which smelled like lilacs to him. He pushed the gown from her body, his palms sliding over her smooth, warm skin.

Jonathan turned her around. He could only see the shadow of her face, but he kissed her, groaning when his lips touched hers. They were Tammy's lips — he knew the taste and shape of them, the feel of her tongue against his.

Things began to move in a blur of hot desire. Her hair fell from its coif, brushing against his cheek and his hands. Tammy's hands caressed him, her light caress arousing him to unimaginable desire. Jonathan could feel his hunger for her swelling in him, and he tried to encircle her in his arms, to press her body against his, to feel her body fit with his one more time, his body gliding in and out of hers, to hear her moans of pleasure, her breath hot on his neck . . .

But as he moved to hold her, he realized he was alone.

Jonathan squeezed his eyes shut and cried out in pain. "*No,* Tammy! I am not letting you go. You hear me? I'm not letting you leave again!" Tears of frustration and longing slid down his cheeks, but Tammy was gone, and in that dreamy fog, Jonathan wondered if she'd ever been there to begin with, or if it was his own sick grief that had led him to imagine this.

The weight of his grief pressed down on him, made him feel sick. He could never touch her again, could never taste her lips or feel her in his arms, and he collapsed to his knees. His head ached; he felt he would be ill at any moment.

Then everything went black.

He awoke to the sound of Sarah's babbling. He opened his eyes and squinted painfully at the first rays of morning sun streaming in through the window. Jonathan felt as if he'd been kicked all over; his head was heavy, his limbs felt even heavier. He pushed himself up to his elbows and glanced around — he was on the floor of Sarah's room. His foot was on top of the small red truck she loved, and he had a vague memory of stepping on it last night.

Tammy.

She'd been so *real.* Had he only imagined it? Dreamed it? Was he losing his mind? But he was here, wasn't he, in Sarah's room, lying at the spot where he'd first seen Tammy standing? How was it possible that he could have dreamed all that?

He drew his knees up, rested his arms on them, and rubbed his eyes. He'd been crying — his eyes felt swollen and his cheeks were still wet. "Great," he muttered into his hands. "I'm losing my freakin' mind."

Jonathan forced himself to stand up on rubbery legs. He dragged the back of his hand across his mouth and cheek, then stumbled to where Sarah stood in her crib and picked her up. "You saw her, too, didn't you, Munchkin?" he asked as she put her hand on his face.

"Ba ba ba ba ba ba."

"Yeah," he said, smoothing her wild little curls. "I saw her, too."

His mood did not improve as he readied himself for his new job, dressing in faded jeans, a long-sleeve T-shirt, and a distressed leather jacket, and prepared Sarah for her first time in day care. By the time he drove up to the yellow building painted with oddly colored animals that housed Bright Horizons Day Care, he was feeling nervous and antsy. He wasn't sure what had happened last night, but it made him feel even more anxious about leaving Sarah with strangers.

There was no way he could avoid it, so he got out of the car and began to gather her things. As he stuffed things into a duffel bag, he heard voices coming from somewhere and looked up. He didn't see anyone in the parking lot, but he noticed a little alleyway between the day-care center and a small but empty office building. He could hear the low tones of a man's voice, but then he heard and recognized a woman's voice.

Now what could Aubrey Cross be doing here? Jonathan stepped away from the car and leaned to his right. He could see Aubrey in that little alleyway, a walkway between buildings that had a bike rack and a bench for smokers. She was standing next to the bench, wearing a denim skirt with black, knee-length leggings, a pair of Doc Martens, a black T-shirt, and a light blue bandanna on her hair, having a conversation with a sheriff.

Maybe she'd decided after all to report the thugs who'd harassed her. Jonathan turned away and resumed gathering Sarah's things.

In the stillness of the morning, Jonathan could hear their conversation.

"Aubrey, I don't think you understand what I am trying to get across," the sheriff said.

"I speak English," Aubrey snapped.

Not the best way to speak to a sheriff, Jonathan thought, but decided it was none of his business. Aubrey was none of his business.

"Well, I can't help but wonder if you do. Now don't say anything, you'll just make a bad situation worse."

Jonathan slowly rose up out of his car with Sarah in his arms. He had no idea what Aubrey had done to attract the attention of the law, but whatever it was, he thought she was treading on dangerous ground.

"I mean, just look at you," the sheriff continued easily. "What do you expect people to think?"

The way the man was talking to Aubrey began to filter into his consciousness, and he felt a little nudge in the pit of his belly. The man's tone was easy, but something was just a little off with what he was saying.

It struck a raw and familiar nerve, and it made Jonathan's skin crawl with anger.

"I don't expect them to think anything!" Aubrey said, her voice rising slightly. "It's none of their business!"

"It's *my* business," the sheriff responded as Jonathan started in that direction. As he neared the entrance to the walkway, he saw the sheriff standing with one foot on a bike rack, leaning on his knee like a man engaged in a simple conversation, the way he might stand if he was talking about sports or a favorite television show. When the sheriff saw Jonathan, he straightened up and smiled. "Good morning! What can we do to help you?" he asked cheerfully.

Jonathan glanced at Aubrey, who was looking at the ground. "Can you tell me where to go to register my little girl? I'm putting her in day care today."

"Well, you've come to the right place. This is the best day care facility in all of Tourmaline," the sheriff said. "Just go inside there and Mrs. Fischer will be happy to help you out."

Jonathan realized he ought to go on, but Aubrey had yet to look up, and he knew something was wrong. "I tried that," he lied, walking deeper into the alley. "The door was locked. I could use a hand. I mean," he said, looking pointedly at the sheriff, "if you're through here."

"We're through," Aubrey said quickly. "I'll help you." She walked away, brushing past Jonathan in her hurry to get away from the sheriff.

"We'll speak later, Aubrey," the sheriff said congenially, but something about his smile did not sit right with Jonathan. It was a cold smile, and Jonathan knew that look — it wasn't the first time a law enforcement officer had looked at him like that. He turned away without another word, following Aubrey.

Aubrey was standing in front of his car, staring off in the opposite direction when Jonathan came around the corner. He didn't speak, and neither did she. He grabbed Sarah's duffel from the backseat and shut the door, then walked to where Aubrey was standing. From the corner of his eye he saw the sheriff striding toward a patrol truck parked on the street.

"What was *that* all about?" he said, skipping over a greeting.

"That?" She flicked a hand toward the alley. "Nothing. Hey, I didn't know you were the new guy who called last week to bring your daughter here," she said, trying to change the subject. "You're in luck, too. We just had two kids move away — to Phoenix, I think. So we've definitely got the space."

He gestured toward the building. "You *work* here?"

"Yes, I work here," she said with a laugh. "Is that so surprising?"

"You don't look like the kid type."

"Neither do you," she shot back. "And anyway, who says you have to look a certain way to work with kids?"

"I didn't say that. I'm just surprised, that's all. So why was that cop speaking to you like that?"

She colored. "You know what?" She reached for the door. "It's none of your business. Let's go inside and register your daughter. By the way, you never told me her name."

He looked at Aubrey closely. Her brows were set in a frown, but her eyes were filled with something else. Sadness.

She abruptly turned away from him. "If you want to register, fine. If not, that's fine, too. But I can't stand out here with you all day while you mull it over." She pushed open the door and walked in.

Man, she had an attitude. But then again, most people didn't start their day being grilled by a cop. With an irritable sigh, Jonathan shifted Sarah's weight, picked up the duffel bag, and walked into the day-care center.

Inside, he found controlled chaos. The walls were painted a bright, sunny yellow, and there was a smattering of little tables and chairs. The kids ranged in age from babies like Sarah to a redheaded kid who looked to be around five. On one wall was a huge eraser board, where several pictures had been drawn by little hands. Sliding glass doors led to a playground with monkey bars, a slide, and several swings. Balls and toys were scattered around the playground.

On another wall were red cubbyholes, with the kids' names prominently placed beneath each. Toward the back was an area fenced with a tennis net around a huge, square floor mat with lots of soft toys. It was, Jonathan realized, a giant playpen. And in the playpen were two babies roughly Sarah's age. One was crawling toward a ball, and the other was seated, chewing on a wooden block.

The noise was extraordinarily loud — kids were playing and shouting and running around the room. Jonathan took a step backward, but Sarah's eyes were riveted on the other kids.

When two kids rushed toward Jonathan, he took another step backward. The boys managed to slide to a stop before hitting him, their curious faces upturned. "Hey," he said cautiously.

"Are you bringing the baby here?" one of the boys asked.

"Yes."

"Yeah!" the kid said, and ran off.

"Did you bring us anything?" the other boy asked.

That confused Jonathan. "Like what?"

"Like a car?"

Jonathan laughed. "Sorry, kid, no car this time."

"Okay!" the boy said, and ran off after his friend.

"Hello!"

Jonathan looked up; a woman in jeans and a sweatshirt that said DON'T BOTHER ME, I'M READING was holding a bunch of bananas and smiling at him.

"I'm Nancy Fischer. And who is this little angel?" she asked, stroking Sarah's cheek.

"Tammy."

"Well, hello, Tammy." Nancy Fischer smiled at Jonathan again. "I assume you are the gentleman who called last week looking for day care?"

"Yeah," he said, shifting Sarah's weight onto his hip and dropping the duffel bag. "We just moved into town. Mrs. Young said this was a good place for Tammy."

"Oh, she's so *sweet*," Mrs. Fischer trilled, and reached for Tammy.

Jonathan instinctively moved back, out of her reach.

Mrs. Fischer smiled patiently and lowered her arms. "We'll be happy to keep Tammy if you can let her go, hon! I don't blame you for being anxious, but you have to let her go. She's just precious, isn't she?"

"She is. To me."

"We'll take good care of her, I promise," Nancy said as Aubrey joined them. "You want me to try and take her?"

"I've got her, Nancy," Aubrey said. "We're already acquainted."

"You know Tammy?" Nancy asked, looking pleasantly surprised.

Aubrey glanced at Jonathan. "Yeah, Tammy and I have met a couple of times."

"Great! You see?" Nancy said to Jonathan. "Tammy will be just fine. So if you want to give her to Aubrey, I'll get the papers you need to sign, Mr. . . . ?"

"Winslow. J. B. Winslow."

"Mr. Winslow. I'll be right back." Nancy went off to fetch the papers.

Aubrey smiled at Sarah. "You want to come play with me, Tammy?"

And as if she understood what Aubrey had said, Tammy extended her arms, leaning away from Jonathan and toward Aubrey.

Aubrey slipped two hands beneath her arms. "Look at you!" she cooed. "What a pretty girl you are!"

But Jonathan didn't immediately let go. Aubrey turned a dark gaze to him. "Let go, J.B."

"Look, she's not used to being left places. She's probably going to start crying the minute I let her go."

"Okay, well . . . you'll be standing right here and can save her from the torture I am going to put her through."

"Are you going to be a smart-ass about it?"

"You're just making it hard for me. And for her." Aubrey looked at Sarah. "What's that?"

Jonathan looked down. Aubrey had noticed the cameo he'd pinned on Sarah's shorts. "A cameo."

"I can *see* that. But it's pinned on her shorts."

"Yeah . . ." Reva had given her granddaughter that cameo before they'd slipped away. "It's a good-luck charm."

Aubrey glanced up expectantly. When he didn't say more, she smiled. "A good-luck charm. I like that."

He frowned. But he let go of Sarah, who laughed with delight when Aubrey settled her on her hip and took her tiny hand in hers. She smiled so broadly at Aubrey that Jonathan felt tightness in his gut. Sarah liked Aubrey.

He swallowed hard and picked up the duffel and set it on top of a child's table. "I've got some instructions for you," he said, and pulled out diapers and the attendant creams and powders. He also retrieved some baby food, some tiny little fish crackers, formula, and apple juice. After that, he reached inside and removed Sarah's favorite blanket, two changes of clothing, and six of her favorite toys.

"She likes the red truck and the kitty the best," he said, holding those both up so Aubrey could see. "Don't let the other kids take them, they're hers. I brought some extra clothes in case you need them. I've got plenty of diapers and baby wipes."

"J.B., it's okay."

"Here." He thrust a thick, little wooden book toward Aubrey. "I read this to her at nap time. She likes the pictures."

"Okay." Aubrey bit down on a smile.

"What's so funny?" he demanded.

"Did I say anything?"

She hadn't — but she was smiling. Jonathan frowned. "You think I'd go off and leave my daughter without the things she needs?"

"No," Aubrey said with a giggle. "I definitely don't think that."

Jonathan's frown deepened. "I wrote down everything," he muttered, showing her a piece of paper on which he'd written twenty instructions.

Aubrey pressed her lips together and took it gingerly. "We'll *all* read it."

"I've never left her at day care before."

"Obviously."

"You're going to watch her, right? Every minute?"

"J.B.," she said softly. "Look around you. Do you see any baby that looks like he or she is being mistreated or neglected?"

Jonathan looked around. She was right — the kids looked pretty happy. A third woman was in the baby playpen now, sitting on the floor with two babies, playing with them. They were intent on their toys, and they all seemed happy. "Yeah, well," he said, "I don't know you people. I could walk out the door and you'll forget she's here."

"Oh, yeah." Aubrey nodded with mock solemnity. "I can see why you'd be so concerned. But I guess the only way you can prove your theory that we neglect children is to go away and come back, huh?"

She had him there. He couldn't suppress a smile. "Okay," he said, stuffing the things back into Sarah's duffel. "I'll take off." He looked up, peered right into Aubrey's eyes, and pointed at her nose. "But I'll be watching you, brown eyes." He handed her the duffel.

"You do that." Aubrey reached for the duffel, her fingers grazing his and sending a weird little electrical shock through him. He

188

held on to the duffel, their hands touching, her fingers on his, sending little shivers of warmth through him.

"So what was that out in the alley?" he asked quietly.

Aubrey tugged at the duffel and freed it from his grip. "You're really nosy, you know that? It was nothing. Nada. Now, if you don't mind, there are a lot of little kids I should be neglecting."

He sighed, grabbed Sarah's face between his hands, and leaned in to kiss her. In doing so, he detected Aubrey's scent, and it confused him that a woman with such a badass exterior would wear the sweet scent of roses on her skin.

Jonathan leaned back and looked at her again, at the wide copper eyes, the full lips, the silky surface of her skin. He could feel the male in him awakening, having been dead for so long. It unnerved him, made him feel extremely uncomfortable.

He glanced at Sarah, who was reaching for the big circle of a silver earring Aubrey was wearing. "Be good," he said, caressing her back. "I'll be back for you. I'll always come back for you. You remember that."

Sarah babbled at Aubrey's earring, so Jonathan stepped back. "Okay." He gestured at Aubrey. "Take her. Go."

"Ta-ta," Aubrey said, and turned away, carrying Sarah to the back of the room where the other babies were playing. Sarah did not look back — she was riveted on the other babies and the toys they had.

Great. In the space of twenty-four hours, he'd seen a ghost, his daughter had gone off with a stranger without even giving him a second look, and he had felt a stirring he'd not felt since before Tammy died.

He was such a traitor to her memory.

"Here you are, Mr. Winslow. You can fill these out at the counter," Nancy Fischer said, appearing again.

Jonathan took the papers from her and walked to the counter, anxious to be away from here, and the sudden need to feel a woman beneath him again.

He needed some air in a very bad way.

"So who was *that?*" Noelle asked excitedly when J.B. had stalked out of the day care.

Aubrey glanced at the door and tried to act nonchalant. "Some guy," she said with a shrug. "Kind of weird, isn't he?"

"Kind of *hot.* If I wasn't married, I swear." Noelle winked at Aubrey. "You're not married."

"Noelle, don't start."

"What?" Noelle asked playfully. "The guy is hot."

"Not two days ago you were desperate to hook me up with Keith, remember?"

"But that was before I knew we had a new guy in town who looked like *that*. Come on, aren't you the least bit interested?"

"Right now, I am more interested in knowing if we have any teething rings. I think she has a new tooth coming in."

"Aubrey, really, you are so hopeless." Noelle opened a cabinet and withdrew a disposable teething ring. "When he comes to pick up the baby this afternoon, just ask him if he needs any help with anything. Create an opportunity to see him."

"Noelle, do you mind? I told you — I'm leaving Tourmaline as soon as I can. The last thing I need to do is hook up with some guy like that. He's weird."

"Whatever," Noelle said airily. "Be a stick-in-the-mud if you want." She moved away, leaving Aubrey with Tammy.

Aubrey looked at Tammy and smiled as the girl bit down on the teething ring. Noelle would never understand that Aubrey harbored a secret desire to be with J.B. in a major way, but she was too afraid to pursue it. Too afraid that Zeke was right, that he would find her stupid. Noelle would push and push and . . . who knew what Zeke would do if J.B. and Aubrey hooked up? No, it couldn't happen.

"But you and I can be friends," she whispered to Tammy, and took her to meet the other babies.

15

The job site was the construction of a large county recreation center that would host everything from concerts to rodeos to fairs. After Jonathan had filled out the paperwork, he was put on a crew that was erecting big metal frames to form the walls of one side of the building. It didn't require as much skill as it did brawn, and Jonathan was happy for that — he was too worried about Sarah to concentrate on anything.

Would she freak out when she understood that he was gone? Would Aubrey be able to handle that? His worry caused him to be a little sloppy a couple of times, and one of the guys — Bob, Jonathan learned — snapped at him, "Hey! Watch what you're doing!"

Jonathan glared back at him but didn't offer a word of apology.

When the work ground to a halt due to the late delivery of some crossbeams, the foreman on the job told them to take lunch. Jonathan hadn't exactly packed a lunch — he'd been more concerned about getting Sarah's things together — so he stood off to one side, his hands stuffed in his pockets.

The other men — five in all — sat on a big metal brace, munching through the fare in their lunch boxes. Two of them eyed Jonathan curiously as they ate. He knew it, he could feel it, but ignored them completely until one of them said, "Hey, Pirate Jack," mocking the length of Jonathan's hair, which he'd tied in a ponytail today. "Where'd you come from, anyway?"

Jonathan looked away. "Around."

"What's the matter?" the man asked, drawing Jonathan's attention to him again. "Think you're too good to talk to us?"

"Left my chitchat at home with my lunch."

That earned him a laugh from four of the five men. But Bob, a big guy with a short buzz cut, a day of stubble on his chin, and a tattoo around his enormous biceps, took a couple of steps toward him. "You know what I think? I think you don't have a lot of respect for your coworkers. I think you got an attitude about something."

Jonathan slowly turned and faced him fully. "I've got plenty of respect if you earn it," he said, ignoring the howls of delight that rose up from the four men who remained seated, watching.

Bob's eyes narrowed menacingly. "You know what, hotshot? You're not going to get along here."

"Come on, Bob," another guy said. "Go easy on him. He just started."

"I don't need anyone to go easy on me," Jonathan said.

That remark definitely caught their attention — another of them stood up. "You sure don't make friends easy, do you?" he said.

"Don't need them," Jonathan said as the foreman stepped in between them.

"Hey, hey . . . what's going on here?" he demanded, looking at Bob. "You better not be causing any trouble, Davis."

"*Me?* Talk to your new hire," Bob said, gesturing at Jonathan.

"Look, whatever is going on here, cut it out. We got another hour at least before the materials get here, so make yourselves useful when you're through with lunch. Clean up the site and move those columns to the other side of the building." The foreman pointed to a forklift and some concrete columns. "And you," he said, pointing at Bob now, "lay off. Don't cause any trouble here."

He started to walk on, but paused to give

Jonathan a look.

When he'd left them, Jonathan glanced at Bob, who was still glaring at him, and shoved away from the wall. He started walking.

"Where you going?" Bob called after him.

He didn't bother to respond. He just kept walking, pretending not to hear the hoots of disapproval from the other guys in his crew. Not that he cared — he had passed the point of being able to bear the uncertainty of how Sarah was adjusting to day care. He could not stop picturing her beautiful face twisted in fear because he wasn't with her. And besides, he had an hour — plenty of time to get over to Bright Horizons and see if she was all right. Maybe he even had time to grab some lunch.

"Hey!" Bob shouted again, but Jonathan had already removed his hard hat and was walking briskly to his car.

He was in town in minutes. He parked down the street a little way from the day care and then walked up the sidewalk, thinking he'd just catch a glimpse of the kids through the big picture windows in the back. If he could just see Sarah and know she was all right, he'd be okay.

Only the little kids weren't inside — they

were on the playground, beneath the shade of big elm trees, playing with their trucks and balls and toys. Honeysuckle vines covered the fence, the fragrant blooms scenting the air. Holly bushes were planted along the back of the building, and the leaves of the shade trees littered the ground around the children.

In the middle of them was Sarah, rocking her red truck back and forth. Beside her, and holding another baby in her lap, was Aubrey. She leaned over to brush a curl of Sarah's hair from her face. She smiled down at her, touched her lovingly.

Jonathan drew up — there was something different about Aubrey, he thought. She seemed . . . *softer* somehow. He stepped behind a tree, watching from behind it, unseen, unnoticed. It fascinated him — he couldn't quite fathom what it was about her that seemed so different.

But then Sarah did something that made Aubrey laugh.

She *laughed.* She cupped Sarah's cheek and kissed the top of her head, and she smiled so beatifically that Jonathan could feel it deep inside him. He realized he'd never heard her laugh before, that he'd hardly even seen her smile. But now that he had, he had a sudden need to see more of it.

Good Lord, Aubrey was beautiful when she smiled! She looked vulnerable and gentle, and the hard shell she usually presented seemed to crumble away. What emerged was a very desirable woman.

That he was even thinking she was desirable confounded Jonathan. That he could have such raw, sensual feelings for anyone other than Tammy seemed impossible because he'd pledged his heart and soul to her. Yet at the same time, he understood why Aubrey had developed such a tough outer shell — it was the only way to keep things from hurting her deeply. He'd had to do the same thing.

He didn't know what had happened to Aubrey that made it necessary for her to try to protect herself, but he could guess, and he suddenly saw her in a different light.

In truth, Jonathan was suddenly feeling things for Aubrey Cross that he had no right to feel, that he did not *want* to feel. Yet she was pulling him to her like a magnet, and it startled him when she suddenly looked up and saw him standing by the tree, watching her.

The softness in her expression shuttered; the hard shell was there again. She glared at him and suddenly stood up, picking up one baby and placing him in one arm, then stooping down to pick up Sarah in the other before marching across the playground. She paused halfway to him and quickly said something to one of the women Jonathan had seen this morning, then continued toward the fence, her stride long and determined, her gaze hard and unwavering from him.

Jonathan straightened self-consciously as she reached the fence.

"*What* are you doing?" she demanded.

He had seen the real Aubrey exposed for a moment, but now *he* felt exposed. "I have a right to check on my daughter and make sure you're taking good care of her."

"Ohmigod," Aubrey muttered as Sarah spied Jonathan and smiled broadly.

"*Ba ba ba,*" she said, reaching for him.

"You want to take her?" Aubrey snapped, shifting so that he could take her over the fence. "Take her."

"What are you doing?" Jonathan exclaimed, throwing up his hands. "I can't take her!"

"No, take her," Aubrey insisted again, allowing Sarah to lean out over her arm and forcing Jonathan to catch her. "You'll feel a whole lot better if you do, because you obviously believe anyone else who looks after her is going to harm her somehow."

He took Sarah and smiled down at her before glaring at Aubrey again. "I told you, she's not used to strangers. I had to make sure you knew what you were doing."

"Oh, I'm sorry. I thought accreditation by the state and three years of child development in college would be enough, but I guess I was wrong. But, hey, if you want to take her out of day care —"

"Cut it out, all right?" He held Sarah out to her again. "I'm not taking her out. Can't a dad check on his kid?"

"Of course you can. But come in the front door next time instead of skulking around the back," Aubrey said, and cocked her hip beneath the weight of the little boy she was holding, who was looking at Sarah and seemed to be on the verge of crying.

"Come on, will you take her?" Jonathan said again, holding her out. "I have to get back to work."

"Will you promise to quit being so paranoid?" Aubrey demanded.

"Yes." He sighed in resignation. But Aubrey didn't look as if she believed him. "I *promise*."

With a suspicious look, Aubrey took Sarah, who began to cry. The moment she began to cry and stretch her arms toward her daddy, the little boy began to cry, too. "Great!" Aubrey snapped over her head. "Thanks a lot!"

She was standing there with a crying butterball on each hip, glaring at him, and Jonathan couldn't help it — he laughed.

"Hey!" Aubrey protested.

He lifted a hand in apology, but he could not stop laughing and the babies wouldn't stop crying. "Got to get back to work," he said. "Just be careful with her."

"Oh my *God,*" Aubrey cried. She whirled around and marched away from the fence, speaking first to Sarah, trying to calm her down, then to the little boy. The other woman emerged from under a patio awning and took the boy from Aubrey, and they both looked over their shoulders at Jonathan.

That was it — he shoved his hands in his pockets and walked back the way he had come.

He caught one last sight of Aubrey when he was back in his car and had come to a stop at the corner — she was sitting on a picnic table with Sarah in her lap, pointing at paper butterflies that hung from a tree. As if she'd always known Sarah. And Jonathan realized that he was looking at Aubrey more than Sarah.

That image was still with him when he entered the diner to grab a quick bite. He settled in at the counter and smiled at Randi.

"You're back!" she said cheerfully. "Where's your little girl?"

"Day care," he said. "You got a burger for me back there somewhere?"

"Sure." She smiled at him. "I think we might even have some fries." She jotted something down on an order pad and glanced up at him. "Don't go anywhere," she said with a wink, and walked away, her hips swinging.

On the counter in front of him were the usual condiments and a stack of homemade coupons. He picked one up — it was advertising free pie on Wednesday nights. Jonathan slipped the coupon into his pocket, then picked up a menu to peruse while he waited. It was something to look at, something to distract him from the image of Aubrey and Sarah, sitting on that picnic table, looking at paper butterflies. But he couldn't get the image out of his head or stop thinking about the way it made him feel.

That inevitably led him to think about Tammy and the weird thing that had happened to him last night. It wasn't a dream

— it couldn't have been a dream — but neither was it real. Was it her ghost? Was he crazy to even consider that possibility? Whatever he believed, he believed Tammy was trying to tell him something. Somewhere in that . . . that dream, she had been trying to give him a message, and he was too dumb to figure out what it was.

It angered him that he'd allowed thoughts of Aubrey to creep in and confuse Tammy's message.

He was so deep in his thoughts that he didn't notice two men who came into the diner until they slid onto stools on either side of him.

He was startled to see the sheriff who had been bothering Aubrey this morning. Jonathan immediately stiffened and glanced to his left. Another cop was sitting there and looking him over.

"Look here, Dan," the sheriff said. "This is the guy I was telling you about, the one who signed up for day care over at Bright Horizons."

That instantly put Jonathan on his guard and he slowly straightened up, bracing his hands against his thighs.

"You must be new in town," the sheriff said, checking out Jonathan's leather jacket.

Jonathan pressed his lips together and

didn't answer.

"So what's your name?"

"J.B."

"J.B.? That it? Is that one of those celebrity names?" the sheriff asked with a snort of laughter. His crony laughed, too.

Jonathan looked him straight in the eye. "Winslow."

The sheriff nodded and smiled. "Well, hello, J. B. Winslow. I'm Sheriff Cross — but most people around here call me Zeke. And this is Dan Gomez, my chief deputy."

It took Jonathan a moment to actually hear the deputy's name, because the sheriff's name had stunned him. That was Aubrey's last name. She was related to this guy? What was he, her father? The man who had spoken to her so disrespectfully this morning was her *father?*

"What's the matter?" Zeke asked, and Jonathan realized he was staring at him. When Jonathan didn't answer, Zeke grinned. "So you just rolled into town, huh?"

"You might say that."

"Looks like you decided to make Tourmaline your home. That's great. We're always glad when good, upstanding citizens decide to live in Tourmaline . . . aren't we, Dan?"

"You bet," Dan agreed.

"Working with Grace Construction, I take it?" Zeke said.

Startled again, Jonathan looked at the sheriff. "How'd you know?"

"Because I'm a cop," Zeke said, his eyes narrowing slightly. Jonathan could feel the color drain from his face, but then Zeke suddenly laughed. "But it doesn't take a cop to figure it out. Just look at you," he said, gesturing to Jonathan's jeans. "You're covered in concrete dust and you're wearing work boots. And if you haven't noticed, there ain't a whole lot going on in this little town of ours. Most people work for the county or Grace Construction."

"Good guess," Jonathan said tightly. "I got a job with Grace."

"Then why aren't you working?"

What was up with the twenty questions? He tried to assess Zeke, figure out what angle he was working. "They're waiting on some materials."

"Ah." Zeke nodded. "I bet that's those trucks we saw out on the highway, Dan."

"I bet you're right, Sheriff."

"You've got time for a quick meal," Zeke said congenially. "But those parts oughta be there in a half hour." He grinned. Jonathan pressed his lips together and nodded.

"So where are you staying, J. B. Winslow?"

Zeke asked, twisting around on his counter stool to face Jonathan.

The man was smiling, but with all of his questions, Jonathan felt the guy was a little in his face. He couldn't tell if he knew something and was sniffing for more or just being nosy. Nevertheless, he'd had enough dealings with cops in his life to know that he was better off answering. "Out on 78."

"Ah. The old Haney place. Glad to see it's not sitting vacant any longer. No one lives out that way anymore, and about every six months we get called out on a vandalism charge there. You know how kids are," Zeke said with a shake of his head. "So you got the baby in day care. That's good. That's a good operation. My late wife was a partner in it," Zeke continued blithely. "Which reminds me . . . where's *your* wife?"

Jonathan gave the sheriff a sidelong look, wondering what made him assume there was no wife. Fortunately, he'd been asked the question so many times he had a pat answer and offered it up now. "Not here," he said simply, which usually silenced most people.

Not the sheriff, however. "Oh, yeah? Where is she? San Diego? Phoenix?"

"Why?" Jonathan asked.

Zeke laughed and looked at Dan. "I think

we've got some domestic issues here."

"Looks like," Dan readily agreed.

Zeke turned his gaze to Jonathan again. He was smiling, but his hazel eyes were as cold as ice. "You can't fool me, J. B. Winslow," he said, and Jonathan's pulse jumped. "I know what's going on with you."

"Oh, yeah. What?" Jonathan asked evenly.

"You're splitting up with your old lady." Zeke waited for some acknowledgment from Jonathan that he did not get. "Hey," the sheriff said with a shrug, "it happens."

"Yeah," Jonathan said with a nod. The man had no idea how it had happened.

"You've come to the right place, then," Zeke said, his eyes still cold. He leaned in a little closer and looked Jonathan squarely in the eye. "We look after our own in Tourmaline. Everyone here gets along real well, and we look out for one another. As a result, we don't have much trouble in this town."

Jonathan didn't know if the sheriff was warning him or merely bragging about his town. "That's great," Jonathan said. "Good to know."

"Yeah," Zeke drawled. "So if that wife gives you any trouble about that precious little girl of yours, you just give us a call. We'll be looking out for you. Hell, we already are, aren't we, Dan?"

"We sure are. That's Tourmaline's way."

Jonathan looked at Dan, then at Zeke, as Randi appeared with his burger and slid it across the counter to him. Zeke smiled, clapped his hand on Jonathan's shoulder. "Good to have you here in Tourmaline, J.B."

"Hello, Zeke. Dan," Randi said cheerfully. "You boys want the regular today?"

"You bet, Randi. We're just going to take a seat in the booth over there and let Mr. Winslow enjoy his burger before he gets back to work." Zeke Cross stood up from the stool, gave Jonathan's shoulder a squeeze that felt a little too hard, and sauntered to an empty booth at the window with Dan Gomez on his heels.

Randi smiled at Jonathan. "Need ketchup, hon?"

"Sure."

When Randi returned a moment later with the ketchup, Jonathan said, "So what's the story with the sheriff?"

Randi blinked. She looked at Zeke and Dan, then at him. "No story that I know. Zeke's a good guy. He's been sheriff here for a hundred years and will probably go on being sheriff another hundred years."

"Why's that?"

"Everyone loves him." Randi nodded thoughtfully. "I have to say, he takes real good care of us and this town. He makes Tourmaline a good place to live." She suddenly laughed. "Only blind spot Zeke's got is his daughter. Everyone knows to steer clear of her."

That certainly piqued his interest, and Jonathan looked up from his burger. "Why?"

"Oh, you know how some men are — they don't like anyone touching their little girl. Zeke's as bad as any of them, just so overly protective of her, especially since her mom died. Everyone knows not to start anything up with Aubrey unless he's approved of him, that's for sure." She leaned across the counter and added in a whisper, "Of course, no one wants to start anything with her because she's kind of cuckoo." She made a whirling motion with her finger at her temple.

"Randi! Are you going to talk all day or are you going to get this order out?" the cook shouted at her.

"Gotta go," she said, and pushed away from the counter.

Jonathan choked down the bite of burger. There was nothing he could point to precisely, but he hadn't had the feeling this morning that Zeke considered Aubrey his precious little girl. And furthermore, he bristled at Randi labeling her cuckoo. Yeah, he'd thought Aubrey was a nut job when he'd first met her. But he knew now that she was just a little different . . . not crazy. She just wasn't a sheep following the herd.

Jonathan glanced over his shoulder — and caught Zeke looking at him.

Zeke pretended to tip a hat and smiled before resuming his conversation with Dan and looking away.

You're being paranoid, Jonathan told himself. Zeke didn't know anything — he'd just asked a few nosy questions the way cops were prone to do. He had nothing on Jonathan, nothing at all.

Why, then, did he get such a bad vibe from the man?

16

Aubrey left the day care center early and wasn't there when J.B. came to pick up Tammy. That was just as well, she thought. He'd confused her completely, and she was feeling irritable about it.

On the one hand, he was gruff and rude and spied on her at work. But on the other hand, she had seen the way he looked at her, had seen something spark behind those gorgeous brown eyes of his that she'd felt deep inside her.

It made no sense and Aubrey had about decided she was as nuts as Zeke made her out to be. So when Nancy needed someone to go to the bank, Aubrey had been more than happy to do it, just so she could get out of there before he came for Tammy and confused her even more.

"Tell the new guy that he needs to bring a mat and some blankets for Tammy to use at nap time," Aubrey said to Noelle.

"I hope he doesn't flip out," Noelle muttered.

Aubrey picked up her satchel and looked at Tammy again. She was chewing on a twisty toy that made noises every time she moved it. So every time she chewed on it, it made noise, startling her. Aubrey smiled and dipped down next to her. "Bye, Tammy." She kissed the top of her head. Next to Tammy, Bryan, a baby boy about the same age as Tammy, looked up at her with soulful blue eyes. She laughed and kissed the top of his head, too.

"Okay," she said, standing up. "I'll see you rug rats tomorrow."

"Have a good evening, Aubrey!" Nancy called to her. "Oh, by the way, if you get a chance . . . the lawyer sent some papers over to your father to sign this week. Could you double-check that he has them and maybe urge him to sign?"

Aubrey forced a smile even as her gut tightened. "Sure," she said as she went out.

No one in Tourmaline knew about her relationship with Zeke — or lack of one. "It's no one's business what goes on in our home," her mother had once said when Aubrey begged her to leave Zeke after he'd accused her of cheating on him and had hit her again.

"But, Mom . . . he could kill you. Why won't you leave him?" Aubrey had pleaded with her. "Why do you let him treat you like that — treat *us* like that?"

"And just where am I going to go, Aubrey?" her mother had asked wearily. "I don't have any money of my own. He'll make sure wherever I go in this county that I am miserable."

"We could go to Grandma and Grandpa's house," Aubrey suggested.

"Honey, my parents would take us in for a time, but do you think they planned to have to look after us in their retirement?"

"But . . . there has to be somewhere we can go," Aubrey had insisted. "What about Aunt Amy?"

Mom had snorted and shaken her head. "I haven't spoken to Amy in fifteen years. I hardly even know who she is any longer."

"Then what about Nancy Fischer?" Aubrey had said, determined. "She's your best friend, Mom. How can she refuse to help you?"

Mom had looked at Aubrey then, and she could see the distress in her eyes. "Honey, do you know what he would do to me if I left him and went to *Nancy?* He'd see it as a blow to his pride and reputation in this town. You know how he prides himself on being the big man around here. He wouldn't stand for it, but that's not the worst of it — I don't know what he'd do to Nancy or her husband."

"Mom —"

"Aubrey, don't worry about me. My life is what it is. You need to think about yourself. Get out of here, honey. Get out of Tourmaline. There's a whole wide world out there and you should just go and never look back."

"But, Mom," Aubrey said tearfully, "what would happen to you if I left here?"

"Don't you worry about it." Mom put her arm around Aubrey's shoulder. "I'm a survivor."

Aubrey hadn't believed her, but Mom really was a survivor. Somehow, she'd convinced Zeke to let Aubrey go to San Diego to school. And then she'd gotten Zeke to agree to put up some money for her half of the day-care center. Aubrey would never really understand how that had happened — Zeke was pretty tight with his money, and he hated Nancy Fischer. Yet somehow, Mom had convinced him to give her the money. Aubrey asked once — Mom just smiled mysteriously and wouldn't answer.

Maybe Mom had thought things were

turning around. Maybe that was why she'd never confided in Nancy — or anyone else, for that matter. Maybe she'd thought she had turned the tide.

But she hadn't been able to survive cancer.

Just when things had been looking up for Mom, just when it looked as if the day care would really make it, she'd found a lump in her breast. It was aggressive — in spite of the chemo and the radiation, Mom had died within two years of being diagnosed.

Aubrey missed her. She missed having someone to talk to, someone who knew what her life was like. She wondered what Mom would have made of J. B. Winslow. Would she have seen the vulnerability in him? Whatever she might have thought of J.B., Mom would have loved Tammy.

The day care had been everything to Mom. It had represented her freedom, her victory of sorts. Aubrey wasn't going to let anything happen to it. And she wasn't going to let anyone know how abusive Zeke was because Mom never wanted anyone to know, and Aubrey would not be the one to tell her secret. Especially not after what she'd seen on 78 that rainy afternoon. So she smiled and said, "Sure," when Nancy asked, and she would figure out a way to ask Zeke about it without angering him and prompting him to do something awful with the papers.

As for her secret, well . . . it was something she had to endure for a few weeks. But the next time she left Tourmaline, it would be for good. She would get in her car and put it in drive and never look back.

Never.

Jonathan's afternoon on the job site didn't go well, given that he had left the site to check on Sarah. The foreman was waiting for him when he came back with a warning about leaving work again. Jonathan was unapologetic.

His crew members were even less welcoming. Bob told him if he ever left the work to them like that again, he'd be waiting for him after work. Jonathan told Bob to mind his own business. It served no purpose other than to make a bad situation worse, which Jonathan had a history of doing before Tammy had changed him into a better man by making him face up to some of his behavior. Without her, he seemed to be regressing.

He was in a foul mood by the time he clocked out. When he arrived to pick up Sarah, Aubrey had left for the day. Jonathan was surprised and frankly a little perturbed that he felt disappointed that she wasn't there. Sarah was fussy, too — it had been a lot of changes for her and a long day. And then, the other young woman — Noelle, she said her name was — told him he needed a mat.

"A *mat*," he repeated, trying to absorb the meaning of that word.

"A mat and some blankets. For nap time," Noelle said, peering at him curiously.

"Okay," Jonathan said slowly. "And where am I supposed to get this mat?"

Noelle smiled and shrugged. "Maybe the department store down the street? You can start there — I'm sure they can tell you where to go if they don't have it. All the kids have one. You can roll them up and carry them like a yoga mat."

That was no help at all.

It was no surprise to Jonathan that the department store didn't have kid mats and had no idea where to get one. It annoyed Jonathan that the day care could require something like this mysterious mat and not tell him exactly where to get one. It annoyed him even more that he didn't know he was supposed to have a mat. *All* the kids had one? He could honestly say he'd never seen a mat. By the time he arrived home, he was thoroughly frustrated with his day, his thoughts, and a crying baby who had a wet diaper and was hungry.

"I'm doing the best I can here," he said as he took Sarah out of the car seat and grabbed her duffel. "But no one ever told me about mats for naps."

Sarah cried even harder.

Neither of them slept well that night — Jonathan could hear Sarah in her crib, moving around, murmuring to herself. It was as if they both were waiting for Tammy to appear again. Every noise, the slightest movement, brought Jonathan up, straining to see in the dark.

But she didn't come.

"Tammy," he murmured over and over.

Still, she did not come.

Sarah was fussy from the moment he got her up until he dropped her off at the day care, where, once again, he felt betrayed by his thoughts. He was disappointed Aubrey wasn't there to take Sarah from him. He wanted Aubrey to watch over Sarah, not the other women.

"Did you bring a mat?" Noelle asked cheerfully.

"No," Jonathan said as he shoved a stack of blankets at her. "Couldn't find one."

"Oh." She took the blankets. Her brows rose almost to her hairline. "We just needed, like, *two* blankets."

"I wanted to make sure you had enough." Jonathan thrust his hand through his hair and looked around the room. "So this is okay? She'll be okay?"

Noelle shifted her gaze to him and looked at him curiously. "Who? Tammy? She'll be fine!"

And Sarah had, indeed, stopped crying. Still, Jonathan felt uneasy, off-balance, as if the world had tilted the wrong way on its axis. "Doesn't look like you have enough people to watch after them all," he remarked.

Noelle glanced around the room as he put Sarah down, then looked at him again. "Aubrey will be here, too. Is that what you mean?"

Jonathan didn't answer, but looked at Sarah, who was at Noelle's feet, trying unsuccessfully to peel Noelle's shoe off her foot.

"She's coming in late," Noelle said. "But she'll be here."

"She better be. I'm not leaving my daughter here if there aren't enough adults to watch her."

Noelle's expression darkened at his harsh tone. "She's thirty minutes late. But she'll be here and there will be plenty of adult supervision, I can assure you."

"Good." Jonathan squatted down, put his hand on Sarah's back. He kissed her head and stood up, glancing at Noelle from the corner of his eye. "Later," he said, and walked out without another word, furious with himself for showing any interest in Aubrey at all and feeling so damn self-conscious about his ability to care for Sarah.

Aubrey had to stop at the supermarket on her way to work to pick up Goldfish crackers, apple juice, and Popsicles for the older kids. As she wrestled the oversize containers into her car, a black pickup pulled in behind her and the tinted window eased down.

"You need some help?" Keith asked from behind his reflective sunglasses.

"No thanks," Aubrey said as she tossed the first gallon carton of Goldfish into the trunk. "I've got it."

"So, Aubrey, I was wondering . . . got any plans for tonight?"

How long was he going to keep this up? "Yep," she said without even looking at him. "And tomorrow night, and the night after that."

Keith laughed. "That's fine. I figure sooner or later you'll get hungry for a little companionship, and when you do, I'm just a phone call away."

Aubrey put the last of the stuff in the trunk and shut it, then turned abruptly and caught Keith admiring her derriere a little too openly. He grinned at her. "Nice skirt," he said, referring to her short plaid kilt. "I like the way you wear it."

She glared at him. "Would you mind moving your truck? I've got to get to work."

Keith's smile faded. "You don't have to be such a bitch, Aubrey. I'm just paying you a compliment. And it seems to me you're practically begging for one in that outfit."

Just like that, he went from potential nice guy to jerk. "The only thing I'm begging is for you to move so I can get out of here."

He glowered at her. "Fine." He punched the window up and hit the gas. His truck roared away, lifting the hem of her skirt.

At the day care, Aubrey struggled inside with the goods. Noelle walked up with Tammy on her hip and watched her. "You missed your boyfriend this morning."

"Huh?" Aubrey asked, confused, thinking Keith had come by here, looking for her.

"That new guy. When he dropped Tammy off, he was looking for you."

Aubrey dropped a gallon carton of Goldfish crackers on the floor. "He was looking for me?"

"Sure was," Noelle said with a smile. "He's sure cute, Aubrey. A little weird — and a little snippy — but cute."

Aubrey laughed nervously and put up a hand. "Okay, Noelle . . . don't even try."

"What?" Noelle asked, grinning, her gaze shifting to something over Aubrey's shoulder. "You can't tell me you're not attracted to him. I saw you with him yesterday, you know. Jakie! Put that block down!" she shouted.

Aubrey could feel herself color and turned partially from Noelle to pick up the dropped carton of crackers.

"Why not explore it, is all I am saying," Noelle blithely continued as little Jake had apparently put the block down.

"Noelle," Aubrey said with some exasperation as she put the crackers on the table. "Why are you so interested in hooking me up with someone? It feels like you're my personal matchmaker."

"I don't know." Noelle shrugged. "Because it is boring otherwise? Because I am dead and married and live vicariously through you? Or maybe because I just want to see you happy?"

"What's that supposed to mean?" Aubrey asked as she wrested the box of apple-juice packages from the hands of a little three-year-old girl.

"Look, Aubrey — I've known you a long time. Granted, we weren't exactly friends in school . . . but the thing is, I've never seen you happy, except when you're around kids. And now that I've gotten to know you a little better . . ." Noelle sighed and pulled her hair from Tammy's grip. "I just think it would be nice to see you happy for once. That's it. I'm just trying to help you out."

Aubrey sighed to the ceiling, then held out her hands for Tammy. Noelle handed her over. "Thanks," Aubrey said. "I know what you are trying to do, but I . . . I don't think this is the place for me. I told you, I'm going back to San Diego as soon as I can. And besides, I don't really think a guy like J.B. could ever be seriously interested in me."

"Are you kidding?" Noelle asked with a snort of incredulous laughter. "What's the matter with you? Look at you, Aubrey — you're the only original thing in this town. You're vibrant, you're pretty, and you're different. It's the same reason Keith is so hot for you. Don't you see that?"

Aubrey laughed. "Ah . . . no. Nothing like that."

"That's your problem," Noelle said, folding her arms and giving her a stern look. "You know, you should really get out of that little hovel of an apartment more. You have *no* self-esteem. You really need to work on believing in yourself."

"What I need to work on is this kid's diaper," Aubrey said with a smile for Tammy, who had grabbed the long spike of her earring and was pulling on it.

"Okay, fine," Noelle said as a toddler ran up and hit her in the leg. "Just a minute, Terrell. I'm talking. Little boys wait until the adults are through talking." She looked at Aubrey. "Stick your head in the sand, but I'm telling you — this is your chance if you want it."

"Okay. Well. Glad we had this little chat. I've really got to change her and get my earring back," Aubrey said, and with a small smile for Noelle, she moved to the changing station.

Noelle was nuts, she reminded herself as she pulled the giant duffel down — and sputtered when the stack of blankets fell on her head — because J.B. was not interested in her. Whatever she thought she might have seen in his look yesterday was just an overactive imagination — it had to be. If he'd been looking for her this morning, it was just to complain about something, she was certain.

Nevertheless, she couldn't help a little fantasy of him from creeping into her mind as she changed Tammy. She could imagine him actually smiling at her, could imagine the feel of his arms around her, the feel of his lips on hers . . . oh, *hell.* What was she doing?

Getting back to reality, that was what. "Come on, sweet pea," she said when she'd snapped Sarah's pink overalls back together and adjusted the cameo good-luck charm he'd pinned on her. "Let's go see what your friend Dusty is doing."

17

After a grueling day at work where Jonathan found himself lifting steel beams by himself more often than not, he looked again for the kiddie nap mat without any luck. It wasn't much of a look, really — the day care closed at six, and after checking in a baby-clothing boutique — "You might have to go to San Diego," the woman said — Jonathan pulled into the parking lot of Bright Horizons at 6:30 p.m.

Only one car remained in the parking lot — they were gone. *Gone!* He leaped from his car and ran to the door, but found it locked. His heart began to race — where was Sarah? The unthinkable crept into his mind — Alan. *Impossible!* No, no, he was just late. He jogged around to the side of the building and hopped over the fence, then ran to the sliding glass doors in back.

Nancy Fischer was inside turning off the lights when Jonathan pounded on the glass doors. It startled her badly — she jumped a foot in the air and whirled around with her hand pressed to her heart. "Mr. Winslow!" she cried, and hurried to the patio doors to open them.

"Where's my daughter?" Jonathan demanded.

"I was just going to leave you a note —"

"Where is she?"

"Hey!" Nancy exclaimed. "Take a breath, mister! You're late. Our facility closes at six and we all have other obligations! We tried to find you, but the number you left is not working —"

"Let me see," he demanded. Nancy Fischer held up the form he'd filled out. Jonathan looked at the number and realized in his haste to get away from Aubrey and the thoughts he was having, the zero looked more like a six. He grabbed a pen and corrected it. "Tell me where my daughter is!"

Nancy pursed her lips and glared at him. "Aubrey took Tammy with her. She volunteers at the YMCA three days a week and can't be late. It was the best we could do given that we had no way to get hold of you."

"Where is it? Where is the YMCA?"

"At First and Elm. Now that you've corrected your number," she said, turning away from him, "we'll make sure this does not happen again."

But Jonathan was already gone. His panic was choking him, making it difficult to breathe. It was insane, but when he'd found the day care closed and Sarah gone, he could only think of Alan Spaulding. That fear never really left him, sometimes expanding inside him, making it difficult to breathe. Alan was capable of doing horrible things, and the slightest hint of him made Jonathan's fear swell.

He raced across town like a crazy man, driving well over the speed limit, weaving in and out of traffic. He found the YMCA in an old school that had been converted into a community center. He hardly bothered to turn off the motor before he was running into the building. As he neared the doors, the kid who had helped him at the department store walked out.

"Hey!" he said when he saw Jonathan. "Hi! Remember me?"

Jonathan grabbed him by his shoulders. "I'm looking for my baby. Remember my baby?" he asked desperately.

"She's pretty."

"Have you seen her?"

"Yes," Mark said, smiling in spite of Jonathan's grip on him. "She's in there with the others."

Jonathan let go of him and started for the door.

"I'm coming, too!" Mark shouted, running after Jonathan as he burst through the doors and strode inside.

But he instantly slid to a halt. Inside the gym, at least a dozen kids were under the supervision of three adults. Two of the adults were working at a table in the back, pouring juice into a line of cups. The kids were all seated in a half circle on the floor around Aubrey, who was sitting in a chair and holding up things like billfolds and coin purses.

His baby was in the lap of a teenaged girl who was listening with rapt attention to whatever Aubrey said. Sarah's attention was on several plastic cups of various sizes scattered on the gym floor around them.

There was one other thing that Jonathan slowly began to notice as his heart stopped pounding. When he looked at the girl who was holding Sarah, he noticed she was like Mark. At least half of the assembled little group was like Mark, with Down syndrome. Others looked both physically and mentally challenged. They were, he realized, all special-needs kids.

As Sarah had yet to see him, Jonathan

slowly eased down onto his haunches, watching them from across the gym.

Mark did, too, just like Jonathan, next to him, and asked in a loud whisper, "What are you doing?"

"I'm watching," Jonathan said, and put a finger to his mouth to indicate Mark should be quiet. Mark nodded, and the two of them remained like that, just watching, as Aubrey told some story about a boy who had gone to school and lost his lunch money. They reviewed all the places people were supposed to keep their lunch money — in their pocket, in their coin purse. Then they reviewed what they should do if they lost their lunch money.

All the while, Sarah chewed on the plastic cups or her kitty. But when one of the adults joined the group and announced the snacks were ready, the girl holding Sarah put her on her feet and ran toward the back of the room where the snacks were waiting. Sarah spied Jonathan then and, with a squeal of delight, started walking toward him on wobbly legs.

Aubrey got up, too, prepared to catch her . . . and saw Jonathan. She blinked with surprise and smiled a little sheepishly.

Jonathan stood up and held out his arms to Sarah. "Come on, baby," he urged her.

"Walk to Daddy. Come on, Munchkin." With a gurgle of delight, Sarah made it almost halfway across the floor before taking a misstep and going down on all fours. The fall stunned her — for a moment she stared at Jonathan. But then her face twisted into a little, red ball and she let out an ear-piercing wail.

"I'll get her!" Mark shouted, taking off before Jonathan could stop him. But Aubrey was there first and had scooped Sarah up and soothed her before Mark or Jonathan could reach her. When he did, Aubrey smiled up at him, her brown eyes sparkling.

"Thanks," Jonathan said, reaching for his daughter. He took Sarah in his arms and held her up, cooing gibberish to her before folding her in his embrace and kissing her face. "I missed you."

"You had us worried," Aubrey said.

"Not nearly as much as you had me worried," Jonathan said with a small laugh. "When I couldn't find — I thought . . ."

"Can I hold her?" Mark asked.

Jonathan looked warily at him, but Aubrey gave him a look. "Okay," he said. "But be careful with her, all right, sport?"

"Yeah, yeah," Mark said eagerly, and held out his hands for her. Sarah shook her head, but after a few soothing words from Aubrey, she went willingly with Mark. A scant moment later, she was laughing at the faces Mark was making to her.

Jonathan looked at Aubrey, taking in her long-sleeved T-shirt, in which she had cut a V-neck, and her plaid skirt, from which two shapely legs emerged. "You're . . . you're really good with my kid," he said.

"Wow," she said, giving him an appraising look. "Coming from you, I consider that a huge compliment." She smiled fully, almost transforming her face. *"Thanks."*

"You're good with other kids, too." With his head, he gestured at the others. "What's all this?"

"This is a program the YMCA funds. We're trying to teach the kids some assimilation skills."

"Night job?"

She laughed. "No, it's strictly volunteer. The program barely has money for snacks, much less paid staff." She gestured to the back and the kids who were snacking. "It's a problem — it's impossible to find good programs for kids like this." She looked at him. "Speaking of jobs . . . how's yours?"

Jonathan avoided her eyes and looked again at Mark and Sarah. Mark had her on her feet now, holding her arms up and prompting her to walk. "It'll do."

"We tried to call you —"

"Nancy told me. I went looking for a nap mat like Noelle told me." He shook his head. "I can't find one anywhere. It feels like a big conspiracy — don't tell the new guy where the kid mats are sold."

Aubrey laughed. "I guess they don't tell you stuff like that when you have a baby. It's not in the manual, right? But I think I can put my hands on one for you."

"As in '*Psst,* hey, man, I'll get you a mat for five thousand dollars'?"

She laughed. "I promise — not a cent over one grand."

Jonathan grinned at her as he stuffed his hands into his pockets. Something about her eyes always drew him in, made him think of her in a very intimate way. A sudden, uninvited vision of her popped into his head, one where she was beneath him, her brown eyes full of passion, her lips wet . . . the vision shuddered through him, and his gaze slipped to her lips.

Aubrey didn't move — she kept her gaze on his face, waiting. And watching.

Jonathan smiled a little. "You know what, brown eyes? You look too hot to be a teacher. Did anyone ever tell you that?"

Aubrey blushed and gave him a shy smile. "Ah . . . no. No, I can safely say no one ever told me that."

"I really dig the skull-and-crossbones earrings." He casually flicked one with his finger, then caught it again and let it drop. His fingers grazed her neck as he removed his hand. Such a small touch, but such a big reverberation in his body.

A slow smile curved Aubrey's lips. "Thanks," she said. "They're really different. That's why I like them."

Jonathan pushed his hand through his hair and glanced at Mark and Sarah — and started. Mark was holding Sarah aloft and attempting to toss her as he'd undoubtedly seen TV fathers do. "Whoa, whoa, sport!" Jonathan exclaimed, lunging toward him and catching Sarah out of his hands. "She's too little to throw."

"Oh," Mark said, his face falling. "I didn't mean to."

"It's okay." Jonathan smiled at him. "You're doing great. But you shouldn't throw her."

"Okay." Mark began to touch the tips of his fingers together. "I won't throw her. I promise."

Jonathan looked at Aubrey. He had no reason to hang around, but he wasn't quite ready to leave.

Aubrey clasped her hands behind her

back. "Well . . . Tammy is ready to go. Her enormous, troop-grade duffel bag with all her worldly possessions is in the corner."

Jonathan grinned. "Better safe than sorry. So . . . thanks, Aubrey. Thanks for taking care of her."

Her smile brightened. "No problem, J.B. Tammy's such a sweetie."

"I took care of her, too," Mark added as he nervously touched the tips of his fingers together. "Didn't I, Miss Cross? I took care of her."

"You certainly did, Mark," she said, and put her arm around the kid. She smiled at Jonathan again. "So I guess we'll see you tomorrow?"

"Right." Jonathan tried to make his feet move, but he couldn't seem to take his eyes off Aubrey. So many competing thoughts were in his head — such as how hot she was, and how he appreciated her style — that he was beginning to feel a little crazy. He'd lost Tammy only seven months ago — how he could suddenly find Aubrey appealing when he hadn't so much as looked at a woman in all these month baffled him.

Besides, it was useless to feel this way. He could never be with her even if he wanted to — which he did not — but if he did, he had too much baggage.

He realized he was holding Sarah tightly to him; she was beginning to squirm, restless to go or be put on her feet. "Okay," he said again. "I better go. Thanks. Really. I mean it."

"You're welcome."

He took another step back and collided with a rack of basketballs, sending a few of them to the floor.

"I'll get them!" Mark shouted, and began to try to round up the basketballs, picking up more than one and then dropping them all again.

Aubrey covered her mouth with her hand, but her eyes were glistening with laughter.

Jonathan waved and hurried out before he did anything else to humiliate himself.

He drove out of town with the gas pedal on the floor, trying to escape those weird feelings he'd had in the gym. Unfortunately, no matter how fast he drove out of town, he could not escape the image of Aubrey standing there looking hot as hell with that beautiful smile and those silly skull-and-crossbone earrings dangling from her ears.

18

"What do you think you're doing?"

Aubrey closed her eyes and braced herself before turning around to face Zeke. She'd known it was a bad idea to come home.

She was in the garage of her parents' home, in a cabinet where her mother had kept supplies for the day care, including several mats for napping. She had hoped to get in and get out before Zeke got home, but as usual, her timing was all wrong as far as he was concerned.

"I was getting some things for the day care," she said, holding the mats close to her chest. "You weren't home but I didn't think you'd mind."

"See, that's the problem with you, Aubrey. You're just like your mother — you *don't* think," he said, tapping his head. "And I guess when you tried to *think,* you thought those things belong to you, huh?"

"These are things Mom had collected for

work. I don't think they belong to me, I think they belong to the day care."

"Don't get smart with me. I know what you thought, but as usual, you thought wrong. Whatever is in this house, on *my* property, belongs to me. Not that damn day care. That was a big waste of money."

Aubrey saw her opening and stepped gingerly into it. "Nancy said the attorney sent you papers to sell it. Maybe you can sign them and be done with it."

That obviously surprised him. He laughed and shook his head. "You never cease to amaze me with the depth of your ignorance. You think I am going to sign a paper without thinking about it first?"

Aubrey glared at him. He returned a smirk as he strolled into the garage, one hand on the butt of his gun in his holster, the other hooked into his belt. "Now what do you call going into someone's house and taking something that doesn't belong to you? Stealing?"

She swallowed and forced herself to ask, "May I have these kid mats, please?"

"That depends," he said, bracing his legs apart and blocking her exit from the garage. "I might see my way to giving you my property. But I want something in return."

She cringed inside, dreading whatever

favor he wanted in return for a few measly mats she'd bet her life he didn't even know were here. "What?"

"I'm having a little barbecue for some of my buddies and their wives this weekend. I want you to come."

Aubrey blinked. There had to be a trick. There was always a trick with him. "That's it?" she asked suspiciously.

"That's it. I'd like my daughter to join me." He smiled, but it was a cool smile that had always made Aubrey's skin crawl. "Keith Stanley will be here. I think you oughta come and be nicer to him than you've managed to be since you came traipsing back from San Diego."

She immediately started to shake her head. "I can't. I —"

"You want those papers signed?" he asked quietly.

"Are you kidding? You will hold those papers over my head so you can pimp me out?"

He laughed, low and snidely. "You talk like a hooker. Call it what you want — but I want you here Saturday night at seven."

She hated him. Dear Lord, how she hated him. He said nothing, just stood there with that awful grin on his face, watching her and waiting for a response. She didn't trust him at all — if she refused, she wouldn't be the least bit surprised if he tore up the papers Nancy was waiting to receive, and all her mother's work would disappear, just like that. "I can't," she said. "I've made other plans."

"You'll unmake them if you want those papers."

She debated it. She wanted those papers, but she had promised Mark and his friends to take them to the fair. She shook her head. She'd promised them. "I'm not coming," she said firmly, and started to walk past him. "I have other plans and I won't change them."

Zeke caught her by the arm. "Did you hear me? I said change them. And wear something that doesn't make you look like a damn freak. Wear some decent clothes."

"Let go of me," she said through gritted teeth.

Zeke laughed and let her go. Aubrey wasted no time — she hurried down the drive to her car, threw the mats into the backseat, then got in the driver's seat and turned the key. Not until she reached the stop sign at the end of the street did she release her breath.

That she had risked even running into Zeke was one more sign that she was half-crazy for doing what she was presently doing — which was going out to J.B.'s house with a few things for Tammy.

Oh, yeah, she was crazy, all right. But she'd been thinking about it, and Noelle was right — she needed to get out more. And J.B. had . . . well, he hadn't exactly *encouraged* her to drive six miles out of town without an invitation or any clue how she might be received. But the way he'd looked at her at the gym? Suffice it to say that she could still feel the effects of it now. She could still see his brown eyes, could still feel how deeply they'd pierced her and how vulnerable and exposed and *attractive* she'd felt.

Somehow, J.B. could make her feel as if her insides were blazing when he was near, and somehow, she was compelled by a stronger force to seek more of that feeling. It was so unlike her — there was nothing in life that could *possibly* compel her to go to Zeke's for anything. But just one look from that tall, dark, and handsome stranger in town, and Aubrey was willing to do the unthinkable.

She'd remembered that Mom had kept some of the little napping mats, and that she'd kept a couple of day packs as well. She thought J.B. might appreciate not having to lug that giant duffel bag around. So she'd risked running into Zeke just to have an excuse to go see J.B. and Tammy out at the old Haney place — a bit of information she'd gleaned from the files this afternoon when he'd failed to show up on time to pick up Tammy.

What made this little trip to the outskirts completely insane was that she really had no idea what she'd find when she got there. For all she knew, he was hiding a girlfriend. Or maybe he'd be mad as hell that she'd come out to his house uninvited — she'd seen him fly off the handle for a lot less.

But then again, maybe he would smile at her the way he had this afternoon, and she could throw herself at his feet and beg him to take her to bed. That's what she wanted to do. Her blood was running so hot that was the only thing she could think of doing.

But whatever he might do — or not do — she would never know it if she returned to her little apartment, popped the frozen dinner into the microwave, and tuned in to some inane television show. "So just shut up and drive," she said to herself.

Aubrey arrived at the Haney place at a quarter to eight. She parked under an elm tree a little down the drive, gathered up the mat and the day pack, and began the trek up the gravel drive. As she neared the house, she could see J.B. in the window of the front room doing something that required he move his arm back and forth.

Curious, she strained to see —

Wait.

Aubrey paused. He was *ironing.* And when he held up what he was ironing, she gasped. He was ironing — and folding — baby T-shirts.

Aubrey had to stifle a laugh. She'd known a couple of people in her life who were anal-retentive enough to iron their T-shirts, but they weren't men, and they weren't ironing baby T's.

She continued up the drive, stepped through the squeaky little gate, then walked up the steps. With the first groan of the porch's wood, the door suddenly opened and J.B. stood there clutching a baby T in one hand.

And he wasn't wearing a shirt. *He wasn't wearing a shirt.*

This wasn't exactly how she'd imagined this scene going — she'd practiced what she'd say: "Hi, I hope you don't mind . . ." But she hadn't thought she'd be completely dumbstruck. Aubrey could not take her eyes off J. B. Winslow. She'd never seen a man who was shaped as well as he was — he looked like one of the Sexiest Men Alive guys they announced every year. He had a five-o'clock shadow that made him look rough and dangerous; his hair hung to his shoulders. His chest was broad and muscular, his pecs looking a little like armor. His biceps were huge and there wasn't an ounce of fat on him — all that muscle tapered into a trim waist. So did a thin line of hair that disappeared into the waistband of his jeans.

Fortunately for Aubrey, J.B. seemed a little shocked and didn't speak at first, which gave her enough time to find her breath, for it was suddenly gone from her lungs.

He squinted at her as if he was trying to make out who she was. And then he looked over the top of her head, down the drive, while he ran a hand over his head.

Aubrey cleared her throat. "Ah . . . *hey.*"

J.B. put his hand on his waist and peered at her. "What are you doing here?"

"I know, I know, I should have called first," she said, throwing up a hand, "but there is the problem with the, ah . . ." She gestured toward her ear. "Your phone number. I had the wrong phone number."

She was babbling.

"Right," he said, but still looked at her curiously. "So . . . is something wrong?"

Only that she was still having trouble

breathing while he stood there practically naked in front of her. Not *naked,* really, but wouldn't it be nice if he were? Oh, God, what was she thinking?

"Aubrey?" he prompted her.

"Are you ironing baby T's?"

J.B. glanced at the T-shirt in his hand as Tammy began to cry inside. "Yeah. Why?" he asked as he stepped inside the house. "Is there some reason I shouldn't be?" he called over his shoulder as he moved deeper into the room.

"No," Aubrey called after him, and stepped to the open door. He'd left the door and the screen open. He tossed the baby T onto the ironing board and squatted down to unlatch Tammy from her swing. Aubrey glanced around the room — it was sparsely furnished, but then again, it was obvious he was just moving in. There was a couch, a chair, a scarred coffee table, and boxes serving as end tables. There was nothing else but the baby swing and a few toys scattered about. "I'm just surprised."

"What? You didn't think I knew how to iron?" he asked, rising up with Tammy in one arm.

"I didn't say that." She smiled as she noticed the neat stack of baby clothes on a box. "But it wouldn't have been my first guess as to your talents."

"Yeah, well, if you saw how many of her T-shirts had burns on them, you wouldn't call it a talent." He picked up a teething ring and gave it to Tammy, then looked at Aubrey standing in the doorway and smiled a little. "Looks like we keep surprising each other."

"Looks like," she said, returning his smile.

He motioned for her to enter. "Come in, if you're coming in."

"Oh. Okay." She stepped across the threshold and closed the screen door behind her. "I, ah . . . I brought you a mat." She held that up. "And I thought you might want something a little more manageable than a duffel bag for the day care."

He looked at the things she held out, then at her. "Why?"

Why? What do you mean why? Why do you always ask *why?*"

"Why would you do that for me?"

Because I like you. Because I want to get to know you. Because I couldn't think of a better reason to drive out here just to see you. "Actually . . . I did it for Tammy."

"Ba ba ba ba," Tammy babbled at her.

Aubrey smiled. "See? She knows."

"So where's this top-secret location where they hide the nap mats?"

"They, ah . . . they carry them at the hardware store."

"The *hardware* store?" J.B. echoed incredulously, and shook his head. "The one place I didn't look. So what do I owe you?" he asked, reaching in his back pocket for his wallet.

"Oh, nothing," she said quickly, waving a hand at him. "My mom had a few of them lying around."

"She's okay with me having one?" he asked as he suddenly dipped to retrieve a lamp that Sarah was about to pull off the end-table box.

"Oh. Sure," Aubrey said, a little disconcerted. "I mean, she's not around anymore."

J.B. glanced at her curiously. "What do you mean?"

"She, ah . . ." Aubrey shifted her gaze to her hands. It had been three months and it was still too raw and painful to speak of. "She died," she said, and frowned at her hands.

"Man. I'm sorry," J.B. said instantly. "I didn't know —"

"No, of course you didn't. I didn't mean to bring it up. I guess it just hasn't been that long ago, and I'm still getting used to the idea."

He nodded, but he kept watching her, as

if he expected her to burst into tears. Which, remarkably, she felt close to doing.

"How'd she die?" he asked quietly.

"Oh." Aubrey gestured to her chest. "Breast cancer." She pressed her lips together and nodded. "Yep. That's what got her."

"Ah," he said, and looked down at Tammy. "My mom had breast cancer, too."

"Really?" Aubrey asked softly.

"Yeah." He frowned a little. "She almost died. But she . . ." He smiled a little and glanced at Tammy, who was now crawling toward her favorite red truck. "She beat it. My mom's a real fighter."

"You're lucky," Aubrey said quietly. "My mom was a fighter, too, but I guess the big C was too big for her in the end." That, or Aubrey had always wondered if her mom had just wanted out, away from Zeke for eternity. "So do you see your mom often?"

Something passed over J.B.'s features. He suddenly swooped down on Tammy again. "Nah. We're not exactly speaking."

"Oh. I'm sorry."

He turned away from her; she could see that the conversation was making him uncomfortable. "So, listen, I've got to give the munchkin a bath."

That was obviously her cue to leave. Aubrey nodded. "Sure. Okay, well —"

"You want to help?"

Aubrey couldn't help her smile. She felt as if she were going to burst wide open with it. "I'd love to . . . if it's all right with Tammy, that is."

"I don't know." He suddenly turned around and held Tammy out to her. "Ask her while I run the water."

Aubrey laughed as she took a smiling Tammy from him.

"I'll be right back." J.B. walked toward the kitchen door. "Have you eaten?" he asked, pausing at the door.

"Ah . . . no."

"I made some spaghetti," he said from the kitchen. "Not exactly gourmet, but Sarah likes it."

"Who?"

J.B. suddenly blanched. But then he smiled, a little too brightly. "I mean Tammy," he said, gesturing to her. "I have a cousin named Sarah. I was thinking of her." He abruptly turned and walked into the kitchen. "So you want a little spaghetti and a glass of wine?" he called back.

Frankly, after many nights of frozen organic foods, that sounded almost too divine. "I would love some!" Aubrey responded, then smiled down at Tammy and kissed her little hand. "Hey," she whispered, shaking her little hand. "Thanks for the leg up."

19

Jonathan grabbed a shirt from the laundry pile and shrugged into it as he entered the kitchen. As he buttoned up, he did a quick look around the kitchen to assure himself he hadn't left anything incriminating lying around. Fortunately, all he saw was a pot of spaghetti on the stove, a bottle of wine that he'd left open to breathe, and Sarah's things.

The pantry, which lacked doors, showed nothing more than the baby foods lined up in alphabetical order. He'd learned early on that it was easier to be organized with a baby. Cans of formula were on the bottom shelf, and four bottles with premeasured formula awaited the juice or water he would mix it with tomorrow before he left for work.

On the kitchen table, he'd left a package of diapers and wipes and now pushed those onto a chair — it looked a little unsanitary, he supposed, but the table was the perfect height to change her. He made a mental note to wash it down with soap and water before he tried to serve a plate of overcooked noodles and sauce from a jar. He wasn't exactly a world-class chef. Frankly, no one was more surprised than he when the invitation had slipped out of his mouth — but Aubrey had looked so damn cute and vulnerable standing there.

Speaking of the devil, she stepped tentatively into the kitchen with Sarah and looked around.

"I just bathe her in the sink," Jonathan said as he turned on the water. He nodded at a bag that looked like a giant pink bunny hanging off the back of one chair at the kitchen table. "Do me a favor and hand me that bag, would you?"

Aubrey picked it up and walked around the kitchen counter to stand next to him. Sarah began to gurgle with delight as he tested the water temperature — she loved baths. As they waited for the water to warm, he opened the pink bunny bag and pulled out the rubber ducks Sarah loved, and the baby began to babble.

Aubrey stood Sarah up on the counter so that she could remove her clothing.

"Thanks for the help," Jonathan said. "It's hard to juggle her and everything else."

"I can imagine," Aubrey said congenially

as she removed Sarah's T-shirt. "You'd think that three adults and a part-timer could handle twelve kids on any given day, but sometimes it feels like they multiply like little aliens."

Jonathan smiled. "You ready, Munchkin?" He lifted Sarah up from the countertop and put her in the bathwater along with her ducks. Sarah grabbed the first one that floated by and put it in her mouth. "You might want to step back," Jonathan said. "She gets pretty wild with her ducks. Help yourself to some wine."

"Thanks," Aubrey said. "Glasses?"

Jonathan snorted. "I haven't exactly had time to stock the fine china and crystal. Look up there." He gestured to a cabinet with his head.

Aubrey reached up to open the cabinet, and Jonathan got a glimpse of the flat plane of her bare belly. That led to other visions — bare breasts. Bare bottoms. He couldn't help himself — she was all curves in all the right places in the funky clothes she wore, and he was a guy. He'd have to be dead not to notice. *Tammy,* he told himself. *Think of Tammy.* He shook his head and made little soapy horns on Sarah's head.

"Oh, hey, this is good," Aubrey said as she tasted the wine.

"You're old enough to drink, aren't you?" he asked. "I don't want to get pinged for contributing to the delinquency of a minor."

"Hey!" she said with mock offense. "I'm twenty-three. I am definitely old enough to drink out of a Tweety glass." She held it up to him. "So this is really good wine," she said again, looking at the bottle.

"I picked it up in Phoenix."

"Oh?" She poured him a glass. "What were you doing in Phoenix?"

Great. Just when he was beginning to feel loose and human again, he had to go and open his big mouth and invite questions. "Just passing through. Would you mind checking the sauce? I turned off the burner, but it might be getting cold."

Aubrey moved to the stove and took the lid off the pot. "It smells wonderful. Where'd you learn to cook?"

"Who said I could cook?"

She laughed. "Looks pretty good to me. Did your mom teach you?"

Jonathan looked at Sarah and smiled sadly. He wanted to apologize to his baby, to tell her this was the way it would always be. They'd find someone they liked, and that person would ask a few questions, and that would be it — he'd have to cut it off. When he'd seen Aubrey in his house, he had believed that maybe, just maybe, after months of being on the road with no one to talk to but a baby — and sometimes a sick baby at that — he could have a little human contact.

But he'd been a fool to think it — and that was okay, really. He'd never been one of those guys who could sit around and shoot the breeze anyway. He sure couldn't be that way now.

"Whoopsie daisy," he said as he lifted Sarah from her bath and sat her down on a towel he'd laid out on the counter. He dried her off, and her hair, then wrapped her in the towel. "I'll be back. I'm just going to put her down." He stopped at the fridge, took out a bottle he'd already made up, and tossed it into the microwave for ten seconds.

When he'd diapered Sarah and dressed her in a sleep outfit, he put her down in her crib with the bottle and leaned over the rail. He stroked her cheek as she fed on the bottle. "Sleep tight, Munchkin. I don't think she's coming back, so you get some sleep." There was no sound from Sarah but the little grunts she made as she sucked her bottle. Jonathan turned on the little carousel above her head. "I love you, baby," he whispered. "Daddy loves you."

When he returned to the kitchen, he was

surprised to find that Aubrey had found the plates and had set them on the table. She was looking in the drawers, and for one insane moment, Jonathan felt a surge of panic — until he remembered there was nothing in the drawers.

"Need help?" he asked.

His question startled her — she smiled nervously. "I was just looking for some cutlery."

"Third drawer on your left."

Aubrey opened the drawer and withdrew two settings and held them up with a smile. "Thanks for inviting me. I'm starving. Is Tammy asleep?"

"She will be. She's like her old man. A couple of bottles and she's out cold."

Aubrey smiled as she put the cutlery on the table while Jonathan took the spaghetti from the pan and heaped two mounds onto each plate.

He put the pan of sauce on a hot pad in the middle of the table and stuck a spoon in it. "Sorry there's not more," he said as he picked up a fork.

"Are you kidding? This is a feast. I usually eat some steamed vegetables and call it a night."

"Oh, yeah?" Jonathan asked, noting the elegance of her hands, oddly juxtaposed against the thick, black leather stud bracelet she wore. "Don't you get out?"

"Not much."

"At least you eat at Dot's Diner, right?"

She snorted as if that were a ludicrous suggestion. "*No.* They don't serve my kind of food, and it's just a little uncomfortable. People in Tourmaline aren't used to women eating alone and they stare. It's like this place is stuck in a 1950s time warp or something."

He twirled some noodles around his fork. "So . . . why do you stay in Tourmaline if you dislike it so much?" he asked curiously.

She gave him a wary look over the top of her Tweety glass. "I'm not *staying,*" she corrected him. "I'm getting out of here soon. I just have to see to a few things for my mom."

"Ah." He turned his attention back to his plate. "I like it here."

"That's because you don't know Tourmaline," she said, drawing a look from Jonathan. "You *don't,*" she insisted. "It looks good on the surface. Nice and clean with big, grassy yards and corny traditions like the harvest fair that's starting up this weekend. It looks really homey, like a place you'd want to raise your kid. But trust me, there is nothing good in this town. Nothing ever changes, and if it does, it just goes backward." She stabbed her fork into her spaghetti hard and twirled noodles with a vengeance.

"Wow," Jonathan said, leaning back in his chair. "You really hate it here."

"You will, too, in time."

"Come on," he said, draping one arm over the back of his chair and extending his leg under the table. "Noelle seems nice. So does her mom."

Aubrey put down her fork and shrugged. "They're nice," she admitted.

"And the lady at the diner — Randi. She's always friendly to me."

Aubrey glanced out the window. "You can go down the list of everyone in this town and say something nice. But there's a lot you don't understand, J.B. Still waters run deep."

Jonathan couldn't help it — he laughed. " 'Still waters run deep'? What's that, from a song?"

Aubrey's copper brown eyes flashed, and she suddenly pushed back from the table. "You really don't get it." She stood abruptly.

"Hey, come on." Jonathan caught her by the arm. "I was just having a little fun."

"I didn't think it was funny." She tried to shrug free of his grip.

"Hey, *hey*," Jonathan said, his smile fading as he gained his feet. Aubrey looked truly distressed — far too distressed, really. "It's just a silly conversation about a silly little town. It's nothing to get upset about."

But Aubrey pulled her arm free of his hand. "I just wish you'd listen to me. Don't stay here. Think of Tammy, not yourself!"

Anger rippled through him and Jonathan caught her arm again. "I *always* think of Tammy," he said hotly. "In fact, she is the *only* thing I think about."

Aubrey's eyes were blazing. "Then prove it. Take her some place safe."

Something came over Jonathan — a rush of surprise, of need, of fatigue from running, always running. His gaze fell to her lips and he felt a swell of desire in him. He slid his palm down to her wrist and wrapped his fingers around it.

Aubrey looked at his hand on her wrist, then at him. "What are you doing?"

"Since we're handing out free advice, maybe you should stop acting so tough. You're not tough. Not inside. You're soft."

"I am not *soft*," she scoffed.

"Oh, yeah, you are. You're soft, and someone in this town has hurt you, and so you've adopted this kick-ass attitude to deal with it."

"You don't know anything, J.B.," she said, pulling away from him.

But he held on to her wrist. "I'm not wrong," he said, shaking his head. "I know the signs. I *invented* the signs."

"Oh, for heaven's sake —"

He caught her chin in his hand and made her face up to him. He could see the truth in her eyes — he had pegged her. He knew exactly what she was, because she was a female version of himself. She was alone in the world and lashing out at anyone who got too close. "Admit it," he said softly.

"Why?" she demanded. "So you can ridicule me? Plunge your knife in and twist it a little? You don't even *know* me!"

His gaze slid to her mouth again. "I may know you better than you think." And he did know her better than she thought — maybe even better than she knew herself in some respects. He'd been exactly where she was, but he'd been lucky. He'd found Tammy. He'd found someone who believed in him, who made *him* believe in himself. Who did Aubrey Cross have?

"Just let go of me," she said, pushing again. But her voice was softer, and he sensed she was on the edge of crumbling.

Jonathan did let go of her — but he caught her by the waist with his arm and drew her into him. The moment he touched her, the moment he'd seen the vulnerability and the desire to be held in her eyes, desire began racing through him like a freight train.

"You've been alone too long," he said. "I know what's inside of you."

Aubrey's eyes glittered with anger and arousal. "What do you know? What do you know about hurt or disappointment or anger?"

Jonathan chuckled. "You'd be surprised," he said, and lowered his mouth to hers. Aubrey gasped at first, her breath warm on his lips — but then he felt her go soft.

He smoothed her hair from her face and said, "I see, Aubrey. I see you. You think you're alone, but I see you."

"You think you know so much. What are you hiding, J.B.? What is it that makes you turn away or get angry every time someone asks something about *you*, huh? Maybe —"

He pulled her closer, kissing her hard, kissing her with what felt like centuries of pent-up desire. He nipped at her bottom lip, then swept his tongue inside her mouth as he lifted his hand to her face and splayed his fingers along her jaw, tilting her head so that he could kiss her more thoroughly.

She grabbed the hand that held her chin, holding on tight to it, her kiss every bit as full of passion as his, every bit as full of need and hunger and loneliness. He could feel the pressure building in him, filling him up.

He moved his hand to the vee of her T-shirt, slipping his hand inside, caressing the swell of her breasts with his knuckles before slipping his hand over a lacy red bra and filling it with her breast.

Aubrey made a sound of pleasure deep in her throat when he did. "This is crazy," she panted. "I don't want to be some mindless conquest."

That sparked a memory in him — *The first time you see a woman in tight pants . . .* Those were Alan Spaulding's words, spoken at Tammy's funeral when he'd accused Jonathan of manufacturing his grief, and they came roaring back to him now.

He paused, trying to banish Alan's words from his mind — and something outside caught his eye. He thought it was a firefly, a small, dim flash of light in the evening sky.

He pulled away from Aubrey and walked to the window, peering outside.

"Ah . . . hello?" Aubrey said.

"Someone is out there."

"It's probably just fireflies," Aubrey said. "There are loads of them around here."

"Don't think so." He headed for the door. He strode out onto the lawn, looking around, trying to peer into the darkness.

He moved around the perimeter of the house, looking at every tree, every shadow, his mind racing through the possibilities. Fireflies. A falling star. Alan.

By the time he'd circled around to the front, Aubrey was standing on the porch, hugging herself. "Did you find anything?"

Nothing. But he knew he wasn't hallucinating — he'd seen something from the window. What if it was Alan? "You'd probably better go," he said, gesturing to her car.

Aubrey blinked. "But . . . but there's nothing out here."

"It's late." He walked up onto the porch.

"Just like that?" she asked, her tone incredulous.

He didn't answer. More was going on here than he could explain now, and besides, looking at her face in the moonlight made him realize how close he'd been to betraying Tammy.

"Okay," she said, dropping her arms, frowning. "I get it." She brushed past him and walked back into the house. He followed her inside as she snatched up her purse, then walked back out the door without looking at him. But Jonathan could see the anger and the hurt on her face.

He wanted to say something, to let her know he hadn't meant to sound so callous. But it was too late. She'd already walked out, letting the door swing shut behind her. The sound of it woke Sarah — she began to wail.

"Great," he muttered, standing in the living room, his hands on his hips, feeling like a heel. As Sarah cried, he watched Aubrey run to her car and get in, then watched gravel fly as she drove recklessly from his drive.

"Coming, baby," he called to a wailing Sarah, and, with a sigh, went to see to her.

She was standing in her crib, and he picked her up. *"Sssh,"* he said, bouncing her gently. "It's okay."

She dropped her head to his shoulder and rubbed her eyes with her fists.

He carefully laid her in the crib, gave her a pacifier, and arranged her kitty next to her body. With a sigh, Sarah rolled onto her side, clutching her stuffed animal.

Jonathan turned around — and almost fainted.

Tammy stood at the door.

20

"Tammy." He glanced at Sarah — the pacifier was hanging out of the corner of her mouth; she was already asleep. He looked at Tammy again.

She turned and disappeared into his room.

He wasn't losing her again — Jonathan went after her, his arms reaching for her. But Tammy had somehow managed to move to the other side of the room and was standing next to the window.

"Don't move," he said, pointing a finger at her. "Don't. *Move.*" Slowly, carefully, he walked toward her. She seemed so real — he didn't want to contemplate his mental state, but he thought he was seeing a ghost. And when he reached for her — so close, within arm's length — she wasn't there any longer, but on the other side of the bed. Jonathan went down on one knee onto the bed, leaning forward, bracing his arms against the mattress, poised to lunge for her if she tried to leave him again. "You're gonna stay this time. You're not going."

"You don't need me anymore. Jonathan, you have to go on. You have to stop thinking of the past and think of the future . . . you owe that to Sarah."

"I owe Sarah *us*," he said desperately. "It was supposed to be you and me, babe, and Sarah — remember? That's what I want for her. That's what *she* wants. Come back, Tammy. Come back," he said, reaching a hand out to her.

Tammy smiled sadly and shook her head. "You know I can't. I'm in the past. You have to go on, Jonathan. Look forward. You've been running all this time, looking back over your shoulder instead of looking ahead to where you should be running."

"I've been keeping Sarah safe, like you wanted. Everything you wanted, I've been doing for you."

"Then do this for me. Move on," she said earnestly. "I want you to be happy. I want you to remember me, not try to live for me."

"No." He shook his head violently. "No." He suddenly moved, jumping up and taking the bed in one stride, desperate to catch her, to feel her in his arms once more. But when he landed on the other side of the bed, she was gone. "Tammy!" he said, twisting one way, then the other. *"Tammy!"*

She was gone.

Jonathan growled with frustration and hit the wall with his fist, then fell back onto his bed, one arm slung over his eyes, squeezing back tears of frustration, of loneliness, of longing for a woman who had died. He thought of how she had looked in the autumn when they stood outside CO^2, the tip of her nose and her cheeks stained pink from the chill in the air. He thought of her holding Sarah in her arms, smiling down at her with eyes full of light and love. And he thought of her in the barn, wearing a skirt and a lacy bra, her face flushed with the heat of their lovemaking.

Jonathan groaned and rolled onto his stomach, but the image did not leave him. Tammy straddled him, kissing him, her small hands cupping his face. "I love you, Jonathan Randall," she said as she kissed him.

Jonathan was lost in the memory. He could feel her body on his, the smooth skin of her legs pressed against him. He could feel her hands on his face, her lips soft and warm on his. He put his hands on her thigh, slid them up to her waist, and up her rib cage. He moaned with pleasure at the feel of her breasts swelling in his hands, and the weight of her body on his lap. He kissed her and felt the familiar heat of need spread through him. He was aware of her body, was imagining how she would feel when he moved inside her.

Jonathan splayed his fingers across her cheek. Tammy sighed with pleasure as they kissed, her hand skimming his shoulders, his chest, and reaching down, between them. But as she touched him, she moaned deep in her throat, and Jonathan opened his eyes.

It wasn't Tammy he was kissing — it was Aubrey. It was Aubrey whose lips he nipped, Aubrey's tongue that swirled around his, Aubrey who moved suggestively against his lap. It was Aubrey whose kiss knocked him back and sent him falling into a pool of desire, and he fell back with a cry of alarm.

It was Aubrey, uninvited, unwanted, smiling down at him.

He heard another cry and shoved away from her, rolling off the bed and landing on the floor next to the bed. He blinked and shook his head, freeing himself from the memory — no, the fantasy. It took him a moment to realize the cry he heard was Sarah's. He quickly gained his feet, stumbling into the nursery.

Sarah was lying on her back, crying. He

picked her up, put a hand to her back to soothe her — but when he touched her, his blood ran cold. She was hot. Feverish. He could feel it through her sleeper.

"No no no no," he muttered, and pressed his lips to her forehead. She was warm, too warm. Fear snaked through him, curling tightly in his belly. How long had she been warm? Had he been so caught up with Aubrey that he hadn't even noticed Sarah had a fever?

"Baby," he said, kissing her again, "you don't feel good, do you? Daddy's going to change that. Daddy's got something to make you feel better." He carried her into the kitchen, where he opened the fridge and dipped down, finding the Ziploc bag with all the medicines she needed.

Aubrey was in a black mood when she arrived at work the next morning in camos, a green SAVE THE EARTH T-shirt, and dark glasses that hid how bloodshot her eyes were.

Last night had been excruciating — just when she would slide into sleep, she would be jolted back to awareness with a memory of J.B. kissing her and sending her home.

Bastard.

What really infuriated Aubrey was that she

considered herself a reasonably intelligent woman. Yes, okay, she'd had her moments, but they didn't usually involve being attracted to insane men.

And J. B. Winslow was insane — totally and completely. One moment he was so sexy and warm with a light in his eyes that made her feel as if he could see all the way through her, right down to the very bottom. And the next minute he was sending her home because he'd seen a firefly.

What in the hell did she *see* in him?

And to think she'd been just moments away from ripping off her clothes and throwing herself at him.

She pulled to an angry stop on the side of Bright Horizons, pushed her hair behind her ears, and squeezed her eyes shut. "Stupid," she muttered to herself. "Stupid, stupid." With a sigh, she got out of her car.

And almost collided with J.B.

She hadn't seen him there, because if she had, she would have backed up and parked somewhere else.

He looked so handsome standing there with his baby that she hated him with every fiber of her being. There were no words to describe the emotions that filled her — she felt queasy and giddy all at once, angry and happy and confused. What was the matter with her? How could she possibly be feeling such ridiculous feelings of desire and longing for this jerk?

"Hey," he said solemnly.

Aubrey threw up a hand. "I don't want to talk to you, J.B." She tried to walk past him.

But J.B. put out a hand. "Hold on, Aubrey."

Something in his voice stopped her, and with an angry sigh Aubrey looked at him sidelong. "Why should I? There's really something not right about you, you know that? Something majorly off."

"Look . . . I'm sorry about last night," he said, and sounded, infuriatingly, sorry.

"Save your breath, J.B."

"Aubrey, I need you. No . . . not *me,*" he quickly clarified at her look of surprise. "Tammy."

Something about the way he said it, the worry in his voice and in his eyes, stopped her. She glanced at Tammy — she had her chubby hands on the collar of his jacket, was trying to put the corner of it in her mouth.

"What about Tammy?"

He pulled out a Ziploc bag full of brown and white bottles and baby medicine droppers that made her eyes widen. "I think she's okay," he said, sounding uncertain.

"She had a fever last night, but she doesn't have one today, which is a good sign."

"Babies get fevers," Aubrey said.

"Other babies aren't like Tammy."

If Aubrey had a dime for every time she had heard that from a concerned parent —

"She's had some . . . problems."

"What do you mean?" Aubrey asked, looking at the Ziploc bag, then at his baby. She instinctively put her hand on Tammy's back.

"It's a long story." He kissed the baby's forehead, his lips lingering there. "I just need you to give her some medicine today."

"Oh, no," Aubrey said, shaking her head. "You can't just drop that on me and then hand me a bag full of medicine and expect me to just smile and start stuffing pills down her."

He sighed. And glanced around. "Okay," he said, shifting closer. "But I don't want anyone else to know this. Will you give me your word?"

She didn't like the tack this conversation was taking. "Know *what?*" she demanded. "And how do you expect me to keep a bag of medicine that big a secret from everyone?"

"Tammy had a bone marrow transplant," he blurted, and shushed Aubrey when she gasped. "She had what is called infant anemia. She's okay, she really is. But sometimes she needs to take medicine to boost her immune system and keep everything up and running."

Aubrey gaped at him in disbelief.

"She's fine, they fixed her. That's all you need to know."

"Why?" Aubrey demanded. "Why is that such a secret? And why are you moving around with a baby who has been so sick?"

"I've got my reasons —"

"There is *no* reason for this," Aubrey said, gesturing wildly at Tammy and the drugs he held. "Unless you kidnapped her. Did you kidnap her?"

His expression turned dark. "Tammy is *my* kid," he said, poking himself hard in the chest. "And the rest is none of your business."

"You owe me an explanation," she said angrily. "If everything has to be a huge secret, then get someone else to play your little game, J.B. I'm not interested."

His eyes narrowed angrily. "And you're so pure, is that it, Aubrey?"

"What?" she said, taken aback. "I'm not hiding anything from you!"

"Oh, no? How about the reason you want to get out of this town so bad? Isn't that a secret?"

"But I haven't done anything criminal — I haven't *kidnapped* a sick baby."

"But maybe you did something, huh?" he said, his voice low and menacing. "Maybe that's why you were so afraid to go to the cops the first night I met you."

Aubrey blanched and backed up a step.

"What's the story there? Your father is the sheriff in this county, and you're afraid to call the cops? Why is that? Maybe *you've* done something wrong."

"I have not!" she cried.

"Then why didn't you tell me your father is the sheriff? You must have something to hide."

"I have *nothing* to hide," she said angrily, knowing as the words came out of her mouth that it was a lie. "You don't know what you're talking about," she said shakily.

"And neither do you," he said, his voice softer. He thrust the Ziploc bag of medicine at her. "I wrote down what she needs to take and when. If anyone asks, will you please tell them it's just allergies?"

Aubrey looked at the bag, then at him. She snatched the bag from his hands. "Wouldn't life be easier if you just trusted me, if only a little?"

Jonathan smiled wryly. "You call me if anything seems strange, okay?"

"Whatever," Aubrey muttered, and took Tammy as he handed her the baby. He dipped into the backseat of his car and pulled out the day pack and sleep mat she'd brought him last night. "I really appreciate this," he said, holding up the two items. He smiled again, a heart-stopping smile that made Aubrey melt inside. Who was crazy now?

On his way to work that morning, as he was driving past the day care, Keith Stanley saw a guy with long, dark hair tied in a ponytail talking to Aubrey on the sidewalk. It was the third time he'd seen her talking to that thug, and Keith was more than a little irritated by it — she treated him like dirt beneath her feet, but then she'd smile at that loser.

Keith picked up his cell phone and called Zeke. "Yo, Sheriff," he said jovially when the sheriff answered. "Got lunch plans?"

"Not really. Dan and I were just doing a little patrolling this morning and haven't really settled on a place," Zeke said.

"How about meeting me at the Brick Oven around noon?"

"Sounds good, Keith. We'll see you then."

Keith was at the Brick Oven, a family-style restaurant on the edge of town, at ten after twelve. He found Zeke sitting in a back booth with his deputy Dan. "Take a load off," Zeke offered, gesturing for Dan to scoot over.

Keith took a seat, told the waitress he'd take a Coke and a California club sandwich.

"Saw your boss this morning," Zeke said, as he shoveled his fork into a plate of lasagna. "Said sales have doubled out there in the last year."

"Yep," Keith said. "We're doing internet sales now, and that has made a huge difference." He looked at Zeke. "And no one's stealing from us anymore."

Zeke smiled. "You must be making some good money then."

"I can't complain. I just bought a new house. And I have a new truck." Keith looked pointedly at Zeke. "The only thing that seems to be missing is someone to fill up that house. It's kind of big for a single guy."

"I hear you," Zeke said congenially. "A man needs to settle down after a time — you know, get married, raise kids. Wouldn't you say so, Dan?"

"Oh, yeah. I've been married fourteen years now," Dan said with a smile for Keith. "Best fourteen years of my life."

Keith nodded.

"You got any plans for settling down, Keith?" Zeke asked as he forked up more lasagna.

"I'd like to. I'd like to have a couple of kids. But it's not that easy. There's not a lot to choose from here in Tourmaline. And besides . . . I've had my eye on someone for several years now."

Zeke smiled. "I kind of thought so."

"I won't lie to you, Sheriff," Keith said, leaning forward. "I was hoping with Aubrey home, we might pick up where we left off."

"So what's the problem?"

Keith glanced around them and leaned even closer. "I'd say a new guy in town is the problem. He's a punk — not the type we want settling in Tourmaline, if you know what I mean. And he damn sure doesn't look like the type Aubrey would want to get mixed up with. He's just a thug, a no-account thug."

"Then maybe he needs to move on," Zeke suggested.

Keith snorted as the waitress slid a club sandwich in front of him. "Easier said than done."

Zeke exchanged a tight smile with Dan. "Well, you know, Keith . . . if someone were to suggest to him that he move on in a meaningful way, Dan here wouldn't object."

Keith looked at Dan.

"Hell, Keith, I'll be patrolling the west side of the county this afternoon. I won't even be in Tourmaline," Dan said.

Keith quickly shifted his gaze to Zeke, who was smiling coldly. "And I've got a three-o'clock tee time," Zeke said with a subtle wink. "I need to run back to the office and finish up a couple of things before I hit the links." He shoved a healthy bite of lasagna into his mouth.

Keith nodded, comprehending Zeke's meaning, and picked up a quarter of his sandwich. "You need me to bring anything to the barbecue Saturday?" he asked, slyly changing the subject.

"Nah, Keith. Just bring yourself," Zeke said with a smile. "I think I've got everything else covered." He lifted his arm and snapped his fingers. "Willa, bring me a check, will you?" he called out, and gave Keith a small smile.

21

Jonathan stopped every hour throughout the day to call Aubrey and ask about Sarah. Aubrey assured him she was fine, and in one of the last calls, she'd grown exasperated with him. "J.B., will you let me work? There are more kids here than just Tammy."

"Okay, fine," he said. But he'd called once more. By the end of the workday, he was convinced that Sarah had had nothing more than a little fever — nothing else, nothing scary.

His relief was like a drug, making him feel deliriously happy — he'd worried all night what he would do if she was getting sick again. He didn't have to face that now, and he was grinning to himself when he strolled out to the back lot where he'd parked his car, away from most everyone else. It was his habit, learned after months on the road. If he stayed too long in one place, people would see the baby carrier in the backseat, and the provisions he'd packed around the seat that would enable him and Sarah to survive a nuclear holocaust, and they'd begin to ask questions.

So he made a habit of parking away from everyone else.

Today, he noticed a big black pickup as he walked across the caliche lot, but he didn't think anything of it — it was a quarter past five, and he figured whoever it was had come to pick up one of the crew.

His head down, he dug his keys out of his pocket. But when he glanced up again, he saw a man standing near his car. It looked like he'd just walked out of the woods that bordered the temporary lot.

Jonathan stopped midstride. He'd been in plenty of scraps in his life, and he knew trouble when he saw it. And as if it had been scripted, another man emerged from the woods and stood beside the first.

Alan. It was his first thought, his only thought. Somehow, Alan had found him. With his gaze steady on the two men, Jonathan slowly put the lunch box he'd picked up at the five-and-dime on the ground. He straightened up and put his hands on his hips. "What?"

The man in front — tall and big, but a little soft — stepped forward. "What's your name, pal?"

They wanted to make sure they had the right guy before they killed him. "Who wants to know?"

The man grinned at his companion. "Most people in these parts are friendly. When a person asks their name, they answer."

Yeah, well, if Alan had found him and sent his goons, Jonathan wasn't giving him any information. Anxiety rifled through him — if they'd found him, had they found Sarah?

"I'll ask you again, politely," the man said. "What's your name?"

"And I'll ask you again, politely," Jonathan said stoically. "Who wants to know?"

The man sighed and shook his head. "Let me tell you something, boy. You don't belong in Tourmaline. I thought maybe you were just passing through with the harvest fair, but looks like you're putting down roots."

Something clicked in Jonathan's brain — these weren't Alan's men. And he'd seen this guy before. But *where?* "What of it?" he asked.

"Well, here's the problem — we're good, decent people here in Tourmaline. We're not a bunch of punks. You'd be better off with your own kind."

Suddenly Jonathan remembered with a

rush of relief — he'd seen this guy talking to Aubrey at the diner. This wasn't Alan's guy — this was a guy with a thing for Aubrey. Jonathan braced his legs apart, prepared to do battle. "Nah," he said with a cavalier shrug. "I think I'll stay."

"Then maybe we can persuade you differently," the man said, moving closer to Jonathan.

"The only thing you can persuade me to do is put a boot down your throat."

"Just what I figured, punk," the man said, and took a swing.

Jonathan ducked and came up swinging with his fists, managing to connect with the man's jaw. He swung again, and again, making contact both times, but the second man jumped him at the same moment the first man got a boot in his ribs.

They knocked him to the ground; Jonathan rolled and managed to get to his feet again, but they were in front of him and behind him. He knew he didn't have a chance, but he gave it all he had. When they knocked him down again, the guy jumped on him, pummeling his face and shoulders, while the second man kicked him. After what seemed like hours to Jonathan, the first man climbed off.

Jonathan was hurting, but he was glad to

see his assailant was panting, his lip busted wide-open, and his shirt stained with sweat from the exertion. "Get out of Tourmaline," he said again, and spit on Jonathan as he stepped over him.

Jonathan groaned and rolled to his side. He heard them jog across the lot and get in the pickup. He heard it start up and tear out of the lot. When it sounded like they were well down the road, he slowly pushed himself to his knees and mentally reviewed all the parts of his body.

He thought they were all there.

He gingerly felt his face with his fingers — his lip was fat but otherwise intact, and it felt like he had a nasty gash over his brow.

"Damn," he muttered, and gingerly rose to his feet, testing all four limbs again before he tried walking. When he was convinced nothing other than his ego was hurt too badly, he picked up his lunch pail with a hiss of pain and stumbled toward his car.

It was five after six by the time he reached the day care. He stepped out of the car carefully, as each step caused a sharp pain to shoot through his side, making him worry that a couple of ribs were broken.

Fortunately, the door was unlocked, which meant someone was still around. He poked his head inside, saw the place had emptied except for Aubrey and Sarah. *Thank God.*

Aubrey hadn't heard him open the door — she held the phone to her ear. A moment later, the cell phone in his pocket went off, startling her. She whirled around. "Hey, I was just calling — oh my God!" she cried, dropping the phone onto a counter. "What happened to you?"

Jonathan slipped in the door and shut it at his back, leaning against it to catch his breath. "The Tourmaline welcome wagon."

"Oh my God," she said, hurrying toward him. When she reached him, she reared back, wincing. "Oh *Lord,* did you pick a fight at work?"

"Thanks," Jonathan said with a snort. "Glad I inspire such confidence in you. More like someone picked a fight with me."

"What happened?"

He put a hand to his temple. "I got the crap beat out of me."

"Okay, come here, come with me," she said authoritatively, and took him by the hand, tugging him away from the door.

"Ouch — it's okay," he said, gasping in pain. "Just let me get Tammy and go — I'll be okay."

"No, you *won't* be okay," she said incredulously. "Have you seen yourself? Come on

— we have a first-aid kit. Tammy will be fine for a few minutes."

He glanced at his daughter — she was in a playpen, concentrating on a Tickle Me Elmo doll.

"Come *on*," Aubrey said again, and tugged him once more.

"Ouch," Jonathan said — but he allowed her to drag him across the playroom and into a large bathroom that had a changing table and two sinks — one low to the ground for kids, one for adults.

Aubrey left the door open so they could see Sarah, then opened the medicine cabinet and pulled down several items — gauze and tape, antiseptic, and hydrogen peroxide. She poured peroxide on a strip of cotton and stepped closer to him. The scent of her perfume was soothing after the smell of blood.

"Close your eyes," she said softly, and touched the cotton to a cut above his eye.

"Ouch, *ouch*," Jonathan protested, lifting his hand, but she caught it with her free hand and pushed it back down.

"The cut on your brow is pretty deep. You really ought to get it stitched."

Jonathan shook his head.

"So what happened?" she asked as she

moved to a scratch on his cheek, dabbing lightly.

"I think your boyfriend doesn't want me around."

Aubrey paused and peered up at him in confusion. "My boyfriend?"

"The big guy you were talking to in the diner the other day." When Aubrey blinked, he sighed. "Tall? Blond hair," he said, touching her hair. "And he has a gut. You wouldn't think a guy could move that fast with a gut."

"Who . . . *Keith?*" she asked incredulously.

"How should I know his name?" Jonathan asked, wishing she would return to fixing him. He sort of liked it when she was fixing him. "All I know is that he wants me gone."

Aubrey didn't speak, but her brows knit in a frown as she lifted his hand and dabbed at the cuts on his knuckles.

"Ouch," Jonathan said when she touched a particularly deep cut.

"Keith did this to you?" she asked again, her voice small.

"Him and another guy. I don't know who he is to you —"

"*No* one —"

"But I'm going to kick his —"

"*No!*" Aubrey exclaimed sharply, and dabbed a little harder at his knuckles.

"What do you mean, no?" Jonathan asked.

"The guy and his friend jumped me."

"Well, it's over. Just . . . just go home and get a good night's sleep. You don't want to start anything in this town. The sheriff won't help you."

It struck him as odd that she should refer to her father that way. "Why not?" he asked, curious, not that he'd ever go to the cops. "Don't I have the same right to his protection as any other person in this county?"

"Theoretically, yes. But that's beside the point."

"How can that be beside the point? What is it, Aubrey — you don't want your old man to know that you're acquainted with a guy like me?"

"Oh, *honestly*," she said with exasperation. "It has nothing to do with that. I mean I *don't* want him to know because it's none of his business —"

"It's his business to know when people in this town are beating up strangers."

"J.B.," she said, looking into his eyes, "you don't understand this town."

"What I don't understand is you." He touched her hair, then traced the line of her ear with his finger. "When I think I do understand you just a little bit, you throw a wrench into it."

"Oh, yeah, I'm the one throwing

wrenches," she said with a snort.

Jonathan sighed. They weren't getting anywhere here. "I'm going to get Tammy and take her home."

"Why do you have to be so stubborn?" Aubrey exclaimed. "Why can't you just listen to someone for once?"

"I can't afford to listen to anyone or anything but my gut," he said as he walked out of the bathroom.

"You are so *infuriating!*"

Jonathan smiled. "I'd rather be infuriating than constantly afraid." He bent over, scooping up Tammy with a moan of pain.

"Are you talking about me?" Aubrey demanded. "You think *I'm* afraid?"

"You're like the groundhog, afraid of your own shadow."

Aubrey dropped her hands and groaned heavenward. "You're unbelievable," she said, as she fetched Sarah's day pack and the Ziploc bag full of medicine.

"I know you are champing at the bit to ask if she's been okay since the last time you called," Aubrey said, shoving the meds at him. "Well, guess what? She's *fine.* She's in much better shape than her father. No fever, no cuts or scrapes, no bruises."

"Good," he said, and kissed the baby's forehead. Tammy laughed and patted his bloodied cheek with her hand. He glanced at Aubrey as he took the day pack and meds from her. "Thanks, Aubrey. I owe you."

"No," she said, holding up a hand and turning partially away from him. "You don't owe me anything. So do you have everything? I really need to get going."

He looked at her curiously. "Are you all right?"

"Me?" She shrugged as she picked up her purse and the keys to the day care. "I'm fine. In spite of what you might think, I'm not afraid to go out in the world. In fact, I am eager to go out in the world. It's been a long day, so if you don't mind . . ."

"Sure," he said, and walked out the door ahead of her. He waited as she locked up the shop. She stuffed her hands in her pockets and walked briskly down the sidewalk. "Hey!" Jonathan called after her.

Aubrey paused and looked at him.

"Good night," he said, peering at her. She seemed different . . . distracted.

"Good night," she said, and turned and jogged the rest of the way to her car.

The last Jonathan saw of her was her little red car driving too fast out of the parking lot, the peace symbol that hung from the rearview swinging with her sharp turn right, into town.

22

"Afraid, huh?" Aubrey muttered as she drove to the sheriff's substation in downtown Tourmaline. "I am *sick* of being afraid!" She pulled into the lot next to the substation, prepared to do battle with Zeke.

She knew he was behind J.B.'s beating. He'd made sure she knew it by calling her shortly after lunch. "Had lunch with Keith Stanley today," he'd said.

"So?"

"So . . . he's looking forward to seeing you Saturday night," he'd said with a sardonic laugh.

"You called me at work to tell me that?" Aubrey had asked, suspicious.

"Just wanted you to know. Have a good day, Aubrey. Looks like a great afternoon."

That bastard — he knew what was going to happen to J.B. J.B. was right — she was too afraid. No more. She was a grown woman, and if she didn't put a stop to this, her father would intimidate her like this for the rest of her life. She knew that — she'd always known that. But for the first time in a long time, she was angry enough to do something about it.

Unfortunately, Zeke wasn't in the office. According to Mrs. Franklin, his secretary, he'd taken a "well-deserved afternoon off for some golf."

Right. While he sent his goons to do his dirty work, he played golf. Aubrey went on, driving past his house. His patrol truck was not in the drive, and the house looked locked up. Frustrated, she drove around Tourmaline, looking for his distinctive truck, but didn't see it anywhere.

An hour later a dejected Aubrey headed home, her bravado and courage having waned when she'd failed to find him. She pulled into the parking lot of her apartment complex and parked. As she walked across the lot to her door, she saw the sheriff's truck parked at the corner of the building.

Aubrey slowed her steps and looked at her door. She knew instinctively that he was in there, waiting for her. But instead of dreading the thought of seeing him as she normally did, she felt a surge of anger. She marched to her door and didn't even bother to put her key in the lock, but turned the knob and threw it open.

Just as she suspected, her father was inside, sitting in a chair, drinking a beer.

Aubrey tossed her purse aside and faced him, her hands on her waist. "You have no right to come into my apartment without an invitation," she said, her voice shaking. She stood between him and the door, intentionally leaving it open — she had a feeling she might need an escape.

"Oh, for the love of — just shut up," he said, as he casually rose.

"I won't shut up, not this time," she said angrily. "I am through with your intimidation and abuse."

Zeke's eyes widened with surprise and he laughed. "Is that right?" He pointed a menacing finger at her. "Don't you *ever* talk to me like that again, do you understand me? I've been saddled with you too long to take that from you."

"You don't scare me anymore, Zeke," Aubrey said, her voice trembling with rage.

But Zeke read her rage as fear. That didn't surprise her — up until today, it had always been fear. His smile was glacially cold as he moved toward her. "You're lying. I scare the shit out of you. Right now, you are shaking in your boots."

She did her best to ignore that, to maintain

her confidence. "Look, I don't care what you do to me, but leave J.B. alone. He hasn't done anything to you. He's a dad, and a good one, and he's just trying to get by."

"Now see, that's what *disgusts* me about you," Zeke said, his voice smooth as ice. "You defending some two-bit punk. You're messed up in the head, Aubrey. You haven't got the sense of a damn milk cow."

"Just leave him out of this."

Zeke laughed at her. "Or *what?* What are you going to do?"

"Tell people who you really are," she said evenly. "Tell this whole town that you aren't anything like what they think, and maybe even a murderer —"

Zeke lifted a hand so quickly that Aubrey faltered; she turned away, grabbing onto the bar to brace herself for the blow she thought would come. But he didn't hit her. "You're lucky I don't slap you into next week," he breathed. "You keep that mouth of yours shut. Do you understand me?"

"What's the matter, Zeke?" she asked, forcing herself to turn and face him. "Are you afraid of the truth? Are you afraid of what will happen if this town knows how you hounded my mother until her dying day? How you used to beat —"

"Damn you." He lifted his hand again as he

lunged for her.

With a shriek, Aubrey whirled away from him and covered her head with her arms. But it sounded as if Zeke tripped or hit something — the commotion that followed confused her — she heard Zeke grunt, heard him cuss. She twisted around, saw that J.B. had come through her door and caught Zeke before he could hit her, shoving him up against the wall.

"You want someone to hit? Hit me, coward," J.B. said through gritted teeth.

"Get your hands off me!" Zeke spat. "I could have you arrested for striking an officer!"

"Is that the kind of coward you are?" J.B. breathed furiously. "You're man enough to hit a defenseless woman, but then you'll pull out the shiny badge when you're confronted by a man?"

"J.B.!" Aubrey shrieked. He didn't know Zeke, didn't know what he was capable of doing. "Don't, don't," she said frantically, wedging herself in between him and Zeke. "Don't, please don't, J.B. — he'll do it, he'll arrest you."

"I don't care," J.B. said, and shoved hard at Zeke again.

"*I* care!" Aubrey cried, and pushed him as hard as she could. But J.B. was glaring at

Zeke with murderous rage. Aubrey caught his chin with her hand and forced him to look at her. "Think of Tammy," she said frantically. "What will Tammy do if you're in jail? *Please,*" she pleaded with him.

J.B.'s eyes focused on her; something flit across them. He slowly let go of Zeke, shoving him again as he stepped back. He was breathing hard, his gaze furious as he dragged the back of his hand across his mouth.

Zeke pushed away from the wall and yanked his shirt straight. "You're in a whole lot of trouble, boy."

"No, he's not," Aubrey said curtly. She turned back to J.B. and gestured to the door. "Just go. Please go."

"I'm not going to leave you alone with him," J.B. said, eyeing Zeke.

"It's okay. You'll make it worse if you stay," she said. But when J.B. showed no sign of budging, she pushed him a little, drawing his attention back to her. She caught his arm, held it tight. "Please go, J.B. I know what I'm doing."

He looked uncertain — his gaze roamed her face a moment before he looked at Zeke again. "Are you going to be all right?"

"Yes," she said, and for once in her life she actually believed it. That J.B. had stuck up for her had infused her with new strength. "He was just leaving anyway. So please, just go. I really want you to go."

J.B. still didn't look convinced, and he did something that was odd for him — he put a comforting hand on her arm and squeezed it lightly. "If you need me, you call me. I'm serious, Aubrey."

Aubrey swallowed. "I will. I promise."

That seemed to satisfy him, and with one last look at Zeke, he went out.

When he'd gone, Zeke glowered at Aubrey, his jaw bulging with his anger. "You're gonna wish this hadn't happened, Aubrey Lynne. You just made a whole lot of trouble for yourself."

"What else is new?" she scoffed. "But if you do anything to him, I will take an ad out in the *Tourmaline Today* and tell the entire town who you are and what you've done."

"How stupid are you? There's not a man in this town who'll believe a word you have to say. People already think you're nuts."

"Oh? Well, it will make for some good trashy fodder, won't it? When exactly are you up for reelection again?"

The color drained from Zeke's face. He clenched his fists and pressed his lips together, and for a moment Aubrey thought she had gone too far. Yet she stood there, her legs braced apart, waiting for the blow to her face.

But Zeke surprised the hell out of her — he stepped back, away from her. He was shaking with anger; it seemed as if it required every ounce of his strength to move away instead of hitting her as Aubrey knew he wanted to do. He made it to the door, where he paused to look at her. "This isn't over," he bit out. "Not by a long shot."

Aubrey stood rooted to the floor, listening to his boots strike a beat down the pavement. When she could hear them no more, her legs gave out and she collapsed to her knees, bracing herself with her hands against the floor, dragging air into her lungs. That was easier said than done — she felt ill, as if she dared breathe, she would be sick.

She was so distraught that she never heard J.B. come in. But she knew the moment his hands wrapped around her shoulders that it was him. She knew it was J.B. who lifted her up and then enfolded her in a strong embrace. Aubrey pressed her face against J.B.'s shoulders and tried to keep the sobs from bursting through the dam she'd built inside her over the years.

23

Jonathan had stumbled on the sheriff and Aubrey in the heat of their argument only by coincidence. After getting Mrs. Young to sit with Sarah for a couple of hours, he'd come back into town to find the bastard who had done this to him. He wasn't quite sure what he was going to do with him if he found him, but the more he thought of it, the angrier he became.

Mrs. Young urged him to go to the sheriff. "We don't abide that sort of behavior in Tourmaline," she'd said angrily as she peered at the cut on his brow and his lip. "You tell Zeke Cross about that, and he will take care of it, you can bet your bottom dollar."

There was no way Jonathan was going to the sheriff, but he was going to find the big black truck that had been parked next to his car. He drove around for about an hour and had finally given up the hunt when he saw a red Jetta that looked like Aubrey's in the parking lot of an apartment complex. He thought about how different and out of sorts she'd seemed after she'd fixed him up.

Jonathan pulled in, thinking he would just stop by for a minute . . . but when he'd gotten out of his car, he'd heard the raised voices, had recognized Aubrey's, and had heard the abusive tone of her father.

That tone had washed over him like acid.

He quickly realized that a door was open somewhere and followed the sound of their voices, alarmed by the vile way the sheriff was speaking to her. He found the right door, spotted the two of them inside at the same moment Sheriff Cross raised his hand as if he intended to strike Aubrey.

Jonathan reacted without thought, shoving the man back against the wall and restraining himself from punching some sense into the slimeball.

He'd left because Aubrey had asked him to. But he hadn't left her alone. He'd waited for the sheriff to leave so he could check on her, and now he stood with Aubrey in his arms.

He could feel the deep tremble in her body, could feel it resounding in the pit of him in a painful way he had not felt in a long time.

"I'm sorry," she said after a moment, and pushed away from him, turning away to wipe the wetness from beneath her eyes.

With his foot, Jonathan pushed the door shut. He shoved his hands in his pockets and watched her as she moved across the room. She was slender, and a little on the small side. He couldn't imagine how a man might lift his hand to her and felt his rage rise up in him again. "How long has he been abusing you?" he asked quietly.

Even though she had her back to him, he saw her shoulders tense at his question, but she instantly shook her head. She made a scoffing sound and glanced at him from the corner of her eye. "He's not *abusing* me — we just had an argument."

"Aubrey. He was about to *hit* you. He *would* have hit you if I hadn't stopped him."

"No, no, J.B.," she said with a nervous laugh. "Okay, yes, he was being an ass . . . but he wouldn't have *hit* me."

He wasn't letting her get away with that and moved closer. "Yeah, you're right." He touched the nape of her neck and ran his finger down her back. "I have no idea. No idea what it's like to wake up in the morning wondering, 'Hey, I wonder what I'm going to do today to piss him off. Will it be me talking back? Rolling my eyes? Hell, maybe today he'll think I'm breathing too loud.' "

"J.B. . . ."

"I have no idea," he said, forcing her around to face him, "what it's like to believe that every time he hits me, he's only doing it for my own good, to make me into a person he can be proud of, and not the horrible, worthless piece of crap that I am."

Her eyes filled with tears and her bottom lip began to tremble.

He stepped even closer, so that they were standing only a few inches apart. Her eyes, the color of pennies, seemed bottomless, a well that should be filled with hope and love, not fear and pain. "And I don't know anything about looking like a grown-up on the outside, then turning into a sniveling, worthless little kid every time my dad so much as raises a hand to take off his sunglasses."

She said nothing at first — her eyes studied his face, as if she couldn't work out how he'd discovered her awful secret. At last, she asked him in a whisper, "H-how do you know?"

He touched her cheek with the back of his knuckle. "My father."

"You got over it, though."

"Sure. Let's pretend I did."

"How?"

"Just kept living. Having a kid of my own, that helped. Showed me I was better than him. Like you're better than Zeke Cross."

"I don't know —"

"You've got to believe it."

"It's not that easy," she muttered, dropping her gaze to his lips.

"You're worth so much more than that man could ever hope to be. You just have to believe it."

She rolled her eyes.

Jonathan stepped closer, took her face in both his large hands. "You have to believe it, Aubrey. You *have* to believe it." He kissed her forehead. "Believe it," he repeated softly, and kissed her temple. "Believe it." He kissed her mouth.

He felt that sink in his belly, the one that told him he was on dangerous ground. He'd meant to keep his distance, but her softness and vulnerability were beguiling and far too enticing to ignore; it seemed almost beyond his ability to control. He touched her lips, just enough to taste her, but the male in him sprang to rapt attention, and he slipped his arm around her waist, drawing her in closer, nipping lightly at her lower lip.

After what had happened between them last night, he expected Aubrey to push him away. But she seemed to need this, to need him, more than he'd understood. She sank into him, opened her mouth beneath his.

Her response was his undoing. He was suddenly kissing her with a passion he had rarely felt in his life, his tongue in her mouth, his hands sliding up and down her body, over her breasts, down her hips.

He caught her by the waist and lifted her up, and Aubrey wrapped her legs around his waist as he twirled her around, pushed her onto the bar. "I don't know what it is about you, but you make me crazy, you know that?"

"I thought it was just me," she said as her hands tangled in his hair.

"Do you know what I want to do to you right now?"

"I can't wait to find out," she said as she dipped her hands into his shirt.

Jonathan was close to losing control — her hands on his body, her lips so soft and wet beneath his — he was on the verge of letting go of himself and of Tammy. And it was the thought of Tammy — the image of her, the memory of her never far from his mind — that brought his head up.

Aubrey gasped and pressed her forehead to his shoulder a moment, then looked up and touched the wound at his brow. "What is it?"

"I don't know," he said truthfully. He was twisting in some emotional eddy. His heart wanted one thing, his mind another.

"I can't do this," Aubrey said, shaking her head. "I can't *do* this, not again."

Her declaration made him feel anxious and relieved all at once. He forced himself to take a small step back. He slid the palms of his hands down her arms as his gaze slid down her body. "Then I'm out of here," he said, suddenly anxious to be gone and away from his desires. "You okay?"

She nodded. But she did not meet his gaze.

"Aubrey, the deal with me . . . is hard to explain," he tried lamely. Aubrey shrugged. Jonathan ran his hand through his hair, trying to think. "I'll check on you tomorrow," he said, knowing it sounded ridiculous.

"No," she said, shaking her head and wiping her fingers at the dampness beneath her eyes. "Don't come back here, J.B."

His hand froze on her arm.

She bit her lower lip at his look and jumped down off the bar. "I mean it. Don't come back. It's not a good idea — for you or me, or anyone."

It wasn't the first time he'd heard that in

his life, but it had rarely been so disappointing.

"You should go now," she added, finally looking at him with soft brown eyes.

He wanted to touch her — he ached to touch her — and to tell her it would be all right, that someday she would meet someone who would make her believe she was worth the effort, just as he'd found it in Tammy.

But he couldn't bring himself to say those words to this woman. He couldn't seem to summon anything but overwhelming guilt. This was different from before — on some level, Jonathan had never wanted a woman the way he wanted Aubrey right there and right now. That feeling was what made him believe he had to leave — he suddenly could not be near her and not want to touch her. He couldn't look into those big eyes and not want to kiss her. He couldn't stop thinking of how many ways he could betray Tammy's memory, and he didn't need a big stage to do it. He could do it with a thought, a look, a touch, all right here in this tiny apartment in this tiny town.

Oh, yeah, he had to get out of there. And when his feet began to move, he really did intend to walk past Aubrey and out the door. But his heart won over his mind, and he instinctively, unthinkingly, grabbed her up, crushed her to him, taking her face in his hands and angling it, so that he could kiss her long and deep. He slid one hand down, filled it with her breast, then down again, feeling the curve of her waist, digging his fingers into the meat of her hips.

"J.B.," Aubrey said breathlessly, but he claimed her mouth again, his tongue tangling with hers, sliding against her teeth, and into her mouth. She smelled so damn good, tasted like heaven — the combination was intoxicating, and it quickly filled him to the point he feared he would burst.

"You have to go," she whispered. "This isn't going to work . . . this can never work."

He forced himself to raise his head, to take his hands from her. It was hard, so hard — she was so damned alluring, incredibly sexy with her lips swollen from their passionate kiss, her skin flushed. He could feel his body responding even further, as if he'd been walking a desert for a thousand years and had just found water again. He realized he was at a dangerous turning point.

He had to get out, now, before he did something he would really regret, and backed away from her.

Aubrey didn't say anything. She shoved her hands into her back pockets, watching him with eyes as big as moons.

Jonathan backed up to the door and stood there a moment, his hand on his mouth as he looked at her, feeling such incredible things that he'd believed he would never again feel for a woman. It confounded him — it made him feel strangely hopeful, but also callous and disloyal to Tammy.

He reached behind him, opened the door, and with one last look at Aubrey, he strode out of the apartment.

He walked as fast as he could to his car, his mind racing as hard as his heart. He drove recklessly, mindless of the traffic signals or posted speed limits, flying down Highway 78 toward his house. He turned so quickly into his drive that the car fishtailed, but Jonathan didn't care — he powered up the gravel drive, spewing tiny rocks behind him.

He parked next to Mrs. Young and climbed out of the car, striding with determination as he fished his wallet from his back pocket to pay her. Mrs. Young was sitting in a chair, reading. She put her finger to her lips when Jonathan entered and then pointed to the back.

"Did she give you any trouble?" he asked quietly as he withdrew a few bills and handed them to the elderly woman.

"Not at all," she said with a smile. "Tammy's such a sweet little girl, she could never be any trouble, Mr. Winslow."

With a sigh, he nodded and anxiously thrust a hand through his hair.

"You know, Tourmaline's harvest fair kicks off tomorrow," Mrs. Young said cheerfully as she stuffed the bills into her purse and began to gather her things. "Mr. Young has a bad knee, so we won't be going. If you'd like me to sit so you can get out for a while, I'd be happy to do it."

"Ah . . . thanks," Jonathan said, distracted. "But I don't think so."

"No? Well, now, a young man ought to have a little time to himself. I know you're devoted to your daughter, Mr. Winslow, but everyone needs to have a little fun." She smiled slyly as she hoisted her bag over her shoulder. "And besides . . . how is little Tammy ever going to get a new mommy unless you get out there?"

"She's got me. She's fine," Jonathan snapped, and instantly regretted his tone.

"You say that now, but one day you'll change your mind. Good night, Mr. Winslow."

"Goodnight." He followed her out onto the porch, watched her walk to her car and eventually drive away. But when the taillights of her car disappeared onto the highway, Jonathan whirled around and stalked into the house.

He had to get out of here. Things — emotions — were spinning out of control. Fortunately, it wouldn't take much effort to get everything together to go — he'd done it enough times before. He kept things semipacked in case he ever had to leave quickly and could be out of here by sunup.

It was the only thing he could do. Something was happening between him and Aubrey, something he didn't want and couldn't afford. Too much was at risk. He had Sarah to think of, after all.

Yep, he had to get out. Tonight.

24

Jonathan dragged two big duffel bags from the closet. In the first, he stuffed his clothes and toiletries, and some of Sarah's things. In the second, he crammed as much baby gear and diapers as he could fit. When he was satisfied, he carried the two duffels to the car and put them into the trunk.

Next, he gathered up the diapers and jars of food and formula, cursing himself for having stocked so much of the stuff. What had made him think he could actually stay here? What planet had he been on when he came up with the idea that he could *ever* settle down? There would always be something — fear of discovery, fear of losing Tammy — to stop him from finding a life.

He put the diapers and food in a box and carried that out to the car. When he came back into the house, he walked to the hiding place beneath the floor and pulled the FOR RENT sign out from under the couch, using the point of the signpost to pry up the floorboard. He was reaching for the briefcase when he heard Sarah's babbling. He paused, hoping that she was only babbling in her sleep — but she began to chatter loudly, as if she were talking to someone.

Jonathan's pulse began to race. Instinct told him Tammy had come back. Maybe she knew — had *seen* — what had happened between him and Aubrey, a thought that made him feel queasy. He slowly rose to his full height, listening carefully.

Sarah's jabbering grew louder as he walked to the back of the house. As he entered his bedroom, he saw the milky light that had surrounded Tammy before, and as he moved closer to Sarah's door, a tiny shiver of anticipation ran down his spine.

His heart soared — Tammy was standing next to the crib, smiling at Sarah, who was talking to her, babbling fast and happily. Tammy stood close — so close — but she did not touch Sarah. She just smiled, her eyes the only thing that didn't seem a little watery to Jonathan.

"You came back," he said hoarsely, drawing her attention from Sarah. Tears suddenly filled Jonathan's eyes. He swiped at them, tried to find the words to express how miserable and confused he felt. "I know," he said hopelessly. "I screwed up."

He moved forward, but Tammy moved, too, without seeming to move, just out of his reach.

"You shouldn't leave here, Jonathan, not like this. You always run. When are you going to stop running?"

"Come with me," he said, feeling the tears slipping down his face. "Please."

Tammy didn't say anything.

"Ba ba ba ba . . . ," Sarah said, banging the flat of her hand on the rail of her crib.

Without thinking, Jonathan picked her up, settled her on his hip. When he turned back to Tammy, she moved into a shadow.

Jonathan didn't want to follow her. He didn't want to see their past play out before him again, each scene heartbreakingly real, each moment so full of the life and love and promise that were absent from his life now.

But neither could he let her go — every moment with her was one he would never again have, and he reluctantly followed.

He stepped into a living room, with overstuffed furniture, thick woolen rugs, and a cheery fire in a hearth. He could smell the scent of spiced apples and cinnamon and spruce. Tammy was standing against a wall, and she pointed to something behind Jonathan.

He turned to look over his shoulder and felt his gut drop. He was seeing himself — as real and alive as he was standing there with Sarah in his arms. Next to him was Sarah, playing with her red truck. And seated in a chair, smiling angelically over them both, was Tammy.

"Oh my God," Jonathan breathed. It was almost as if she'd reached inside his head and pulled out his thoughts. He'd envisioned this very scene a dozen times after falling in love with Tammy. When they married, he had believed they would be a family, the three of them, and that they would have the sort of Christmases he'd never had as a child.

He was so enthralled with what he was seeing that he walked toward the scene. But when he and Sarah got too close, everything suddenly changed, and he was walking in a park, not a living room. And Sarah, who looked about three, was running ahead of him. He was walking hand in hand with Tammy. They were watching Sarah, and as they moved along, a yellow Lab appeared, carrying a stick in his mouth. He ran to the side of the path and dropped the stick, then began to dig furiously before nosing the stick into the hole.

Sarah watched the dog with rapt attention, delighted with its antics. When he began to cover the stick with his nose, her laughter rose up and rode on the wind.

Jonathan glanced at the baby he held in his arms. If she saw anything that he was seeing, he couldn't know, but she seemed to be watching the same scene he was watching.

"Don't," he said, looking at Tammy's watery figure standing a few feet to his right. "Don't show me what could have been."

Tammy ignored him and stepped behind a pine tree. When Jonathan followed her, he walked into what looked like a country dance. There were dozens of people — women, men, and children. He didn't know any of them, but he saw Sarah. She was standing, and an older child was holding her hands, leading her around in a circle in time to the music a band was playing. Jonathan was there, too, talking like a regular guy to other adults he'd never met.

But Tammy was not there. He searched the crowd for her and couldn't see her anywhere.

When he looked at Tammy's ghostly figure, she smiled sadly. "Jonathan," she said, her voice amazingly clear and soft in spite of the loud band music. "We had a lot of dreams for our future."

"We did," he said eagerly, reaching for her, but as always, she was just beyond his grasp.

"Our dreams of a happy family — you and me and Sarah — are never going to come true. We can't have that future."

"You don't think I know this?" he demanded angrily. "You don't think I know it every damn second of every damn day?"

"You can still have a future with Sarah. She deserves that future. But you will never have it if you keep running."

"I don't want it. Not without you," he said, gesturing wildly behind him.

"You have to stop running," Tammy said, and it seemed to Jonathan that she sounded far away. "You're running toward the past when the future is standing still, right here, waiting for you."

"Not without you," he insisted.

She was gone. Just like that, she was gone and he was standing next to Sarah's crib with Sarah sleeping on his shoulder.

25

The one consistent thing about her life in Tourmaline these last couple of weeks, Aubrey decided, was that she wasn't getting a lot of sleep. Last night had been the worst — between worrying what Zeke would do to her or, worse, what he'd do to J.B., and wondering what the hell she was going to do with this raging desire she had for the one guy in Tourmaline who was all wrong for her, she couldn't sleep at all.

She drifted off just before dawn and slept through her alarm. She didn't have the energy to dress creatively the next morning. After a quick shower, she pulled on a white T and a pair of jeans, then called work.

"Bright Horizons, Nancy Fischer speaking!" Nancy sang cheerfully into the phone when she picked it up.

"Hey, Nancy," Aubrey said as she searched her cabinets for something to eat. "I'm not feeling very well and slept through my alarm. So I'm running a little late."

"Oh, I'm sorry to hear that! Don't worry about it, Aubrey. Half the kids aren't here anyway. Take the day off if you want. Noelle and I can handle things here."

It was an enticing offer . . . Aubrey wasn't really up to a bunch of kids this morning. "Is, ah . . . is Tammy Winslow there today?" she asked meekly.

"Tammy? Yes! Her father dropped her off a half hour ago."

Aubrey closed her eyes. She'd missed him. It infuriated her that she even cared. "You know what, Nancy? I think I'll take you up on your offer to take the day off. I really appreciate it." Nancy had no idea how much.

"Sure thing. Before you hang up — did you get a chance to ask Zeke about the papers?"

Oh, *man.* "Ah . . . yes. But he, ah . . . he hadn't looked at them yet."

"Oh," Nancy said, sounding disappointed.

"I'll check with him again," Aubrey said quickly.

"Okay!" Nancy said cheerfully. "That would be great — if you get a chance, that is. I better run now — Katie Reynolds is eating chalk again." She clicked off.

Aubrey put down the phone. Finding no food in her cabinets, she decided the first order of business for her day was a strong cup of coffee and something to eat. Getting out of the apartment, getting out of the day care, was just what the doctor ordered.

It took a few hours, but after a coffee, a run in the park, and then a little shopping, Aubrey was feeling much improved. She honestly believed that she could put J. B. Winslow behind her, that she could leave Tourmaline in a month or so and never look back.

She honestly, truly believed it.

That afternoon, when she returned to her apartment after some impulsive shopping with a pair of strappy sandals that she had absolutely no place to wear, a new skirt that flounced around her knees, and some dangly earrings, Aubrey ran into J.B. and all her hard work of the morning evaporated. Feelings of longing and fear and disquiet quickly filled her to the point she was swimming in them.

He was standing under the covered entry to her apartment, in the shadows.

"Ack! You *scared* me!"

"Sorry." He glanced at her door, then at her. "I was going to leave a message . . ."

"But I specifically told you not to come back, remember?"

He grinned as his gaze drifted over her,

lingering on her chest a moment. "Yeah, I remember." He lifted his gaze to hers again.

"So," she said as she squeezed past him. "I'm obviously fine. See?" She held up her shopping bags. "There is nothing to be concerned about, so you can go." She fit her key into the lock.

"No. I don't think so."

"Come on, J.B. What are you doing here?" she demanded, glancing at him suspiciously.

J.B. laughed. "Hey, we knocked off early, and I have a couple of hours before I pick Sarah up. So I thought I would just check in and make sure you're doing okay. You've been shopping. That's definitely a good sign. But I would like a little more confirmation. After all, you weren't at work today."

"Occasionally I get a day off and I *am* doing fine," she said as she opened the door. She glanced at him over her shoulder. "Really."

He gave her a look that said he knew better, which Aubrey ignored as she walked into her apartment. She didn't look back to see if he followed her — she knew he would. Just as she knew she wouldn't stop him.

Aubrey placed her packages on the counter and turned around. J.B. was leaning against the doorjamb, watching her. The way he looked at her made her nervous —

she felt uncomfortably exposed on many levels, so many that she couldn't even count them all. He was a perceptive man, had guessed more about her than she would ever have volunteered to anyone. But something else was in his eye — an attraction to her that seemed mixed with a bit of uncertainty. About her, or himself, she had no idea.

She wished he wasn't so good-looking. She wished he were scrawny, someone whose eyes didn't seem to reflect every emotion, every longing, she felt inside herself.

"You've been shopping," he said again, looking at her bags.

"Yep." She removed the shoes from a sack for something to do with her hands, for some place to put her eyes. She opened the box and removed one sandal, staring at it.

She realized that he had moved, was standing right behind her. "Put them on. Let me see them."

She snorted at that and began to put the shoe back in the box, but J.B. put his hand on top of hers. His fingers curled around her wrist. "Put them on," he said low.

His voice had a strange catch, something that sounded a little like teasing and a little like lust. Whatever it was, Aubrey was strangely compelled to do as he asked. She never took her eyes from him as she kicked off her shoe, bent her knee, and slipped the strappy sandal on.

J.B. handed her the other shoe, and Aubrey slipped that one on, too. The heels lifted her up, so that her eyes were level with his mouth. That was a mistake — she couldn't take her eyes off his lips, couldn't keep the memory of them on her skin from flushing hot through her.

J.B.'s gaze flicked to her feet and he slowly smiled, one corner of his mouth tipping up. "You look *hot,* brown eyes."

"Wait just a minute, pal," she said, putting a hand up between them.

"Aubrey," he said, cutting her off as he took her hand in his, folded his fingers around hers, and pressed her hand against his chest.

He didn't finish. His eyes darkened as he took her in. There was no need for him to explain himself; the way he was looking at her made her believe he could see inside her, could see the desire raging, could see how much she *wanted* him to look at her.

It made her feel more desirable than she'd ever felt in her life, made her feel like a woman, capable of inspiring lust in a man.

J.B. drew a breath and with a small shake of his head smiled a little lopsidedly. "I'm a guy who usually sizes people up in ten seconds. But you, I can't figure out who the hell you are. The tough chick in the combat boots who thinks she could take three losers in a parking lot?"

"I could've."

He smiled. "The girl who knows how to handle my daughter better than I do? The one who spends her free time with kids who got knocked down before they ever started? I can't figure you out and it freaks me out. . . . But I can't stop thinking about you," he said.

She didn't know what to say. She didn't know if she could even move. J.B. didn't seem to want a response — he touched his lips to hers and kissed her, passionate and deep, snatching the air from her lungs. He cradled her face; his finger stroked her brow, her temple, and fluttered to her neck. Feeling a little weak at the knees, Aubrey grabbed his wrist and held so tight that she could feel his pulse, could feel it pounding in rapid time with hers.

And then she was sliding, drifting down, J.B. with her. Somehow, they had made their way to the couch. Somehow, they were on the couch, his hand on her knee, then her thigh, slowly sliding up beneath her skirt, his tongue dipping between her lips as his fingers brushed against her panties.

A feeling of warmth, thick and molten, spread through Aubrey. Her hands were suddenly around his neck, her lips moving across his, urgently feeling and tasting them, then her tongue was inside his mouth, feeling his teeth, the smooth skin of his mouth. When his finger slipped inside the silk of her panties, dipping into the damp cleft, she gasped into his mouth, and her hands fell to his shoulders, clinging to them, then his muscular arms, and his waist . . . and his erection.

He pressed it against her, moved seductively against her leg. She could feel him sliding her panties down her leg, excruciatingly slowly. A fog had enveloped her brain, shrouding her mind and common sense. All her doubts were gone, all her questions, all her fears. She was heedless of anything but his body, his strong, hard body. J.B.'s hand tangled in her hair as he stroked the wet heat between her legs. Purely sexual instincts took hold — she couldn't think, couldn't feel anything but the hunger for him to sink deep inside her. She suddenly sat up, pulled her T-shirt over her head, and tossed it aside.

J.B. stilled. He looked at her breasts, at the black bra she wore. He touched her breasts reverently, but as Aubrey leaned forward to put her arms around him, he drew back just a little.

It was hardly even noticeable, really, but something in the way that he moved gave her pause. She suddenly leaned over and grabbed her T-shirt.

"Wait," he said, clearly confused. "What are you doing?" He reached for her, his hand on her breast, his mouth on her neck.

But the moment had been lost, Aubrey could feel it. There was something off, something not quite right between them. She couldn't say what it was — the passion was there, but something else was missing.

"No, stop," she said, pushing him off her. She scrambled up from beneath him and pulled on her T-shirt. J.B. fell back against the couch, his legs splayed, watching her with disbelief.

"What's the matter? Is it the other night?"

"No," she said instantly, then winced a little. "Maybe. I don't know what it is, but it doesn't feel right."

"Come here and I'll make it feel right."

She smiled a little and shook her head. "Whatever you might think about me or have heard about me . . . I'm not into casual sex."

"Who said it was casual?" He sat up, bracing his arms against his knees as he watched her take off her shoes.

"Look, J.B.," she said as she tossed the sandals into the shoebox. "It's probably pretty obvious to you that I like you. But I'm not looking just for sex. I don't want to get hurt."

He snorted at that. "You think I do? I've had enough of that to last a lifetime and then some."

She glanced at him curiously. "What do you mean? What happened to you, J.B.?"

He looked at her intently a moment, then abruptly stood. "You want to know what happened to me?" he asked curtly.

"Yes." She turned to face him, her hands on her hips. "I want to know what happened to you."

His eyes narrowed. He clenched his jaw, ran his hand over the top of his head, then put his hands on his hips as he considered her. He opened his mouth, drew a breath . . . and then promptly shut his mouth again.

"Okay. Whatever this thing is between us," Aubrey said, waving a finger between the two of them, "it's never going to amount to much if we can't at least trust each other."

"It's not that I don't trust you, exactly."

"Then what is it?"

J.B. sighed and lowered his head, looking

up at her as if she were being petulant. "I have to go pick up my kid."

Aubrey shrugged a little and turned toward the bar again, trying to be nonchalant about it, trying to act as if she didn't care. But she *did* care. She cared a whole lot more than she should.

J.B. must have sensed it, because he walked up behind her, slipped his arms around her waist. "Just give me a little time, okay?" he asked softly, his breath warm on her neck. "I'm trying."

Aubrey closed her eyes and leaned back against him, feeling his strength at her back, the warmth of his body wrapped around hers. "Maybe," she said, her voice little more than a whisper. "Maybe we need to go slow and see what happens."

"Maybe."

"So . . . are you willing to try?" she asked carefully. "I mean, you're not going to freak out on me, are you?"

She could feel him draw a breath that filled his lungs and slowly let it out again. "I'm willing. That's why I'm here."

She smiled and put her hand over his. "I'm taking some of the kids from the after-school program to the fair Saturday night. That seems like a good place to start. You could bring Tammy. You want to come?"

He said nothing at first, just nuzzled her neck. But then he lifted a hand to her forehead and held her against him. "Yeah," he said softly.

Aubrey twisted in his arms and looked up at him. She could see so much in his eyes — warmth, desire, trepidation, secrets. She was inexplicably drawn to this man. Something about him seemed so familiar, something that almost seemed a part of her. She caressed the breast of his jacket and smiled up at him. "You should go and get Tammy."

"Yeah," he agreed, and touched his finger to the tip of her nose. He kissed her softly, then dropped his arms from her waist and walked to the door. He opened her apartment door, then paused and looked back at her. Aubrey thought he would say something, but he gave her an uncertain smile and went out.

26

Fortunately, Mrs. Young was true to her word — she was available to babysit Saturday night. Jonathan left his number posted on the fridge, in the living room, and in Sarah's room, and plenty of food and diapers on the kitchen table. As always, Mrs. Young assured him they would be all right and encouraged him to go on and have a good time.

He had arranged with Aubrey to meet her at the fair entrance. He arrived a little early and sat on a picnic bench, watching the denizens of Tourmaline arrive with kids and grandparents in tow.

He saw Aubrey long before she saw him. He was a little surprised; she looked different tonight — not so hard on the outside. She was wearing a blue skirt with tiny flowers on it that swung around her knees, a T-shirt, and a denim jacket. And on her feet were the sandals he had made her put on yesterday. Her legs, long and shapely, looked outstanding in the skirt and sandals. Her hair, short and wavy, was held back by a scarf that she'd folded to the size of a wide ribbon and had tied at her nape.

She was laughing as she walked up the road with Mark and two young women with Down syndrome. Even from this distance, he could see the sparkle in her eye. She was beautiful when she laughed. It was little wonder the men in Tourmaline wanted her. The only person who didn't see her beauty was Aubrey.

He stood up as they approached, and her face lit up at the sight of him. His body's visceral reaction to it surprised him — he felt a warmth surround his heart, and contentment, a feeling of being in the right place at the right time, filled him up.

"Hey, you!" she said as the four of them walked up.

"Hey," he said, smiling at her.

"Hi, J.B.!" Mark shouted.

Jonathan smiled at him. "Hey, sport."

"J.B., this is Sandra and Allison."

He looked at the young girls and smiled. The two of them exchanged wide-eyed looks and high-pitched giggles.

"Where's Tammy?" Aubrey asked brightly.

"I got a sitter."

"But what about the Texas Tornado?" Mark asked. "She can ride the Texas Tornado."

J.B. laughed. "I think she's a little young for the Texas Tornado."

"I'm not. I'm going to ride it ten times!"

Aubrey beamed at Jonathan. "I think he means it."

"He won't ride it," Sandra said. "He's afraid!"

"No, I'm not!" Mark shouted, and began hurrying toward the gate.

"Mark!" Aubrey cried.

J.B. winked at Aubrey. "I got it," he said, and hurried to catch up with an overly eager Mark.

J.B. had not expected to enjoy the outing to the fair. He'd never been to a fair as a kid, and it seemed a little foolish for an adult. He was as wrong about that as he'd been about so many other things — he had the time of his life.

It started with the rides. Mark was so determined to ride the roller coaster, the Texas Tornado, that he couldn't wait for the girls to figure out their finances for purchasing tickets. J.B. offered to buy them all tickets, but got a look from Aubrey and realized she was teaching them the art of spending money. The girls' learning curve was too much for Mark, so Jonathan went with him, climbed into the little car, squeezed beneath the metal bar the attendant slammed down, and looked at Mark. "Scared?" he asked.

"No!" Mark said. "I've been on these before."

As it turned out, Jonathan yelled louder than Mark. But it was exhilarating, and Jonathan happily volunteered to ride with each of the girls. After they had gone, he coaxed Aubrey to ride with him.

"I can't leave them," she said.

"We'll stand right here!" Mark said, gripping the rail of the fence around the roller coaster. Sandra and Allison immediately did as Mark did, gripping the rail of the fence, watching Mark.

"I don't know," Aubrey said uncertainly.

"You know what? I think you're chicken," Jonathan said.

"I am not and you know it," she said with a laugh.

"Bok, bok, bok," he said, flapping his imaginary wings to the delight of the three teens.

"Okay, that does it," Aubrey took her purse from her shoulder and handed it to Mark. "You promise you will stand right here?"

"I promise," Mark said.

"Sandra and Allison? You, too?"

Allison giggled, which prompted Sandra to shove her. "We'll stay right here!" she promised.

Aubrey looked at Jonathan. "Okay, pal. You're on," and she pivoted about, marching to the gate.

"Watch this," Jonathan said with a conspiratorial wink to the three kids, and quickly strode after her.

They loaded into the front car. Jonathan squeezed in and looked at Aubrey. She was looking up, at the loop-de-loop above their head. "Don't be afraid," he said, and put a hand on her knee, squeezing it. "I won't let you fall."

Aubrey looked at him, then at the hand on her knee, and burst out laughing. "Are you kidding? I'm not scared! I've ridden this thing a million times."

"Yeah, right," he scoffed.

As the ride started, Mark, Sandra, and Allison shouted and waved at them. Aubrey leaned over Jonathan and waved back. She gave him a look as she settled back into her seat. "Think you're man enough to go no hands?"

He grinned. "Is that a *challenge?*"

"Oh," she said with a mischievous grin,

"it's *definitely* a challenge."

Jonathan snorted. "No hands, then."

Aubrey smiled with all the power of a woman who knew she had the best of a man. "No hands."

Jonathan made it no hands until the last downslope. Beside him, Aubrey laughed and thrust her hands straight in the air, threw her head back, and screamed. Jonathan tried, but it felt as if he would pitch right out of the car, and he grabbed the bar as they picked up speed. When they hit the flats, Aubrey howled with laughter. "Chicken!" she cried.

"That's not fair!" he insisted. "I'm a big guy. I could have gone flying out of the car."

"That's okay, J.B.," she said with mock condescension. "We'll try the teacups next."

With a laugh, Jonathan grabbed her in an embrace and kissed her on top of her head. "Here's what I think of your damn teacup," he said, and began to tickle her.

They went on, the five of them, through the hall of mirrors, where they made funny faces and contorted themselves for a laugh. At the shooting range, Jonathan pinged enough ducks to win Sandra and Allison matching pink stuffed bears, which delighted them no end. At the basketball toss, it took him fifteen tries, but he won Mark a hat. And at the baseball throw, where he had to knock over bowling pins, he refused to leave until he'd won Aubrey a giant stuffed dog.

They ate hot dogs, then Jonathan and Aubrey sat outside the Whirly Bird on a picnic table sharing a funnel cake while Mark and the girls rode. "I haven't been to the fair in so long," she said as she popped a generous piece of funnel into her mouth. "I had forgotten how much fun it could be, you know?"

"Not really," he said, as he swatted her hand away from the cake and tore off a piece.

"Come on, you don't remember? When was the last time you were at a fair?"

He glanced at the Whirly Bird and shrugged a little. "Never."

"Never?" Aubrey cried with disbelief, then laughed. "You're kidding! How did you miss going to a fair when you were a kid?"

He smiled warily and looked away.

"Come *on,*" she said, punching him playfully in the arm. "Even *I* got to a fair."

"Never in the right place, I guess," he said, and crumbled up the empty paper plate that had held their funnel cake and tossed it into a can.

He could feel Aubrey looking at him,

could almost hear the wheels in her head turning. But he was having too good of a time to let her dwell on how it was a man could have missed going to a fair in his life and grabbed her hand. "Here they come. I told Mark we could do the Hammer."

"Oh, you *didn't*," she moaned, but tucked the dog securely under one arm, then slipped her hand into his and allowed him to pull her along to gather up their charges.

Jonathan insisted on accompanying Aubrey to deliver the kids safely home. When they were all inside their homes, he drove her back to the fair parking lot and her car. It was a quarter after eleven, but few cars were left in the lot and the lights were off on all the rides. The fair had shut down for the night. "Wow. They fold it up early in this town," Jonathan remarked as he pulled in next to Aubrey's car.

"That's Tourmaline for you," Aubrey said with a sigh. "The only thing that stays open past midnight is the Quickie Pick on the highway and Benji's outside of town."

"That's what I like," Jonathan said. "Not a lot of opportunity for trouble."

"For you . . . or Tammy?"

He smiled a little. It was dark in his car, the only light coming from streetlamps, but

Aubrey looked luminous. "I've had my share of run-ins," he said, and picked up her hand, held it in his palm. "Thanks. Thanks for inviting me tonight."

She gave him a sexy smile. "Your share of run-ins and yet you've never been to a fair. You are a mysterious man, J.B."

He stroked her hand with his finger and debated telling her what sort of life he'd had. It was hard for him to speak of those things — he'd told only a handful of people in his life. Tammy, of course, and he'd even spared her some of the worst of it. His mom, Reva, knew a little, and he might have told Dinah, an old girlfriend, a couple of things. But most of it was too close, too personal, and too deeply buried to talk about.

"So . . . who are you really, J.B.? What has gone on in your life? Where are you from?"

Jonathan groaned and leaned his head back against the seat. "Listen . . . it's been a great night. Let's not mess it up with a lot of questions."

"You know, sometimes I have a hard time talking about things, too," Aubrey said softly, her gaze on him. "There was a lot going on at home that I never wanted anyone to know about. Not then, and not now."

"Why not now?" he asked. "You're out of the house. You don't have to take anything from him."

"Oh." Smiling sadly, she shook her head. "You don't know him. He can be mean in so many ways. Like tonight," she said, entwining her fingers with Jonathan's. "Tonight, he pretty much commanded me to come to his house, to a barbecue. But I'd promised Mark and the girls I would take them to the fair."

"So?" Jonathan asked.

"So . . ." She looked down. "So he will make me pay for it. One way or another, he will make me pay for skipping his barbecue."

"Hey," Jonathan said, and slipped two fingers under her chin, lifting her head up. "You don't have to worry about that. If he even thinks of touching you, I'll take it from there."

She laughed a little. "That's very nice of you, but . . . but I'm not talking about that," she said, making a nervous gesture with her hand. "It's bigger and deeper than that. Maybe I'll even tell you one day. Maybe one day, you'll even tell me," she said hopefully, and carefully touched the cut on his brow.

Frankly, Jonathan didn't know if he could ever tell her everything — he wasn't sure he'd ever told anyone everything — but he thought she was right, that if he was ever going to tell anyone, it would be her. "Maybe." He reached for her, but Aubrey leaned back.

"I told you — I'm not into casual relationships. Maybe one day you can open up and let me in."

He laughed self-consciously. "You planning on sticking around that long?"

Her smile was a bit of soft light in the dark interior of his car. "I am leaving Tourmaline in a couple of weeks. Just think how much better we could get along in those two weeks if you'd just relax and let your guard down a little bit? And after that . . . who knows?"

"You talk too damn much," he said, and pulled her into his arms as he kissed her deeply.

27

While Aubrey was riding the Texas Tornado and eating funnel cake, her father was watching the road for her while he tried to play host to fifty people in his house. Normally, he wouldn't give a rat's ass if Aubrey showed up or not. To him, the girl was so worthless that he saw nothing but someone using up available oxygen that other, worthier people needed. But what really had him irritated was that he'd told Keith she'd be here, so now, she was making him look like a goddamned fool.

He'd *told* her to come if she knew what was good for her.

Zeke did not like her disregarding him in any way, shape, or fashion, and he'd been watching out for her for more than an hour. He'd worked up a good head of steam when Keith found him in the kitchen and handed him a beer. The barbecue was in full swing — guests had spilled out onto the patio and backyard, and the house was packed to the rafters. Everyone knew when Zeke Cross threw a party, it was a *party.*

"Looks like a great turnout," Keith said, and tapped the neck of his beer bottle against Zeke's.

"So far so good. Although I'm still expecting a couple more," Zeke said as Steve Peters wandered into the kitchen.

"Who else are you expecting, Sheriff?" Steve asked casually as he helped himself to some brisket Zeke had just cut up and was about to carry to the dining room.

"The Millers. And my daughter."

"Who, Aubrey?" Steve asked like an idiot, as if Zeke had been unfortunate enough to have been saddled with more than one. "She took Mark and a couple of other kids to the fair tonight."

Zeke's hand stilled in stirring the potato salad. He felt the slash of fury across his chest, as if it had opened him up. He looked at Steve just as Belinda, a woman who'd been trying to get in Zeke's bed, walked into the kitchen.

"To the fair?" Zeke echoed as Belinda went up on her tiptoes to kiss his cheek. That was Aubrey's big, grand other plan?

"Yep," Steve said, about to shove more brisket into his mouth. "Took him and two of the girls from that class she runs."

"You don't say." Zeke forced a smile and looked at Belinda. "Sugar, why don't you run that brisket out to the table and tell everyone it's on?"

"Sure, Zeke," she said. "Want me to mix you a martini?"

"That would be great." As Belinda went out carrying the platter of brisket, Zeke exchanged a look with Keith, who was standing against the counter, his head down.

"Sometimes I wonder what's in that girl's head," Zeke said with a laugh. "She's just like her mother, so scatterbrained." *So goddamned annoying.* "Anyone else go with them?"

Steve had turned to the relish tray and was munching on some baby gherkins. "Dunno for sure, although Mark was talking about some J.B. guy. Could be a counselor or another kid in the class. Who knows?"

Zeke knew exactly who he was. So did Keith, judging by the way he looked at Steve, his jaw tight from the clench of his teeth. Zeke picked up the relish tray and shoved it at Steve. "Do me a favor and put that out on the table, would you, pal?"

"Sure," Steve said, and walked out of the kitchen, still munching on the pickle.

"I thought we were going to run that thug

out of town, Keith," Zeke said congenially as he turned to the sink to wash his hands.

"I sure thought we had."

Zeke wiped his hands on a dish towel, then turned and clapped Keith on the shoulder. "Maybe he's just a little dense. Could be he needs a strong reminder."

Keith looked warily at Zeke.

"Did you happen to notice any suspicious activity while you were near him?" Zeke asked, squinting at Keith. "Anything like drugs or a lot of cash? Something that might make a visit by the sheriff worthwhile?"

"As a matter of fact," Keith said, nodding, "I think I smelled pot."

"Marijuana!" Zeke said with mock alarm. "We can't have that, not in Tourmaline. Come on, let's have a drink. Then I think I'll take a quick drive out to the Haney place and have a look around for some marijuana plants."

"I think you should, Sheriff," Keith said as he pushed away from the counter. "I really think you should."

Zeke left Keith in charge of the party before making an excuse of going for more beer. Several of his guests offered to do it for him, but Zeke assured them that it was better if he went. "Don't want anyone getting pulled over," he'd joked.

The sun was just setting when he pulled up the drive of the old Haney place. He recognized the Buick in the drive and smiled to himself. Edna Young owed him a favor or two.

Speak of the devil — as he got out of his truck, she walked onto the porch carrying the baby, looking surprised and, he couldn't help noting, a bit apprehensive. "Sheriff?" she said, shielding her eyes from the setting sun.

"Edna Young," Zeke said pleasantly. "How the heck are you?"

Edna slowly lowered her hand as he walked through the rusted gate. "Well . . . I'm fine. How are you?"

"I'd be a whole lot better if I knew where my daughter was. I need your help to find her."

She looked confused. The brat she was holding started to fuss. "I'm sure I can't help you, Sheriff," she said with a small smile. "I haven't seen Aubrey in three months, since your wife's funeral. And certainly not tonight — I've been babysitting the last couple of hours and haven't seen anyone."

He'd figured as much and looked past her, to the house. "So what do you know about this guy, J. B. Winslow?"

The baby began to cry and squirm in her arms. Edna patted her on the back, watching him warily. "I know he seems to be a good man."

He could tell she wasn't going to be helpful, which annoyed him, particularly in light of the enormous favor he'd done her at one time. "Look, Edna, why don't you put the kid down or give her a bottle or whatever while I have a look around."

Edna braced her legs apart as if she thought she could take him. "Now, Zeke, I'd rather you come back at another time, when Mr. Winslow is here. I told you the last time I wasn't going to do that again."

"I know what you told me, Edna, but I told *you* that I can pick up that boy of yours and throw him into jail even now, even though it's been eight months since he robbed the gas station. Evidence is evidence, and it's still as good today as it was then." He smiled. "So let me ask you again — do you want to go and do something with that child and let me have a look around? Or do you want me to pick up your son and put him in jail for what I'm figuring will be about ten to fifteen years?"

Edna Young pressed her lips firmly together and glared at him. A few moments passed while the baby screamed and twisted in her arms. Just when Zeke thought he was going to have to make good on his threat, if only to shut up the baby, she turned abruptly and walked back into the house.

He grinned. "There's my Edna," he said, and followed her inside.

The house was sparsely furnished and looked like a bachelor pad. It didn't look permanent, either. Edna had disappeared somewhere in the back, so Zeke took his time walking around. In the living room, he didn't notice anything out of the ordinary and moved to the kitchen. That room was a bust, too — he found nothing but a whole lot of baby food, a six-pack of beer in the fridge with three beers missing, and some frozen dinners. Under the sink were a few cleaning supplies, and in the cabinets, some dishes that looked as if they'd come from a garage sale.

He slammed a cabinet door, put his hands on his hips, and looked around. People didn't live in a house day in and day out without leaving *something* around that provided a little information about them. A piece of mail, a receipt — *something.* He bent over the trash can and looked inside. Nothing but some dirty diapers and the packaging for a Hungry-Man frozen dinner.

The more he looked, the more he realized that there was nothing in the house — no mail, no pictures, no phone numbers jotted down on a paper — and it raised Zeke's suspicions even more.

He wandered to the back, to the master bedroom and the adjoining nursery, where Edna was leaning over the crib, changing the kid's diaper or something. "Have you noticed any mail, Edna? Any letters?"

The old bag of bones refused to answer him.

Zeke opened the closet door and rummaged around, going through the few shirts and jackets hanging in the closet, and kicked through the shoes in the bottom of the closet. He picked up a pair of work boots and knocked his fist against them, hoping to dislodge something hidden inside. There was nothing.

He stood up, reached up to the shelf above the hanging clothes, and moved his hand around. His fingers brushed against something — a box, he thought. He rose up on his toes and got hold of it, bringing down a shoebox that had been pushed out of sight.

"Here we are," Zeke said with a grin as he pulled off the lid and carelessly tossed it aside. Inside were a few pictures of the baby as a newborn. No one else — just the baby.

No mother, no father, no set of beaming grandparents. There were a couple of other items, too — an arrowhead, a small, wooden car from which the paint had flaked off, and a pair of wings like those they handed out to kids on airplanes. That was it.

Zeke carelessly tossed the box and its contents aside, then stalked to the adjoining room, where Edna Young had finished changing the brat and was holding her tight.

"What's in here?" he demanded.

"There's nothing in here, Zeke," Edna said with a definite tone. "Trust me — I've been all over this room and there's nothing here but the baby's things."

"Edna? Don't you have something you need to do?" he said, pointing to the door.

With a huff, Edna picked up the kid and let him proceed with his investigation. Zeke went through everything — the diapers, the baby clothes, the toy box. He opened the door of the closet, but came up empty again.

With a sigh, Zeke glanced at his watch. He had to get back to his house and the party before anyone started to talk. He didn't like this at all — he was certain with enough time, he'd find the something he needed to bring in J. B. Winslow for questioning. He supposed he was going to have to think of an inventive traffic stop.

He stalked back through the house. Edna was in the living room, sitting in a rocking chair, the baby in her lap with a bottle. She didn't look at Zeke as he walked through, but kept her head down. He stood in the middle of the living room, looking around. "You know what bugs me, Edna?" he asked casually, as if they were conversing over dinner. "People don't live without a single piece of paper. There's gotta be something."

"He just moved to town, Zeke," she said, her voice full of indignation.

"Why Tourmaline?" he asked as he thoughtfully stroked his chin.

Edna refused to speculate. She put the baby on the floor, and she instantly crawled toward a red truck and some other toys.

"Well," he said, sighing a little and glancing at his watch. "Looks like you lucked out tonight, Edna. I just don't —" He was about to say that he didn't see anything to keep him here, but his gaze fell on a stick or something sticking out from beneath the couch. He walked across the room and pulled it out — it was a FOR RENT sign. He stood up, staring at the sign, wondering why it was under the couch. As he stood there contemplating the FOR RENT sign, he noticed that one of the floorboards looked higher than the others.

Zeke was on his knees in a moment, knocking his fist against it. It sounded loose. Using the stake on the sign, he pried up the floorboard and looked below.

Nothing but dirt and cobwebs. Zeke sighed and sat back on his heels, thinking. The baby, who was moving the red truck back and forth, back and forth, hit a miniature basketball, sending it across the floor, toward Zeke.

Zeke absently watched the ball roll across the floor. But as it neared him, it dipped and rocked back and forth a moment before settling in the slight depression the floorboard made.

It was worth a shot, he figured, and moved across the floor with the FOR RENT sign, which he used to pry up that floorboard. When he had it up, he leaned over to have a look beneath it.

"Eureka," he muttered, and pulled up a briefcase wrapped in a shirt. It was locked with a combination, but Zeke gently worked the lock with his pocketknife until he unlatched it. When he opened the briefcase, he felt a surge of elation. This was it, the mother lode. Whoever or whatever J. B. Winslow was, it was all here, he was certain.

An awful lot of paper was inside, some of it legal, some of it letters, all of it incriminating. "Well, what do you know, Edna?" Zeke said with a grin. "Our boy's been in a little trouble."

Edna gathered up the baby and walked into the kitchen as Zeke flipped through the papers, soaking it all up, his mind racing as to how he might use this information. But then his eye caught something that made his pulse race. It was just a name, but one he instantly recognized.

Alan Spaulding.

Zeke knew that name — anyone who was alive and breathing knew that name. He was rich, he was powerful, and he might just want to help a guy like Zeke get a state office in exchange for the information he was holding. Oh, yeah, judging by the papers he was looking at, Zeke figured that Alan Spaulding would be very interested in knowing where Jonathan Randall was living.

Jonathan made it home a little after midnight, his step light, and a smile on his face. When he walked in the front room, Mrs. Young already had her things together and was standing at the door.

"Sorry to keep you so late, Mrs. Young," he said cheerfully.

"It's quite all right," she said, and reached for the door.

"Tammy's okay?" he asked, looking at her curiously — she seemed to want out of there in a hurry, and Mrs. Young always wanted to chat.

"She's fine. She went down about nine." She gave him a quick glance and a quicker smile. "All righty, then —"

"Wait!" Jonathan said with a bit of a laugh. "Your money." He reached for his wallet.

Mrs. Young stood at the door, staring at her feet. It was almost as if she didn't want to look him in the eye. Jonathan pulled out a few bills and handed them to her. "Is something wrong?"

"Nothing," she said curtly. "I suppose I'm a bit tired. It's been a long evening."

"Right, I stayed out a little longer than I'd thought," Jonathan said, and couldn't help the goofy smile on his lips. He'd had such a great time with Aubrey. For the first time in months, he was doing exactly what Tammy had told him to do — he was looking forward, not back. "I'm sorry, Mrs. Young," he said again. "Thanks."

Mrs. Young looked up at him; the expression in her eyes startled Jonathan. She looked worried and sad and tired all at once. "You okay?" he asked again.

She didn't answer that, but she put her

hand on his arm and said, "You take care, Mr. Winslow." And with that, she went out into the night.

Jonathan followed her out onto the porch and watched her go. He didn't know what was bothering her, but he made a mental note — he would not keep her up so late next time. With a yawn, he went back inside, turning off lights as he made his way back to his room. When he walked into his bedroom, he saw on the floor the shoebox where he kept some keepsakes, the contents scattered around the room.

For a moment, Jonathan tried to understand how the box had gotten there, but he quickly realized Mrs. Young must have found it. And if she'd found this up on the shelf, out of sight . . . His stomach lurched; he wheeled around, running to the living room. He fell on his knees next to the couch and pulled the *for rent* sign out from beneath it, then used that to try and pry up the floorboard where he kept the briefcase. But the board was wedged tight — had it been this tight the last time? He clawed at it with the sign's edge for a futile moment, then clambered to his feet, ran to the kitchen for a hammer, and back again. He dug at the floorboard with the hammer until it came up, tossed the board aside, and pulled out his briefcase. His anxiety led to several attempts at the combination lock, but when he finally got it open, he sank back on his heels and stared at the contents.

Had he left the birth certificates on top? He couldn't remember! He quickly went through the contents. Everything seemed to be there, every bit of paper he could recall. But was this how he'd left it? He wasn't sure at all. Jonathan took a deep breath and replaced the briefcase. One thing was certain — he'd just lost his babysitter. He wouldn't risk having Mrs. Young in his house again.

28

In Springfield, Reva carried in her mail to have a look before she went out. She had a stack of catalogs and two bills, which she tossed onto a console near the front door. She almost missed the white envelope with the distinctive printing, then grabbed it up.

Tourmaline, California.

He was in California. She turned away from the console, walking into her living room as she tore open the envelope and pulled out a slip of paper. It was green, had been photocopied, and was cut at an uneven angle along the bottom.

DOT'S DINER
Tourmaline, California
Wednesday Night Summer Special!!
Brisket, potatoes, dinner salad, and rolls.
Bring this coupon in for a free slice of pie.

Where the hell was Tourmaline? Reva dropped the coupon on the coffee table, but took the envelope, intent on Googling Tourmaline. She had just turned on the computer when she was startled by the sound of the doorbell.

"Just a moment!" she shouted, and ran to the kitchen. She quickly lit one of the gas burners and set the envelope on fire, holding it over the sink while the address and the stamp cancellation burned.

The doorbell rang twice more.

"Coming!" she yelled, then put the envelope on the counter and slapped it with her hand to put out the rest of the fire. She threw it in the trash can, straightened her clothes, smoothed back her short blond hair, and walked to the door, just as the doorbell rang a third time.

Who *was* it who couldn't wait a few seconds for her to get to the door, for heaven's sake? "I said I was coming!" she called irritably. But just as she reached for the door, she remembered the coupon. She whirled around, ran back to the living room, snatched it up, shoved it in her pocket, and ran to the door again. She paused, caught her breath, and opened the door with a cheerful smile.

Oh dear *God.* "Haven't you plagued enough people today, Alan?"

He started to respond, but caught himself

and sniffed the air. "Do I smell smoke?"

"No," she snapped, but it was useless denying it — she could smell it, too. "Yes. I had a little kitchen mishap. But you didn't come here because you smelled smoke, Alan."

"No," he said, clasping his hands behind his back. "May I at least come in, or will we have this conversation on your doorstep?"

"I choose C, none of the above," she said, and started to shut the door.

Alan threw up a hand, stopping the door. "The doorstep it is then."

Springfield had such big ears. With an irritable sigh, Reva turned away from the door. "Make it brief and let's start with assuming whatever you say, my answer will be no."

"Why must you always be so melodramatic?" Alan groused as he walked into her house and shut the door. "I haven't come here to argue."

"Then why have you come?" she asked as she walked into her living room. "I can't imagine any *good* reason for you to show up at my door, unannounced."

He strolled to her hearth and looked at a picture of Jonathan, Tammy, and Sarah on the mantel. "Why have I come? Unfortunately, there's not an easy answer to that."

"Well *try.*"

Alan gave her a thoughtful look. "You know how some people believe New Year's Day is a new beginning? And for others, it's the new growth of spring or the change of season that marks the beginning of a new time?"

"I guess," Reva said, wondering where this was going.

"What time of year represents new beginnings for you?" he asked idly as he traced a finger over the top of the picture frame.

"That's what you came here to ask me? Is Spaulding in the poll business now?"

He ignored her. "You know what represents a new beginning to me?"

"I couldn't possibly guess," Reva said with a roll of her eyes. "But I'm sure you're going to tell me."

"September," he continued casually. "The beginning of a new school year. The start of school is so full of promise and possibility, isn't it? All the children marching back to school with their books and their lunches and their eagerness to learn. It's such a great sight to see the little kids climbing on the bus for their first day of school."

"Very poignant," Reva said with a snort. "But I think I am missing your point . . . assuming you actually have one."

"My point?" He shrugged a little, looked at the picture on the mantel a long moment. But when he looked at Reva again, he surprised her — he actually looked distressed. He looked like a man on the verge of tears. His eyes were red, his lips pressed together. And he looked at his hands as if he didn't know where to look or what to say.

They had their history, but Reva couldn't ignore his obvious anguish. "Alan?" she asked, carefully putting a hand on his arm. "What's wrong?"

"I can't help . . . I can't stop thinking of Sarah," he said mournfully.

"What?"

"Sarah, my great-granddaughter," he said, turning away from Reva. With his back to her, he rubbed his forehead.

"I know *who* you mean," she said, watching him curiously. In all the years she'd known Alan, of all the things they had been through, together and apart, she'd never seen him so tearful. "I just don't understand *what* you mean."

"I mean . . . I had a dream last night about Sarah . . . all I can think of is Sarah. I think . . . I think how I will never get to see her climb on that school bus." He gestured vaguely to the street. "I will never see her at a birthday party, or at Christmas. I will never see her go to a prom or walk down the aisle at her wedding . . ." His voice trailed off and his shoulders started to shake.

"*Alan?*" Reva said softly, flabbergasted. She stepped closer, put her hand on his back. "We *all* miss Sarah." Frankly, he had no idea how much — her heart ached every day with the knowledge that she was out there, and Reva couldn't see her, couldn't touch her. "We all live with knowing we'll never see her again."

Alan pressed his fingers to his eyes. "Are you sure?" he asked quietly.

"Am I *sure?* Of course I'm sure, Alan. She's *dead.* You have to face the fact that she is dead!"

"You're certain?" he asked again, and turned, looking her in the eye. "In my dream, she didn't die. She's still alive."

The mournful great-grandfather was gone, and in his place was the ruthless millionaire Reva knew Alan could be. Something in his eyes, something cold and hard, made Reva step backward, away from him.

"Just . . . just tell me once more what you saw that day, Reva."

"Oh, for the love of Pete!" she cried, throwing up her hands in exasperation.

"Not again! We've been over and *over* this!"

"Tell me, please."

Just his asking made her want to throw something. "Do you think you are the only one who hurts?" she cried.

"If there is a chance that they are alive —"

"There is *no* chance!" Reva cried angrily. "When will you get that through your head?"

"Just tell me what you saw on the cliff that day!" he insisted.

"No," she said heatedly. Her pulse was racing, her palms getting damp. She had relived that day a thousand times if she'd relived it once, and it was never easier, never less painful. How could she forget the terror, that horrible feeling of her heart ripping open the moment she believed her son and granddaughter were dead? "I'm not some filly you get to put through its paces for your own amusement."

"Reva —"

"Using me to get your own way is like a hobby for you. From the first time we met —"

"You aren't seriously going to twist this around to an event that happened almost twenty-five years ago?"

"You even made me believe you loved me

360

just to use me!"

"Well, at least that's a little progress. That happened only twenty years ago. Come on, Reva. Don't you believe a man can change?"

"No," Reva said low.

That got him — she could tell by the wince in his eyes and the clench of his fist.

"You want to know what I saw, Alan?" Reva continued angrily, moving toward him now. "I saw a car that had plummeted off a cliff, one hundred feet to the bottom of a quarry. I saw a car engulfed in flames. I saw *my* son and *my* granddaughter burn because there is no possible way they could have gotten out of that car. There is no *possible* way they could have survived. So you need to bury this sick obsession once and for all and *leave me alone,* because the next time you ask me to tell you what I saw, I won't be held accountable for what I may do to you."

They were standing almost nose to nose. Reva's heart was pounding so hard it was making her breathless. Alan stared down at her, his expression inscrutable.

"Perhaps you are right, Reva," Alan said quietly, surprising the hell out of her. He looked down, moved away from her. "I've been thinking a lot about Sarah lately. I don't know . . . I just can't seem to focus. I can't keep my thoughts on my work, I can't remember things." He sighed and ran a manicured hand over his hair. "Maybe I should get out of town."

"That would be a *great* idea," Reva snapped.

"Maybe I'll go to the Himalayas to meditate at a Buddhist temple for a while." He looked at Reva. "Or maybe I will go and see about the new business I've been thinking of pursuing. I've been thinking of investing in a mine."

"A *mine?*"

"Yes," he said, turning to face her fully, watching her closely. "There's one in California that mines tourmaline. What do you think of that?"

Reva felt as if she'd been kicked square in the gut. She could feel the blood drain from her face, could feel her knees quiver. But she remained standing, remained as stoic as she possibly could, knowing that Alan was watching her for any hint that she knew.

"No opinion?"

"I don't know anything about tourmaline," she said evenly.

"It's a semiprecious stone. Some cultures believe that it has magic properties that offer protection and even love to those who possess the stone."

"How interesting, Alan. Good luck with that."

Alan smirked. "Perhaps tourmaline will take away all my troubles. What do you think?"

Reva thought she would be sick. She could feel her revulsion and fear mixing like a bad brew in her. But somehow she managed to smile. She walked to the front door and opened it. "Have a nice trip, Alan."

Alan did not respond, but his gaze was riveted to her with every step he took, as he walked to the door.

"Do me a favor," she said as he stepped over the threshold. "Next time you want to drop by? Call first so I can arrange to be somewhere else." Reva pushed the door shut in his face as she should have done when she first saw him.

She stumbled into the living room, her head reeling from the knowledge that Alan knew something — or did he? Could it be a weird coincidence? No, no, nothing was ever a coincidence with Alan.

Reva stood in the middle of her living room, her knees locked, her heart beating.

She'd let Jonathan down once before, by giving him up to stay with his father and unwittingly giving him a life of pain. It had been her mistake, and it was as she'd once told Jonathan — her guilt was her problem. She didn't know what to do with it and never had. But she did know this: she would not let her son down a second time. She had promised him at Tammy's funeral that they would fix this thing with Alan.

Alan.

She could still feel his cold blue eyes on her, boring through her, seeing all the way down to her secrets.

Reva knew she had no time to waste. She had to find Jonathan before Alan did. She had to warn him. And the only way to do that was to get to Tourmaline first.

29

"What is up with you?" Noelle asked Aubrey the following Friday. "You've been grinning like that every day this week." Noelle nudged her a little as they washed finger paint from the kids' hands.

Aubrey grinned. She'd seen J.B. and Tammy every day since the night of the fair, and while she didn't really want to put a name to it, Aubrey thought she might be falling in love.

She didn't have a lot to compare it to; she'd never really been in love. She didn't trust love. She didn't trust that men who said they loved her wouldn't hurt her. There had been the one guy in San Diego Aubrey believed she'd come close to loving. Franny had introduced them. He was a musician and had the soul of a poet. But even that had felt nothing like this. Aubrey didn't think about that guy every waking moment the way she thought about J.B. She didn't feel the same sort of connection with him as she felt with J.B.

It was a preternatural experience for Aubrey. She'd never had so much in common with another human being before, had never felt such a bond. They were truly cut from the same cloth, their personas derived from the same sort of life experiences.

"Come on, Noelle. Haven't you guessed?" Nancy asked, popping in between them with a broad smile.

"Guessed what?" Noelle asked, looking at her mother.

"When J. B. Winslow comes to pick up his daughter this afternoon, notice how he looks at Aubrey."

"*Stop,* Nancy," Aubrey said, and to her horror, she giggled. She couldn't remember the last time she'd giggled! Apparently, it had been a really long time, judging by the way Noelle was gaping at her now.

Nancy laughed as she walked by them.

"Get *out,*" Noelle cried. "You and that hot, hot new guy? The guy you said you would not date?"

"Get out!" echoed Dusty, the little boy whose hands Noelle was washing.

Noelle grabbed a towel. "Okay, kiddo, you're done. Wipe your hands." She then pointed him in the direction of the playroom and zeroed in on Aubrey. "Okay, *spill.*"

"There is nothing to spill," Aubrey insisted with a smile she couldn't seem to keep off her face as she dried Mariah's hands.

"Don't be coy, Aubrey," Nancy called in a singsong voice as she walked by.

"Okay, fine." Aubrey pushed her hair behind her ear a little self-consciously. "We've been seeing each other a little —"

Noelle squealed and clapped her hands. So did Mariah.

"But it's nothing to get excited about!" Aubrey said, grabbing Noelle's hands before her gleeful clapping propelled her into the stratosphere. "We're just hanging out. I'm leaving in a couple of weeks, so it's not going anywhere."

"Who cares? At least you're hanging out! You're not sitting in that little apartment by yourself eating a veggie carry-out from Dot's."

Aubrey laughed. The truth was, she hadn't had much appetite at all the last few days.

"What about Keith?" Nancy asked from the refrigerator, where she was collecting juice boxes to hand out.

Her question instantly sobered Aubrey. "What about him?"

"Just that I heard you two were seeing each other."

"No," Aubrey said quickly. "God, no. I mean, *he* wanted to see me, but I . . . my head is somewhere else."

"Not only her head," Noelle said with a snigger.

Aubrey laughed again and gave Noelle a playful shove. "Okay, so I am going to get our lunch now before you become completely unglued."

"Oh, sure, run away when we get to the good stuff!" Noelle called after her as Aubrey grabbed her purse. Honestly, she thought she could run to the diner and back, she felt so buoyant. But she intended to walk, because the moment she got back to the day care, she would be counting the minutes and hours until J.B. came to get Tammy. She laughed and waved at them as she walked out into the bright sunlight.

She'd just stepped into the parking lot when she saw the sheriff's patrol truck pull in.

Aubrey felt herself go cold. That thing inside her began to coil as it always did when she saw him, and today, it coiled a little tighter. She knew he was probably pissed she hadn't come to the barbecue as he'd commanded, and frankly, she was a little surprised it had taken him a week to look her up and give her grief about it.

"Well, well," he said as he got out of his truck and looked her up and down. "So you aren't dead after all."

"Don't sound so disappointed."

He chuckled. "Do you really think you're in any position to get an attitude with me? I'm about a minute from knocking your fool head off, you know that?"

"I figured as much. It's your response to everything."

His smile widened, almost as if he was amused by her. But then again, she was not in the habit of provoking him.

"Didn't that whore of a mother of yours teach you anything?" he asked, disregarding her remark. "Where were you last Saturday night?"

"I told you I had plans."

"Yeah, I heard about your plans," he said, his tone dripping with acid. "At the fair, huh? Is that where whores go these days?"

Aubrey's blood ran colder. She could see nothing but contempt and disgust in his eyes, the same way he'd looked at her when she was a kid and would tell her she had to be somebody else's kid, that she damn sure wasn't his. *What had she ever done to deserve him?* "Look, Zeke," she said with a wave of her hand. "If you're just going to call me names, I'm going to go. I have to get back to work."

"Then go." He moved slightly, giving her just enough room to pass. "By the way," he said, catching her arm at the elbow as she passed him, digging his fingers into the crook of her arm at the same time he smiled at her. To anyone passing by, it would look like a father who had a hand on his daughter's elbow, nothing more.

"Let go," she said with a hiss, trying to peel his painful grip from her arm.

He didn't let go. "You and I aren't done yet. Not here, not today. But soon."

Aubrey bit her lip. "Let *go, Zeke.*"

He let go of her. Aubrey gasped with relief as Zeke leaned in, his face only an inch from hers. "*Soon,* Aubrey Lynne," he repeated through gritted teeth, then turned and strolled back to his truck.

Aubrey watched him go as she rubbed her elbow. Lord, how she despised that man. She felt nothing for him. Absolutely nothing. Except maybe the fear she'd worked so hard to banish.

She walked on, to the diner, the smile gone from her face.

Jonathan and Sarah pulled up in front of Aubrey's just after lunch on Saturday. Jonathan had attached a flag depicting the sun and surf on his antenna. At the department store, he'd bought Sarah a yellow sunsuit and a matching yellow hat that looked like a bear with ears. He'd also brought along a cooler full of gourmet treats — champagne, two packages of weenies, buns, mustard and relish, and for dessert, New York–style cheesecake. In the trunk, he had a picnic blanket, a sand pail and shovel for Sarah, and a Frisbee for the grown-ups.

He was really looking forward to this outing, in spite of the guilt he couldn't seem to shake. But it was as he'd told Tammy last night, as he'd looked up at her star while he and Sarah lay on a blanket beneath the late-summer sky: he would always love her, no matter what.

"I'm trying, Tammy," he'd said as Sarah tried to crawl over him. "I'm trying."

He knew he didn't imagine her star blinking at him in response.

This morning, he hadn't thought of Tammy at all as he'd gotten Sarah ready, and he grinned when he saw that Aubrey was waiting for them. She was wearing a goofy straw cowboy hat, a pair of board shorts that rode low on her hips, and a short halter top that gave him a great view of her cleavage.

Oh, yeah, the girl was hot.

She was dragging an enormous tote bag, too. Jonathan had never seen anything so big and got out of the car to give her a hand. "What is all this?" he asked as he hoisted the thing onto his shoulder.

"Oh, you know. Towels. Sunscreen. Scrabble."

"Scrabble?"

She laughed and pointed at him. "Gotcha. I know you better than that. Actually, there is a portable baby swing in there, in case Tammy gets bored. And I brought a couple of books in case you get bored."

Jonathan looked at those copper brown eyes and a pretty face transformed by a prettier smile. "No chance in hell of that."

He wasn't lying — once they'd found their own private little part of the beach near San Diego and had set up their camp, complete with an umbrella Aubrey had found at a thrift store, it was midafternoon. While Sarah played on the blanket, Jonathan and Aubrey threw the Frisbee around, until Jonathan tackled Aubrey in the surf and she got his head underwater. But when they came up for air, Jonathan noticed that Sarah had crawled off the blanket and was trying to put handfuls of sand — sand that thankfully fell through her fingers — into her mouth.

They spent another hour playing with Sarah, helping her build a sand castle that Sarah kept pounding with her little shovel. When the sun began to sink into the ocean, Aubrey put Sarah in her swing with a teething ring while Jonathan built a pit and a fire. They drank Cristal champagne from paper cups and stuck weenies on wire coat hangers and held them out over the fire. When Sarah began to tire, Jonathan changed her diaper and dressed her in something a little warmer.

The sound of the surf finally lulled Sarah into the peaceful sleep of a baby. She lay on the edge of the blanket with her pacifier, clutching her kitty.

Jonathan stretched out on the blanket and propped himself on his elbow. Aubrey sat facing the ocean. She'd pulled on a sweater when the sun had gone down and had her legs drawn up and her arms wrapped tightly around them. She'd long lost the hat, and the sea air had made her hair curl around her face. Her eyes were closed, her face lifted to the darkening sky above.

"What are you thinking?" Jonathan asked, poking her with the end of a weenie wire.

She laughed. "I was thinking about you, actually," she said with a smile.

Jonathan couldn't deny it — that smile

made him feel like he could leap across the ocean. "Oh, yeah?" He poked her again.

"I was just wondering where you came from. What you're like."

Jonathan laughed. "You know what I'm like."

"Not really," she said. "For starters . . . where are you from?"

"Not anyplace close to here."

She frowned playfully. "How old are you?"

He wondered if he should even admit to that, but could not resist her big eyes. "I'll be twenty-four in a couple of months."

"Oh!" Her face lit up with a smile of pleasure. "Information!"

"Don't get excited," Jonathan said with a laugh, but Aubrey had already scooted around to face him.

"What's the best thing you ever did?"

"Made Sa— Tammy," he said.

"Sarah, Tammy. When are you going to pick a name?"

He smiled.

"Ah. Nothing on the name front. So . . . where is Sarah— Tammy's mother?"

Jonathan groaned and fell onto his back. "What's with all the questions?"

"I want to know you better. How can I know you better if I don't know anything about you? And what's the big deal? I mean, you're obviously divorced, or she's dead —"

"She's dead," he said quietly. Tammy may not have given birth to Sarah, but he considered her Sarah's true mother.

"Oh," Aubrey said softly. "I'm so sorry."

"Next question," he said, gesturing impatiently.

"Well. Okay," she said, composing herself. "What is the worst thing you have ever done?"

He suddenly sat up and leaned forward. "Are you sure you want to know that?" he asked, and kissed her.

But Aubrey put a hand on his chest and pushed him back a little. "I really do."

He looked into her eyes and thought of all that he'd seen and done. She'd probably seen more than her fair share of ugliness in life, but nothing like what he'd been through. She was too sweet, too good, to know more. He pushed a curl behind her ear. "You ask a lot of questions about stuff that, trust me, you don't want to hear."

"Why is everything such a mystery with you?" she asked with playful exasperation. She frowned down at the blanket. "Do you miss her?" she blurted.

The question felt like a sucker punch. He hadn't been expecting it, wasn't ready for it. When he didn't answer right away, she slowly glanced up, assessing him.

He sighed and pushed his hand through his hair. "I'm trying to move on."

She looked at him with soulful eyes. "Okay," she said sheepishly. "I get it. So," she said, trying to put a bright face on it. "Do you have any questions about me?"

A million questions. He wondered about everything. What she did for fun. What did she look like in the morning when she was waking up? What sort of things did she think about? Had she ever been in love?

But one question stood out from the rest. "Why are you still in Tourmaline?"

She sighed. "Talk about complicated." Unlike Jonathan, Aubrey was not so reluctant to talk anymore. She told him about her mother's day care, and the transfer of ownership to Nancy Fischer. She told him how she had been enrolled in school in San Diego, her goal to get her degree in child development and then go on to be a pediatric nurse, how she had put that on hold when her mother had died from breast cancer.

"But I am moving on, too," she said.

"Oh, yeah?"

She nodded. "Nancy's on her feet, whether she knows it or not. As soon as I can get the papers out of my dad, I am getting out of here."

"Good to know where I rate," he joked.

Aubrey laughed and shifted to her side, propping her hand beneath her head to better see him. "You rate much higher than you know."

"Oh, yeah?" He came down on his stomach and propped himself up to face her. "How high?"

Her smile faded a little, but her eyes sparkled in the firelight. "Really high."

"Higher than a no-hands roller coaster?"

"Higher than the stars," she said, looking at his mouth. She reached for his hand and made him lift it, then pressed her palm to his. "Whatever happens between us, however long this lasts," she said softly, "you will never know what you have meant to me."

The way she touched him, looked at him, made Jonathan's blood churn. He was swept away by the soft timbre of her voice. He was feeling all those things he'd felt when Tammy had whispered to him — that urge to hold her, protect her — but he felt them a little differently for Aubrey. With Aubrey, he didn't have that niggling doubt that he wasn't good enough for her, that he was a drag on her life. With Aubrey, he felt — for the first time in his life — that someone besides his baby daughter needed him. *Really* needed him.

Aubrey needed him. She needed him as deeply and fully as he'd ever needed Tammy.

"Come here," he said gruffly. "Don't make me wait anymore."

Aubrey gazed at his lips for a moment, then looked up, to his eyes. "Are you sure? You know how I feel."

"Aubrey," he said, sitting up. In the firelight, her eyes were dark, like tea. He impulsively grasped her hand and kissed her palm. But then Aubrey withdrew her hand and laid it tenderly against his cheek. Something flowed between them, something that only two people as damaged as they were could possibly understand, and Jonathan was lost.

He reached for her, grabbed her really, and pulled her against him, bearing her down to the blanket. He pressed his mouth against her cheek, then her eyes, and slid to her lips, tasting the champagne on them. "I've been fighting it," he said. "I've been fighting wanting you."

Aubrey drew a breath, as if he'd startled her, then put her hand on the nape of his neck and pulled him down. Her tongue dipped between his lips, touching his tongue, and Jonathan was drifting out to sea.

He rolled onto his back, pulling Aubrey on top of him, his hands on either side of her head, his lips covering hers, and her face, her ears and neck. He devoured her soft lips, inch by extraordinary inch. Then he touched her tongue, the inside of her mouth. With one hand, he caressed the slender column of her neck, then down to her breast, cupping the pliant weight of it.

He was suddenly unaware of the ocean, the sand, the stars, the fire. He was heedless of anything but Aubrey's body, her scent, and the feel of her skin. He slipped his hand under her sweater and inside her halter top, felt the warm, smooth skin of her breast, swollen with desire, and taut nipple.

Aubrey gasped softly in his ear as he squeezed her nipple between his fingers and pressed herself against him.

Jonathan twisted again, rolling her onto her back and coming over her. She was so soft, her skin so smooth and fragrant. He touched his lips to her neck, felt the purely male instincts grab hold of him. He was without conscious thought, filled with a longing so strong and powerful that he felt completely out of control.

And then Aubrey pushed him over the

edge by sliding her small hand down his rib cage, to his shorts, cupping his erection. Jonathan kissed her wildly, deeply, his heart and mind raging to be inside her.

He suddenly sat up, clawed his T-shirt off his body. Aubrey slowly sat up, and holding his gaze, she plunged her hand into the tote bag, dug around, and produced a condom, which she wordlessly held up, then handed to him. And then, heedless of anyone else on the beach, she took off her sweater. And then her halter top.

She was beautiful. He'd known it instinctively, but seeing her on the beach, in the firelight . . . He caught her hand, held it away from her so he could look at her.

"You're beautiful," he said in genuine appreciation. "I knew you were." He palmed a dark areola that stiffened quickly with his touch; his fingers splayed across her breast and nipple and squeezed gently.

Aubrey smiled with pleasure. "You're not so bad yourself." She gave him a seductive smile that was almost his undoing. Jonathan lunged for her, rolling on top of her, catching his weight with his arm as he covered her mouth in a stupefying kiss. Aubrey's arms went around his neck; she pressed her breasts against his chest and giggled when a groan of pure pleasure escaped him.

Aubrey lifted her hand, touched his face. "You're driving me crazy," he said, and reached for her board shorts, unlacing them, then pulling them down her hips. When she had kicked them free, he smiled with appreciation. "Oh, man." He shed his shorts, kicking them off into the sand, and lowered himself to her, kissing her, his hands running over her body.

His pulse was beating too fast, making his heart pound in his chest. He moved lower, to her breasts. One hand floated down her side and across her flat abdomen as he moved against her. When his fingers brushed deliberately against the inside of her thigh, she inhaled softly.

Lying beneath him, Aubrey was not conscious of anything but his touch. She gasped with delight when he took her breast in his mouth, but moaned with pleasure when he slipped his hand between her legs and stroked her. She was about to burst with the burn for him and parted her thighs, inviting him to touch her.

It felt as if it had been an eternity since she'd been so turned on, since she'd actually felt a man's hands on her body. But when Jonathan muttered something incomprehensible against her breast and slipped his fingers deep inside her, Aubrey moved against his palm and thought that it had never been like this. It had never been so intense, so deeply overwhelming, or so sensual.

As his fingers moved inside her, his mouth on her breast, Aubrey rocked against him, until he withdrew his fingers and began to stroke her. Aubrey groaned, but Jonathan buried his face in her neck. "No," he said breathlessly. "I won't let you get off that easy, lady. Do you know what you're doing to me?"

"If it's anything like what you're doing to me, I think I have a pretty good idea," she said, raking her fingers over his back.

"No, you don't know." He kissed her passionately. "You can't know — I didn't know until a few minutes ago."

She was losing control — she couldn't wait for him to figure out how long and abruptly rose up on her elbows, cupped his face, and kissed him hard and deep. "Stop talking about it and show me. Show me what this is doing to you *now*," she demanded.

And with that, he moved his thigh in between her legs, pushed them apart, and pressed himself against her. Aubrey sighed with pleasure; Jonathan laced his fingers with hers above her head, and with his other hand, he guided her hand to feel him.

He was so hard, so hot. Aubrey shuddered at the primal sensation as he shifted against her, pressing inside her, moving slowly, easing in. She grabbed his hips, pushing him deeper inside her. "You feel so good," he said low.

So did he — waves of pleasure were already crashing through her. But Jonathan seemed to enjoy tormenting her and watched her as he slid slowly into her depths, adjusting himself to her body surrounding him, then sliding deeper with small, rhythmic movements.

Aubrey's control was at an end; she did not think she could contain the explosion that was building in her a moment longer. He felt hot and thick inside her; she arched her pelvis against him and instinctively demanded more as she gasped for her breath. Jonathan gave in, covering her mouth with his and thrusting powerfully into her. She cried out with pleasure against his mouth, then let her head fall back as her body rose to meet him, with the next thrust, and the next.

His strokes lengthened within her; her knees came up on either side of him, and she lifted her pelvis to match his rhythm. She felt herself falling swiftly away, falling from this world and everything but Jonathan's body. His breath was hot on her shoulder, his grip of her hand almost painful, his body long and deep within her.

"Oh, God," she moaned, wildly anxious as the pleasure began to mount toward its inevitable, explosive end. She gripped his shoulder, lifted herself higher, meeting his hard strokes.

It happened — wave after wave of pleasure erupted within her, carrying her swiftly away from even Jonathan. She threw her head back and arched her neck as the release flooded from every pore.

"Aubrey," he groaned, and sank his fingers into her hips, lifting her up, and drove into her once more, erupting powerfully inside her, filling her completely as the waves of sexual gratification continued to wash over her. She collapsed backward, tightening around him, never wanting the incredible experience to end. Somewhere, above her, Jonathan called her name on a soft groan.

Aubrey opened her eyes. He was holding himself above her, his arms muscular and strong, an unfathomable look in his brown eyes. Carefully and tenderly he lowered himself onto his elbows and cupped her face in his hands while his gaze roamed her features. *"God, Aubrey,"* he whispered, and sighed with a contentment he had not known in a very long time.

30

Aubrey spent most of the drive back from the beach stealing glimpses of J.B. as he drove and reliving their incredible lovemaking on the beach. She had never made love like that, had never experienced anything so explosive. She'd never felt so alive as she did now, never more desirable or, more important, *wanted.*

She hadn't intended to stay overnight at his house, but after what they had shared, it was impossible to leave him. J.B. woke her the next morning with his hands and his mouth, taking his own sweet time to lift her to the height of pleasure again. And then he gave her one of his shirts to wear while he and Tammy made her breakfast.

The beautiful morning was ruined, however, when Zeke called Aubrey on her cell phone.

She stared at the display a moment, then looked at J.B. "It's Zeke."

"So don't answer it," he said instantly.

"I have to." It was difficult to explain, but Aubrey knew that if she didn't answer, he'd wonder where she was and come to his own conclusions — and then she'd never hear the end of it.

"Where the hell are you?" he shouted when she answered the phone.

She turned away from J.B.'s intent gaze. "What do you want?"

"I'll tell you this once, Aubrey Lynne — just once. You are not going to be the town slut, you understand me? I will make sure of that."

"Is that why you called me?" she asked stiffly, trying to keep her voice even, trying to keep J.B. from knowing how vile her father could be.

"I *called* you because that idiot you work for keeps leaving messages asking me to sign the papers giving her the day care."

"Why don't you just sign the papers so she won't have to call?"

"Shut up," he snapped. "You don't tell me what to do, I tell *you*. And I am telling you to get that idiot woman off my damn back. I can't decide what I'm going to do about it. It's bad enough your mother saddled me with that albatross when she was alive, but now she's gotta go and hand me the burden while she's dead."

Aubrey's stomach dropped. "Zeke —"

"I am *talking!* You tell that woman she better lay off if she knows what is good for her. And you better get your ass home before decent people see you," he added angrily, and hung up.

Aubrey slowly closed her phone.

"What?" J.B. asked.

She sighed heavenward. "Remember the papers for the day care I told you about?" When Jonathan nodded, she repeated the phone conversation. "I don't think he is going to sign," she said quietly. "I think he is going to ruin what Mom and Nancy worked so hard to build."

J.B. didn't say anything, but he took Aubrey's hand, brought it to his lips, and, looking her in the eye, kissed her knuckles. "Don't worry. He'll sign the papers."

She appreciated the sentiment, but he couldn't possibly understand how mean and vindictive her father was. "No, he won't. You don't — you *can't* — understand."

"Yeah. I do. And I'll fix it. Are you going to trust me?"

She looked up again, at the eyes so intent on hers, at the handsome face with a day's growth of beard, the long, dark hair. She *did* trust him. As impossible and improbable as it seemed, she trusted him completely. She nodded.

"Good," he said, and leaned forward to kiss her before standing up and twirling the chair around in one fluid movement. He clapped his hands, then rubbed them together. "Do you like blueberries with your pancakes?"

"Wouldn't eat my cakes without them," she said, and stroked Tammy's cheek as J.B. returned to the kitchen to bang around, making pancakes.

The weekend ended too soon for Jonathan. It felt like a lifetime since he'd been so happy and so full of hope for the future. Something had turned in him this weekend, and he'd honestly begun to believe that he and Sarah really *had* a future. A future that didn't seem like one long trip, but something real, something meaningful.

It was a tenuous hope, but it was hope all the same.

On Monday, he was late to work because he couldn't seem to walk away from Aubrey and Sarah when he dropped Sarah off at Bright Horizons.

The foreman was waiting for him when he walked onto the job site. "Glad you could join us today, Winslow," he said without looking up from his clipboard. "Since you're the last one in today, you can do the overtime work we've got this evening."

"The what?"

The foreman looked up with a frown. "Not familiar with the concept? You work longer hours than the average workday and make a little extra money."

"I've got to pick my kid up after work."

"Oh. A kid."

Jonathan nodded.

"Well, a," the foreman said, holding up his thumb, "this isn't a request. And b," — he held up his forefinger — "you think you're the only father on this job?" he asked with a snort. "So make a phone call like everyone else and arrange for someone to pick up your kid. You're working late."

He walked away, leaving Jonathan grumbling and digging for his cell phone in his pocket. He thought about calling Mrs. Young, but after the last time — he still didn't know what had happened that night she'd sat with Sarah, but he knew he couldn't trust her anymore.

That left Aubrey. He dialed the number of the day care. "Hey," he said when Noelle called Aubrey to the phone.

"Hey." He could hear the smile in her voice. "What's going on? Did you forget to

leave me a list of instructions?"

He laughed. "Can you do me a favor? Can you sit with Tammy after work?"

"Sure," she said instantly. "Why?"

"I gotta do some overtime," he said with a sheepish laugh. "Take her to the house. When I get off work, I'll bring a pizza and some beer."

"I've got a better idea. I will make you dinner."

Jonathan smiled. "That sounds great." It sounded like heaven, actually. "I should be home by eight or so at the latest. There's a key in Tammy's bag. At the bottom, there's a small tear in the lining. The key is inside there. You'll have to work it out, but it's in there."

Aubrey laughed. "You and your secrets. Okay. I'll see you later. And, J.B.?"

"Yeah?"

"I . . . I can't wait."

He smiled. "Me either." He clicked off and was still smiling as he went to meet up with his crew.

As Aubrey was leaving for the day, Nancy stopped her. "Aubrey, I hate to be a pain, but I can't get your father on the phone."

Oh, Lord. This was the last thing Aubrey needed right now, especially after the phone call from Zeke yesterday. She shifted Tammy's weight on her hip and forced a smile. "No?"

"I hate to ask . . . but could you call him? We could wrap this thing up if I could just get him to sign the papers."

Nancy looked so hopeful that Aubrey couldn't refuse her request, even if it made her stomach turn. "Sure!" she said brightly. "I'll call him tonight." With a cheery wave, she went out, her stomach roiling.

She waited until she was at J.B.'s house to call Zeke. For some strange reason, Aubrey felt safer there. When she'd situated Tammy beneath an activity gym on a quilt in the living room, she took a deep breath and dialed her father's number.

He picked up on the first ring. "What?" he asked, without the courtesy of a hello.

"Ah . . . well, I was talking to Nancy Fischer today, and —"

"I know why you are calling, Aubrey. I'm not stupid."

Every fiber in her body tensed. "Okay," she said evenly, "if you know why I am calling, then maybe we can cut to the chase. Will you sign the papers for Nancy?"

"Why should I?"

"Why shouldn't you? You hate that day care. She's paying you a good price for it.

What is the point of holding it over her head?"

"Aubrey, you haven't figured out that I am holding it over *your* head."

Aubrey stilled. She felt herself floundering as she always did when he began to harass her. But, by some miracle, in J.B.'s house, with his things around her, she found her bearings again. "Then it's a worthless piece of paper, Zeke. I am leaving in a couple of weeks, whether or not you sign the paper. You're only hurting yourself."

"Where are you?" he demanded out of the blue.

"What difference does it make?" she shot back. If he thought he could come to her house and intimidate her, he was wrong. She was done with that.

"I need to know where you are so I can bring you the papers."

"Take them to Nancy. She's the one who needs them. Look, I have to go, I'm babysitting. Just . . . just do the right thing for once, Dad. Please."

"Oh, for chrissakes," he said with disgust, and hung up on her.

Aubrey put the phone down and smiled at Tammy. "Hey, baby. You want some apple juice?"

She spent an hour with Tammy on a quilt

on the living room floor, playing with various toys. The baby laughed with delight when Aubrey had the kitty ride the red truck. A little after seven, Aubrey picked Tammy up and carried her to the kitchen to make her dinner. "How about some strained chicken and peas?" she asked idly as Tammy babbled and tried to put Aubrey's earring into her mouth.

Aubrey put a bowl and a baby spoon on the kitchen counter, then turned around to select a couple of containers of baby food from the pantry. When she turned again, the bowl and the spoon were gone. Aubrey frowned and looked around the kitchen. She was sure she'd just put them on the counter. They were not there, however. Then she glanced to the table just beyond the counter and saw them.

"That's weird." She walked to the table. "I didn't put these here, did I?" she asked Tammy. "I know *you* didn't put them here." She shook her head. "I'm losing my mind, kid." She deposited Tammy in the high chair, gave her a pair of plastic rings to chew on, and picked up the spoon and bowl.

With her back to the baby, Aubrey mixed up the food. Tammy babbled, telling Aubrey a story. Aubrey smiled as she listened to her. She'd be talking soon. J.B. swore she'd said *da da* to him a few times already. "You're going to be a talker, huh?" Aubrey called out as she finished mixing the food. "Are you hungry, kiddo?"

Tammy responded by gurgling.

Aubrey laughed and turned around and started in Tammy's direction, but froze midstride. Tammy's high chair had moved from one side of the table to the other. Tammy was laughing and babbling — not at Aubrey, as she'd thought, but at the back door. And as Aubrey watched with the sickening realization that they were not alone, Tammy continued to babble, her little head moving as if she was watching something move across the floor.

And then Aubrey felt whatever it was pass before her, pushing her back against the counter. She dropped the bowl of baby food and spoon; food splattered across the cabinet doors. She felt a strange pressure, some unseen force trying to hold her there. In a wild panic, Aubrey fought to push past the pressure and ran to the table, grabbing a laughing Tammy up from her high chair.

"Who are you?" she cried, whirling around and facing the kitchen. Everything was still, perfectly still. Something had changed — she didn't feel that weird energy any longer. Tammy had changed, too — she was fascinated with Aubrey's earring again. But Aubrey knew, without a doubt, that Tammy had seen a ghost.

She wrapped her arms around Tammy and walked into the living room — she had to collect herself before she tried to feed the baby again. Was that real? Had something just happened? Or was she losing her mind? Fortunately, she'd made up a bottle before she had attempted to feed Tammy, and she gave Tammy that, laying her on the quilt. The baby quickly settled into the bottle, holding it with one hand and reaching for the little fish that hung over her in the activity gym.

When she had Tammy situated, Aubrey stood up and turned toward the kitchen once more, debating whether to clean up the mess and try again. Frankly, she was a little spooked.

And then the kitchen door suddenly slammed closed, followed instantly by the hallway door slamming closed.

Aubrey gasped and backed up a couple of steps. Whatever was happening, whatever this thing was, it wanted her to leave. She could feel it, she could feel it pushing her to leave. She was definitely going to oblige it and picked Tammy up. She grabbed her purse, too, but was interrupted by a loud knock on the door.

Aubrey's panic had her panting — she quickly looked back at the kitchen door, and it suddenly opened, and she felt that thing brush against her again, pushing her toward the kitchen door. The knock came again, and in her panic, in her hope that this was a living breathing person, Aubrey ran for the door and yanked it open. But it wasn't J.B. coming to her rescue. It was Zeke. And he looked as dangerously angry as she had ever seen him. Somehow, on some level, Aubrey suddenly understood that the thing, the ghost, had been trying to save her from Zeke.

31

"Well, well, well," Zeke said, roughly pushing past Aubrey as he invited himself in. "Look who we have here — Tourmaline's biggest slut."

"I am not a slut," Aubrey said, instinctively covering Tammy's ear with one hand.

"What else do you call a skank who jumps into bed with a guy she hardly knows? What's this, he's already pushed his kid off on you?"

"Why are you here?" Aubrey demanded as Tammy began to whimper.

"I brought you the papers." He held them up, and when Aubrey reached for them, he snatched them out of her reach and stuffed them into his back pocket.

She glared at him. "How did you find me?"

"Don't be such a moron," he said as he walked into the room. "Who else would you be babysitting?"

"Well, you need to go," she said, holding the door open. "If you aren't going to give me the papers, you need to go."

"And leave you with some loser and his love child?"

That raised her hackles. He didn't even know J.B. but was going to run him down just because Aubrey was seeing him. And she definitely would not stand by and let him degrade Tammy. "Whatever you have to say to me," she said, seething, "leave him and the baby out of it. J.B. is a good man, and a good father —"

"Spare me the defense of a thug," Zeke said, and Tammy suddenly wailed. "*Do* something with her," he snapped, flicking his wrist at Tammy. When Aubrey didn't move immediately, he frowned at her. "Do you really want her to see this?"

Aubrey felt sick. His expression, his posture — everything about him told her this was not going to go well. Without a word she turned and walked through the door leading into the hallway, which was, like the kitchen door, suddenly open. She took Tammy to her crib and put her there, but Tammy wasn't having it. She began to scream.

"Baby, you have to stay here," Aubrey said. "I promise I'll be back in a minute —

but I have to leave you here." She hastily kissed the top of Tammy's head and tried to give her the bottle. Tammy threw it down and gripped the rail, wailing. And then suddenly, Tammy stopped and looked at the closet door. So did Aubrey. Nothing was there, but Tammy began to babble in her gibberish, and Aubrey felt the weird energy surround them again.

"Oh, God," she whispered. "Oh, God."

Tammy laughed.

"Aubrey Lynne!" Zeke bellowed from the living room. With one last look at the closet door, Aubrey reluctantly left Tammy there, holding on to the rail, bouncing up and down as she jabbered away at whatever was at the door.

Zeke was standing at the far end of the room, his hands holding the top of a FOR RENT sign, the tip of the stake on the floor. She tried to understand the significance of the sign — did he bring it? Had it been in the house? "You don't have any more sense than a gnat, you know that?" he snapped.

She drew a breath and held out her hand. "May I have the papers, please?"

"Do you have any idea what kind of winner you've hooked up with?"

Her hand curled into a fist at her side, and she looked down. She couldn't bear even to look him in the face. "I know him a lot better than you."

"Oh, yeah?" he asked with an ugly laugh. "So do you know that he is a kidnapper?"

Aubrey jerked her gaze to him.

"That's right. A kidnapper."

"I am not going to listen to your lies. May I please have the papers?"

"What, kidnapping is not enough for you? How about arsonist? Or thief? Any of those catch your attention?"

"He's none of those things!" Aubrey cried. "Why are you doing this? You don't even know him! If you want something from me, just say so, but you don't have to drag him into it!"

"Good God, Aubrey," Zeke said with a sigh. "You're so stupid it hurts. Let's start with the obvious. His name is not J. B. Winslow. It's Jonathan Randall."

"No, it's not," she said, but Zeke wasn't listening. He squatted down and, using the sign's stake as a lever, pried up a floorboard.

"Hey!" Aubrey cried.

Zeke went down on one knee, stuck his hand below the floor, and pulled out a bundle. He unwrapped it, discarding a man's shirt, and revealed a briefcase. "Let's see what else Mr. Winslow is hiding from you." He fished his pocketknife from his pocket and picked the lock on the briefcase, opened it up, and picked up the first paper. "Would a birth certificate convince you? How about the white-blood-cell count for Sarah Randall as of last month?" he asked, tossing a paper onto the floor.

At the mention of that name, something twisted inside Aubrey. No one could know J.B. had called his baby Sarah but her. There was no way Zeke could have known it, and Aubrey realized she was moving closer, straining to see inside the briefcase.

"Your boyfriend has been accused of arson, embezzlement, drug dealing — you name it, Jonathan Randall of Springfield has done it," he said, holding up several papers. "And here's the fun part — he faked his and his daughter's deaths and went on the run with her. He kidnapped that baby from her mother, Lizzie Spaulding, who, to this day, believes her daughter died in a car wreck."

"That's not true! His wife died!"

"She didn't die! She's alive, grieving a daughter she thinks is dead!"

Aubrey couldn't make sense of it. She didn't know what was in that briefcase, but she knew J.B. wasn't the man Zeke would have her believe. "Why are you doing this?" she asked angrily.

"Because that baby is Alan Spaulding's heir!"

Aubrey's eyes grew wide. There wasn't a person in the country who hadn't heard of Alan Spaulding.

"He's a very wealthy man, and he's more than willing to pay an awful lot of money to get that baby back," Zeke said, his eyes glittering with avarice. "Do you know how much mileage I will get when I crack this case wide-open?"

"You're crazy," Aubrey said. "He didn't kidnap the baby! She belongs to him — you can tell by looking at them that she belongs to him! And if he did take her, he had a good reason!" Aubrey insisted.

Zeke responded with a bitter laugh. "You got your stubborn ignorance from your mother. But I'm smart." He tapped his head. "I'm on my way up. I might get enough out of this to run for state legislature. Maybe even Congress. Who knows? People love a happy ending. We'll see what Mr. Spaulding is willing to support when he arrives in Tourmaline to claim his great-granddaughter and watch me cart Jonathan Randall's sorry ass to jail."

Aubrey's head began to spin. She didn't believe any of it. J.B. was not the villain here, Zeke was, and she'd finally reached her limit. Whatever the reason he'd taken Tammy — Sarah — from Springfield, Aubrey was certain it was a good one. But Zeke would try to destroy him, just as he tried to destroy everything that Aubrey loved and valued.

"So what do you think of your thug now?" Zeke asked almost gleefully.

Aubrey kicked the briefcase; it slid across the floor to the wall. "Leave him alone!" she shouted. "You think I don't have the guts to tell the whole world what sort of man you are? People may like a happy ending, but I'm very sure they will not like having a wife beater and child abuser in office!"

Zeke's eyes narrowed with indescribable anger. He stalked toward her, matching her movement when she tried to slide to one side, until he stood in front of her. "I am sick to *death* of your superior attitude," he said, poking her hard in the chest with each word. "It's high time you learned a lesson." He unfastened his belt.

Aubrey tried hard not to show him any fear, but she knew what was coming next — she still had the scars on her back from years ago when he would use a belt to "teach her a lesson." Her self-preservation instincts reared up; she looked frantically about for something with which she could defend herself and spied a hammer on the mantel. With her eyes and thoughts on getting that hammer, she didn't see Zeke lift his arm to backhand her. He sent her sprawling across the floor and crashing into the couch.

The blow stunned her, and what happened next was a blur. Aubrey heard J.B.'s shout, saw his boots as he flew across the room. By the time she'd managed to right herself, he'd thrown Zeke up against the wall and was holding him there with one arm to his neck. *"Don't touch her!"* he roared, and pressed against Zeke's neck. "Don't you *ever* touch her!"

Choking, Zeke clawed at J.B.'s arm.

"J.B.!" Aubrey cried, and in that moment J.B. looked at her, Zeke threw a punch to his abdomen, knocking J.B. backward. He hit the mantel, knocking the hammer and a little travel clock to the floor. Zeke threw himself at Jonathan, and the two men crashed to the floor. Aubrey shrieked as a lamp was knocked over. The two of them were landing blows with frightening speed, but Zeke seemed to gain the upper hand and hit J.B. twice in the face before rising to his feet and kicking him in the gut. J.B. rolled to his side, coughing. Then he stilled.

"J.B.!" Aubrey screamed, and fell to her

knees beside him. "Oh my God, you killed him!" she said breathlessly as she cupped his face. "J.B.! *J.B.!*"

"Get out of the way, slut," Zeke said breathlessly.

Aubrey looked over her shoulder and gasped at the sight of the gun trained directly on J.B. "What are you doing?" she cried.

"It's called self-defense," Zeke snarled, and gestured with the gun. "Get out of the way."

"Dad . . . don't," Aubrey said, pushing herself to her feet, standing between him and J.B. "I will tell them it wasn't self-defense. I will tell them you attacked him and killed him."

Zeke laughed. "Stupid bitch, move out of the way or die with him, I don't care." The look in his eyes was wild — Aubrey had no doubt that he meant it.

"You are making a huge mistake," she said, moving slightly, shifting the gun sight off J.B. "You might have gotten away with murder once, but you won't get away with it again."

"Get out of the way, Aubrey!" he shouted.

She shifted again and pointed at the briefcase. "You don't need to kill him. You've got everything you need right there."

Zeke turned his head and looked at the briefcase and snorted. "If you don't move," he said, swinging the gun around and pointing it directly at her, his back partially turned to Jonathan, "I will kill you, too, I swear I will."

He shocked her. Of all the things she believed of him, she'd never believed he would kill *her.* "But . . . I'm your *daughter.*"

He snorted with pure disdain. "You aren't my *daughter.* Your mother was a lying, cheating, whore — you think I don't know that? You think I don't know she got herself knocked up while she was cheating on me? You're not my daughter — you're no one, Aubrey Lynne. *No one.*"

It was the last thing he said before J.B. suddenly surged to his feet with a roar, swinging the hammer. He caught Zeke square in the temple with it; Zeke stumbled backward as blood erupted and ran down his chin. He went down, striking his head on the fireplace mantel.

Aubrey gasped, clamping both hands over her mouth as terror filled her. J.B. gaped at Zeke, then slowly turned his gaze to Aubrey.

"He's not moving," she whispered, her voice trembling. "W-what do we do?"

Almost as if in answer to her question, the

front door was suddenly thrown open, and a woman with short blond hair and expressive blue eyes stepped across the threshold. She took one look at J.B., then at Zeke, with the blood coming out of his mouth.

And then she looked at Aubrey. For a long moment no one breathed, no one said a word, until the woman looked at J.B. and said, "You have to get out. You have to leave now, Jonathan."

"What are you doing here, Mom?" he asked, and Aubrey collapsed onto the couch, her knees having at last given way.

32

Jonathan dropped the bloodied hammer he was holding.

Reva said, "No time for explanations. There's a dead man on your floor. Grab Sarah and get out of here. Take *her*," she said, pointing to the young woman, "and *go*."

"Yeah, about that," Jonathan said. "Reva, this is Aubrey Cross."

Reva looked at Aubrey Cross — the young woman looked to be in shock. Not surprising — she'd just seen Jonathan kill a man. At least Reva thought he was dead — she knelt beside him and felt for the pulse in his neck. She couldn't find one. Good Lord, he *was* dead.

"And that's her father, Sheriff Cross," Jonathan added shakily.

"Oh, Jonathan," Reva said. Things were never easy when it came to her son, and unfortunately, there was no time to ask what had happened. She pressed her hands to her face for a minute to think. All she knew was that he had to leave before Alan caught up to them, and he couldn't be far behind. Reva had planned to warn Jonathan, maybe see Sarah for a few minutes. She hadn't planned on there being a body.

"The sheriff?" Reva asked, and looked up at the young woman. She was pale, her eyes as big as saucers as she stared at her father. Reva sighed. "Well, that really complicates things."

"No," Aubrey said softly. "No, it doesn't. J.B. . . . J.B. did what someone should have done a long time ago." She looked down at the crumpled figure of her father. "What goes around comes around in this town," she muttered, and looked up at Jonathan. "You and Sarah go. I'll stay here. I'll make sure you aren't charged with anything. I'll . . . I'll think of some way to explain it. It was self-defense, after all."

"She's right, Jonathan," Reva said quickly. "I'll stay and help her, but you need to go!"

"No way. I'm not leaving the two of you to —"

"You *have* to go, J.B.!" Aubrey cried. "What about Tam— Sarah? You have to do it for her sake! If you're accused of murder, what will happen to her then?"

410

Reva clambered to her feet and stood beside the dark-eyed girl. "Sarah can't lose you, Jonathan."

Jonathan stared at Reva. Then he looked at Aubrey. "I am not leaving Aubrey here to take the fall for my screw-up." He held out a hand to her. "Come with me."

"I can't just *leave!*"

"This is not a good time for an argument, kids." Reva was hustling them toward the door. "Go now, before matters get a whole lot worse! Jonathan, listen to me. Alan is on his way. He knows you're here! You have to go as soon as possible!"

"We can't leave Zeke in the middle of the floor!"

"I'll take care of it," Reva said.

"How?"

"I don't know," she said, pushing him away from the sheriff. "But I've handled much worse. Please, Jonathan! I am begging you! Sarah needs you! *I* need you!"

Aubrey suddenly moved past them and knelt by her father's body. With a grimace, she pushed her father's body onto his side and pulled papers out of his back pocket. She quickly went through them, the pages stapled together. When she reached the last page, her shoulders sagged. "He didn't sign it."

Jonathan seemed to know what she was talking about and bent over her, stroking her head with his palm as he looked at the papers she held. "We'll forge it," he said instantly. "Reva, do you have a pen?"

"I suspect I'll sleep sounder," she said as she thrust her hand into her purse and found a pen, "if I don't ask what you're forging."

"That's my mom," Jonathan said. He took the pages from Aubrey and knelt down, spread them out on the coffee table.

"Wait!" Aubrey cried as he put pen to paper. "Let me. I practiced his signature a million times." She grabbed the pen from Jonathan and scribbled a signature on the page, then stood up and looked at Jonathan. "Let's get out of here."

"Are you sure?" he asked, studying her face.

"Yes, yes, she's sure!" Reva cried. "Please, go!"

Aubrey caught his face in her hands and looked him in the eye. "I am sure, J.B. I've never been more sure of anything in my life. Let's get out of here."

They threw everything onto the quilt and bundled it up, running it out to the car. While they picked up everything they could find, Reva clung to Sarah. She was asleep now, and it was just as well — Reva could hardly see her through her tears. She looked good, and healthy. Reva had worried so much —

"She's beautiful, isn't she?"

Reva turned at the sound of Aubrey's voice. "She is," Reva said, smiling through her tears. She cocked her head to one side as she assessed this young woman. She was dark, like Jonathan and Sarah. She was wearing clothes that made her look street tough, but in her eyes was a vulnerability Reva had seen once before in her life — the day Jonathan had stood in her living room, trying so desperately to hurt her after having endured so much pain himself. There was vulnerability . . . but also shrewdness, which Reva instinctively knew came from tough living.

She'd seen the same in Jonathan's eyes.

"You love him, don't you?" she asked softly.

Aubrey blushed. "Yes," she said shyly.

"Then take care of him. Promise me that you will."

Aubrey looked Reva squarely in the eye. "I promise," she said solemnly. She held out her arms for the baby. "We have to go."

Tears spilled down Reva's face, and she hugged Sarah to her. "God, I've missed

413

you." She kissed Sarah one last time before handing the baby to Aubrey. As Aubrey started to leave, Reva stopped her and bent over Sarah once more, smelling her baby-scented skin, kissing her forehead.

When Reva raised her head, Aubrey smiled. "I promise to take care of her, too — as if she were my own." She turned away from Reva, just as Jonathan entered the room.

"We're ready," Jonathan said as Aubrey quietly left them alone. "I put the crib in Aubrey's car. We're going to dump her car in a lake."

"Good idea," Reva said, and swiped at the tears that slid down her face.

"Reva," Jonathan said, taking her hands in his, "I can't believe you're here. And I can't believe this is the way we have to say good-bye again. You look good, Mom."

"Oh, so do you, Jonathan," Reva said through her tears. "And so does Sarah."

"I wish you could have seen her take her first steps. Or hear her talk." He laughed a little. "She says *no* a lot, just like her grandma."

Reva managed a smile. "I wish I could see her, too. Maybe someday, huh? Maybe someday this will all seem like a bad dream. But . . . but it has to be this way, Jonathan.

I am so proud of you." Reva spoke in bursts, trying to shove a lifetime of meaning into the few seconds they had left. "For protecting your daughter. And for protecting that young woman from her father. I wish I could have been as brave and protected you from your father. I'm inspired by you."

"Mom . . ."

"Honey, you have to go," she said, squeezing his arm. He nodded, then suddenly grabbed her in his arms, squeezing her tightly to him, holding her as tightly as Reva held him. She did not want to let go — she thought she'd lost her son, and to have only these few moments with him were impossible to bear. But she forced herself to push away from him after she kissed his cheek. "Go," she said.

Jonathan kissed her, too. "You'll know where we are," he said, as he backed out of the room.

"I know." She put out her hand. "Take care of yourself."

"I will. I guess this is it." He shoved a hand through his hair. "I'm no good at good-byes."

Reva knew that, too, and she turned away from him. A moment later, he was gone.

When she heard their cars moving down the drive, Reva drew a steadying breath and walked through the house, wanting to see every inch of the place Jonathan had believed he could finally put down roots. When she returned to the living room, she walked to the sheriff's crumpled form. She picked up the hammer Jonathan had hit him with and paused, noticing the FOR RENT sign lying on the floor.

She was still holding that bloodied hammer and pondering the FOR RENT sign when Alan walked through the open door. He glanced at Zeke Cross, then at her, and judging from his expression, he thought she'd killed him. For a moment, they did no more than just look at each other. And then, because Reva couldn't think of a good enough answer to give him, she went with a question. "Alan? What are you doing here?"

"I suppose I could ask the same. But the answer appears fairly obvious."

"Don't be so smug, Alan," Reva said irritably. "You can't imagine what a rotten day I've had."

"Not nearly as rotten as his, I presume." Alan indicated Zeke's inert form.

"I did not kill that man!"

"Honestly, Reva, I don't give a damn. Where are they?"

Shaken from the events of the last hour,

Reva tried to think of something quickly, some viable explanation, and drew on every bit of acting skill that she had. "Who?" she asked, hoping her expression was as innocent as she was trying to make it.

"*Now* who is being smug?" Alan moved again, to stand directly across from her, over the body. "Where is my Sarah?"

"*What?*" she exclaimed, trying to think. "Sarah?"

"I know they're here, Reva!" he said angrily. "Ezekiel Cross, the sheriff of this county, called and *told* me they're here! But why am I wasting precious time talking to you? I'm going to call Sheriff Cross and —"

"Alan, you idiot, that *is* Sheriff Cross!" Reva cried, pointing to the body with the hammer.

Alan shifted his glare to the body, then looked at Reva with surprise. "You *killed* the sheriff?"

"No! I mean — yes. Yes!" she blurted, her thoughts racing. "Did you say Sheriff Cross called you, Alan? Because he called me, too. He told me the same thing. That he knew where Jonathan and Sarah were. Of course I came at once — but it was a lie, Alan. He brought me here to extort money from me." The tears falling from her eyes weren't hard to summon — emotionally, the night had taken its toll.

"You mean they're not . . . ?" Alan demanded skeptically.

"They are *dead,* Alan!" Reva cried. "Don't you get it? *Dead!* You have got to stop hanging on to this foolish hope that somehow Jonathan and Sarah escaped that car, because they didn't! They died in Springfield, and you and I are both fools for letting an extortionist make us think otherwise!"

"I don't believe you!" Alan protested angrily.

"Oh, Alan," she said mournfully, the tears flowing freely now. "Don't you think I want them alive, too?" She pressed her free hand to her heart. "But they're dead, and this sonuvabitch made up a rotten story to squeeze money out of both of us!"

A look came over Alan that Reva had rarely seen on him — only once before, in her living room. It was the look of complete despair. He looked down at Zeke Cross. "I thought . . . I *believed* him," he said, his voice weaker. His knees seemed to buckle; he sat heavily on the coffee table, staring down at the sheriff, incredulous. "I believed him. I had this insane hope . . ." His voice trailed off.

As much animosity as Reva had for Alan, her heart went out to him. He was a bastard, and everything he did was wrong. But Reva had never doubted that he loved Sarah.

Alan rubbed his mouth and looked up at Reva. "But why did you *kill* him?"

"I didn't," she said, wiping tears from her face. "He . . . he said he could tell me where they were if I gave him money. He told me they were nearby. But I knew, Alan . . . I knew it was a lie and refused to give him the money. He got angry and I . . . I was just trying to protect myself."

"Do you want me to believe you killed him in self-defense?"

Reva glared at him. "Yes! I'm not you! I don't go around killing people when I don't get my way. It's not like —"

The glint of gunmetal caught her eye as Zeke Cross pushed himself up on one elbow and pointed the gun at Reva. He cocked the trigger and looked at her with such hatred that Reva screamed.

He never saw Alan, Reva thought. He never saw Alan grab the hammer from her hand or saw it coming down on him a second time. Alan hit him in the back of the head just as he pulled the trigger. The shot went high and Zeke fell back. The gun scudded across the floor.

Reva looked, wide-eyed, at Alan. He was standing perfectly still, staring down at

Zeke. He lifted his gaze to Reva.

"Alan Spaulding," Reva said softly, reaching across the divide and putting her hand on him. "I do believe you just saved my life!"

Alan didn't say anything, but bent down on one knee and pressed two fingers to Zeke's neck. "By cutting short his." He stood up and looked frantically about. "Killing a law enforcement officer is a capital crime, and I don't imagine they will care that it was self-defense." Alan looked at Reva. "We have to bury him."

"What?"

"In the backyard. Somewhere." Alan motioned vaguely to the back of the house as he looked at the hammer. "We have to bury him, dispose of his car, and get out of here, Reva. We have no choice," he said earnestly, anticipating her objection.

He had no idea, Reva thought. If anyone in Tourmaline were to find out about this, Alan would find out about Jonathan and Sarah, and Reva couldn't bear to think what might happen then. "Okay," she said. "Let's bury him."

"We need to dig a grave. Look around and see if you can find a shovel," Alan said as he quickly moved to the front door to shut it, still holding the hammer.

■ ■ ■ ■

In a shed out back, Reva found three shovels. Alan pulled his rental car around to the back of the house and shone the lights. They discovered a ditch of some sort about one hundred yards from the house. By the light of a gas lantern Reva had found, they dug a shallow grave.

They were exhausted by the time they'd dug it, but conscious that it would be light in a couple of hours, so they had to move quickly. They wrapped the sheriff in a bedspread, cleaned the floor and the house, and were careful to wipe down any surface that might have their prints — and therefore, Reva thought with relief, Jonathan's and Aubrey's, too. When they had finished, they began the chore of lugging the body to the grave.

"Faster. It's almost sunup. We can't afford to be seen," Alan chastised Reva as they struggled with the dead weight out the back door.

"We'd have been done a lot sooner if you hadn't taken so long to find the right spot," Reva groused.

"And I suppose you would have buried him in the front yard — 'Here he is, Tourmaline! Here's your sheriff!' "

They maneuvered the body, dragging it through the unkempt backyard. When they reached the fence, Alan paused, dropped his end of the quilt, and put his hands to his back.

"Open the gate," Reva prompted.

"It's stuck. It won't open all the way. We'll have to lift him over the fence."

"We'll make him fit. Just open it!"

"We're going to have to go over the fence —"

Reva walked around to where Alan stood, pushing him out of the way, and picking up his end. "Fine. I'll do it myself."

Alan watched her for a moment. "I must say, you're very good at this, Reva. Now that I think of it, I seem to remember a murder trial. *Several,* as a matter of fact."

"Ditto," Reva snapped. "So how about we both put our wealth of experience to use and just get this done!"

At that, Alan smiled. In the middle of one of the most horrible moments of her life, Alan Spaulding actually smiled, and as he got down to doing it Reva's way, he told her, "You know, we're more alike, Reva, than you've ever admitted."

She merely let out a yelp of laughter in response, then guiltily covered her mouth with her hand. There may have been no one around, but that was still no reason to press their luck.

"Think about it," Alan said as they transferred Zeke through the pried-open fence and then into his makeshift grave. "For both of us, our families are our greatest priority."

Reva brushed the dirt off her hands. "Okay. We've got different ways of showing that, but, yes, all right, maybe we do have that in common."

"In addition, neither of us particularly cares what others may think of our — granted, *different* — methods of protecting our own."

This time, Reva covered her mouth so Alan couldn't see the slight trace of a smile his observation provoked.

"No one can ever accuse us of trying to please everyone," Alan said. "Or anyone for that matter."

"No," Reva agreed, straightening up. "No one would ever accuse either of us of that."

Several hours later, having left the sheriff's car in the parking lot of a seedy-looking bar, Alan and Reva boarded his private jet for the trip back to Springfield. As they took off over San Diego, Reva glanced at a brooding Alan from the corner of her eye.

"You think he'll be found?" she asked quietly.

Alan shrugged. "Eventually. But I think it will be next to impossible for anyone to connect us to his death." He looked at Reva. "This is our little secret, Reva. The only way anyone could discover our involvement is if one of us should talk."

"But neither of us will," Reva said pointedly. "For the sake of our families."

Alan lifted the cocktail the attendant had served them just before takeoff and clinked it against Reva's glass. "For the sake of our families," he said.

33

Jonathan and Aubrey crossed the border into New Mexico sometime the following night.

Aubrey was staring out the passenger window at the darkness, which is what she'd done since they had pushed her car into a quarry.

Frankly, neither of them had much to say. They were both lost in their thoughts about the extraordinary events of the last twenty-four hours. It was incredibly difficult for Jonathan to absorb. Just when he'd thought he was going to make it, that he could look forward to the future he'd always wanted, everything had been turned upside down. Now a man was dead, and he and Sarah were on the run again, only this time with an innocent woman.

He wondered what Aubrey was thinking. She didn't deserve this, to be a fugitive with a guy who had more baggage than American

Airlines. He should have left her in San Diego. He should have given her some money to get on her feet and then run like hell with his daughter, but he hadn't been thinking clearly. Everything had happened so fast, and then Aubrey had wanted to leave the forged papers at the day care giving Nancy Fischer ownership of Bright Horizons, and he'd been frantic someone would see her.

Someone would eventually put two and two together and figure out Zeke Cross had gone missing about the time Aubrey and Jonathan had disappeared. As long as she was leaving the papers, Jonathan made Aubrey write a note to Nancy telling her that she had to get out of town, that she'd broken up with J. B. Winslow after a fight and realized Tourmaline wasn't for her. She implied she had returned to San Diego and to school.

As for Jonathan — he hadn't been there long enough for anyone to know anything about him or care he was gone. The guys at the construction company had never trusted him and wouldn't be surprised he'd suddenly taken off.

He thought they'd covered their tracks as well as could be expected, given their shock and the timing, but eventually, someone would begin to put the pieces together. He just hoped Reva knew what to do. And he hoped she got out of there before anyone saw her or before Alan arrived. If Alan had found Reva there with Zeke —

He couldn't think about that now. If he did, he'd go crazy with worry, and he had his hands full as it was.

He glanced at Aubrey from the corner of his eye. Did she hate him? Was she mourning that bastard? He was still her father, and Jonathan knew better than anyone else what a hold that was on a person. Maybe Aubrey had been in such shock she hadn't been able to think, but now, after the fact and the hours she'd had to absorb it, she realized she was in a car going nowhere with the man who had murdered her father.

The more he thought about it, the more Jonathan thought she needed to get away from him. He was bad news, always had been, always would be. Whatever had made him think he could live like a normal person? Just thinking of it now made him furious — he hit the steering wheel with the palm of his hand as hard as he could.

Aubrey looked at him, her eyes luminous in the glow of the dash lights. She looked worried and exhausted, and the light in her eyes had gone out. Jonathan had done that to her. He had snuffed the light right out of those brown eyes. When she'd hooked up with him, she had hooked up with the worst trouble of her life.

The best thing he could do for Aubrey now was to force her to go back to San Diego. She was scared, and she wouldn't like it, but it was the best thing for her.

So when they reached Albuquerque later that night, Jonathan drove straight to the bus station and pulled into the parking lot.

Aubrey was sleeping; when the car stopped, she lifted her head and looked around, blinking. When she realized where they were, she sat up. "Hey," she said, frowning. "What's going on?"

"You're going back to San Diego." Jonathan killed the engine and got out of the car.

Aubrey scrambled out, too, gaping at him over the hood of the car as he went to get Sarah out of her car seat. "Why?"

"You don't need this baggage in your life, Aubrey. You don't need to saddle yourself with a guy like me. And I don't want you slowing me down."

Sarah did not want to wake up and began to cry as Jonathan lifted her out of the car seat.

"Are you *kidding* me?" Aubrey cried, and

marched around the trunk of the car, blocking his path. "You're not going to do this to me, Jonathan Randall!"

"Hey!" Jonathan said, taking a quick look around the parking lot. No one was close enough to hear them. "Keep your voice down. No names, remember?"

"I will not keep my voice down," she said heatedly. "And what difference does it make? You have more names, I'm sure. Do you have any idea what I have been through this last week, Jonathan? I have put my faith in you, in spite of knowing *nothing* about you, and now you're going to *dump* me?"

"I'm not dumping you, I'm saving you! You don't understand, Aubrey."

"What else is new?" she cried, swinging her arm wide. "You've been nothing but one giant secret since I met you! But I am still here, aren't I? Did it ever occur to you that I love you and I *need* you now more than ever?"

"Yes," he bit out, and paused in trying to get Sarah's sock back on her foot to think, but his heart was reacting ahead of his brain. His heart was swelling like a shriveled vine given water. "What about Zeke?" he demanded.

Aubrey blinked. Sighed. And folded her arms over her middle as she sagged backward against the car. She looked, he thought, completely exhausted. "I haven't thought of anything else since . . . since that," she said, wincing a little. "I have tried and tried over eight hundred miles to summon something other than relief. But you know what? No matter how hard I try, I can't seem to find anything in me *but* relief. I am so *relieved!*" she cried, shaking her hands at the night sky. "I never have to deal with him again. *Never!*"

She dropped her arms and looked sheepishly at Jonathan. "Do you think that's awful?"

"No."

She nodded and looked at her hands. "I'm not happy about it. It was awful. But I can't find a single tear inside me for him."

Sarah began to cry, rubbing her eyes and squirming. Jonathan bounced her in his arms as he looked at the bus station. "Cut your losses, Aubrey," he said low. "Get out now, before it's too late."

"Maybe, instead of pushing me away, you ought to let me in," she said, and pushed away from the car. She brushed Sarah's hair from her face and whispered for her not to cry, then looked at Jonathan. "Maybe you ought to give us a chance, huh? All I know is that I have never felt so alive until you came into my life. I have never felt so . . . desirable, or interesting, or wanted. I've never felt so protected. I don't want to give you up, Jonathan. I need you. I need you more than you can imagine."

"You're making a mistake," he said, wanting her to acknowledge it, wanting her to leave, but hoping madly that she wouldn't.

"Maybe," she said, and took Sarah from his arms. "But it's my mistake to make, so let me. And I don't think it's a mistake. I think that maybe, finally, I am on the right path."

Jonathan looked at the terminal again and sighed. He didn't want her to go. He had to admit, it was nice to be needed instead of being the one who was always needing. He looked at Aubrey again and those big, copper-brown eyes that had captured him the first time he'd ever seen her and smiled sadly. "Let's get a room somewhere and get some rest."

The light returned to her eyes. "And a shower!" she exclaimed. "Oh my God, a *shower.*"

They took a room in a motel on the interstate. Jonathan lay on a bed with Sarah, watching Aubrey move around the room, unpacking the few things she'd grabbed

431

from her apartment. She was wearing a camisole and bikini panties, walking back and forth between the bathroom and the bed.

Jonathan watched her, his body reacting to the sight of her, his mind warring with his heart over the things he was feeling. He got up, walked into the dressing area, and got a glass of water out of the tap. Aubrey squeezed past him, glancing up at him with dark eyes. Her body brushed against his, stirring something hot and wild within him. She must have sensed what she did to him, because she smiled a little lopsidedly and paused with her body touching his.

He could feel his desire for her thrumming through his body, and it was all he could do to keep from grabbing her in his arms and throwing her onto the bed. The last twenty-four hours had charged him up, made him feel things he hadn't allowed himself to feel in a long time — fury, desire, affection, hatred. It was coursing through his body, filling him up. He was about to burst.

They'd made an unusual commitment to one another, he and Aubrey, had embarked on this journey with no idea of where they were going. It could have been exciting, yet something held him back, something that felt like guilt. Only it was not the usual guilt he felt, the sense of being disloyal to Tammy's memory or the vows and commitments he'd made to her.

It was guilt over not feeling disloyal enough.

He didn't feel that ache for Tammy the way he once had. He missed her, but he didn't feel it coursing through his veins, squeezing like a vise around his heart. He felt something changing in him, and he didn't like it.

He gave Aubrey a tight smile, clenched his hands in fists at his sides, and walked out of the little dressing area, past the beds and Sarah's sleeping form, and out the door. He walked out to the pool and sat on the end of a chaise longue, his head in his hands, trying to work through it.

A sound brought his head up. He knew she would be here — he'd felt it in his bones. And there Tammy stood across the pool from him, her image eerily lit by the light of the swimming pool. He stood up, his hands on his hips, staring at her.

"Tammy."

She shimmered in reply.

"Tammy . . . what do I do now, babe?"

"You know the answer," she said. "You just have to admit it to yourself. And when you do, you will be set free."

"Yeah, see, there's the problem. I don't *want* to be free of you."

She smiled. "I'll always be a part of you, Jonathan. But a part of your past, not your future."

"Jonathan?"

The sound of Aubrey's voice startled him; he jerked around as she walked through the gate wearing a pair of shorts and a sweater.

"Sarah —"

"Sleeping," she said. "I left the door open so we can hear her." Aubrey nodded over her shoulder. She looked across the pool, her expression confused. "I thought I heard you talking to someone."

Jonathan looked across the pool. Only Tammy wasn't standing there — she was suddenly standing next to him, looking at Aubrey.

Aubrey suddenly rubbed her hands on her arms, as if she were cold. She squinted as she looked across the pool. "Who was it?"

"It's Tammy," Jonathan said, drawing her attention back to him. "My wife."

"Your late wife," Tammy reminded him. "I'm gone, Jonathan."

"Don't say that," Jonathan said.

"Jonathan?" Aubrey asked, squinting into the night.

He turned back to Aubrey. "She's . . . she died, Aubrey. She's not really here . . . but she is," he said, fumbling to explain.

To his surprise, Aubrey did not react. She cocked a brow as she looked past him. "Hello, Tammy. I think we've already met."

"What?" Jonathan asked.

"In your house," Aubrey said, and looked at Jonathan. "She tried to get me to leave before Zeke came."

"Wait — what?" Jonathan asked. "You saw her?"

"Not really. Not in the way you can see her. But I felt her. And I see her in you. And I think she would have wanted you to be happy."

"Listen to her, Jonathan," Tammy whispered. "She's a smart chick. You know she's right. You've known it since the minute we said good-bye. If I thought you couldn't do this, I'd stay. Nothing could make me leave. But you're okay now. You're going to be okay."

Tammy looked toward Aubrey. "She needs you. More than I do."

"No!" Jonathan cried. "Hold on, Tammy. I'm not ready for you to go yet. I just —"

Something warm and tender touched his lips. He gasped, but the pressure increased slightly, the warmth of it radiating through him. And then there was nothing. She was gone.

"What happened?" Aubrey asked.

"She's gone."

"Are you certain?" she asked, peering past him.

He was certain, but he couldn't find his voice. He merely nodded.

"Maybe she'll come back."

He shook his head. "No. She's not coming back." It was clear to him now. He'd been released from his own demons, from the guilt and remorse and the fear of loving someone else.

"How do you know?"

"I can feel it," he said, as he slipped his arm around Aubrey's back. He leaned down and touched his lips to hers. Aubrey instantly softened in his arms, pressing against him, her hands snaking up and around his neck. He broke the kiss, bent down, and swept her up in his arms, then carried her out of the pool area and across the threshold of their cheap, little room.

When he laid her on the bed and came over her, she brushed his hair back from his face. "Is this real, Jonathan?"

"It's real," he said, as his hand floated down her side to her hip. "Are you okay with that?"

"I'm okay with that." She smiled up at him with eyes soft and full of light. "I think I've been okay with it almost from the moment I met you."

Jonathan caressed her hip and kissed her forehead. "You know our future is one big question mark, right?"

Aubrey lifted up, bracing herself on her elbows, so that her lips were a moment from his. "Not to me," she said. "Granted, we don't know what lies before us, but I can't wait to find out with you."

He kissed the tip of her nose, then her lips. He could feel his desire rising like a tide in him and stroked her body, tracing a long line from her collarbone to the apex of her thighs. An understanding flowed between them. There weren't any ghosts or bullies hanging over them, nothing but a man and a woman who had found each other in spite of improbable odds.

Aubrey's gaze dropped to his mouth. Her lips parted and she drew a soft breath, full of yearning.

In the dim light of the bathroom vanity, Jonathan could see the creamy skin of her cheeks, the smooth column of her neck, the rise of her breasts, and a look in her eyes that he felt deep to the very pit of himself. He slipped his arm around her, slowly lowered her to her back, and at the same time put his lips to hers.

Her fingers threaded through his hair, then fluttered down his ear, to his shoulder, gripping him as if she feared he would float away.

He wasn't floating away. He wasn't going anywhere. Reverently, he kissed her, sinking into the scent of flowers in her hair, the smoothness of her skin, the heat of her body, which was radiating through his.

His hand slipped beneath her sweater, sliding across bare skin, up to her breasts. Desire, lust, and a surprising amount of affection swirled through him, tightening in his groin. When he touched his tongue to hers, she opened her mouth beneath his. He had an image of her body opening much like that, and he kissed her ravenously, his hand drifting to her hip, drawing her leg up around him, squeezing and holding her against him.

Aubrey ran her hands down his back, panting with a desire as stark as his. He pressed against her, letting her feel what she did to him, and she responded by moving seductively against him, her pelvis sliding against his, her breasts pressed to his chest.

As he kissed her body, touching and tasting every inch of bare skin, taking his time

438

to memorize every curve, every scar, every muscle, he felt an abiding sense of happiness.

And when at last he slid deep inside her, he felt peace. This was where he was supposed to be now. This was home.

When they'd both found fulfillment, they lay on the bed, whispering long into the night while Sarah slept. Jonathan told her who he was, where he'd come from, and most of what he'd done. He told her about Tammy and Lizzie. About Reva and Alan and a whole lot of other people in Springfield. In return, Aubrey told him about Zeke, the terror she'd known growing up as a girl, the terror her mother had lived with until her dying day, unable or unwilling to ever escape it, and her suspicions that he and Keith had killed a man.

When the sky began to pinken with the morning sun, Aubrey knew who Jonathan was. She knew that his heart had beat in time with hers, long before she'd ever met him. And Jonathan had, at last, found the light to guide him from here. There would never be anyone to take the place Tammy occupied in his heart — but he realized there was still a bit of room for someone else.

They piled everything into the car after

they'd showered and dressed, then situated Sarah in her car seat. Jonathan started the car and smiled at Aubrey, both wearing their Radiohound T-shirts.

"Where to?" she asked.

He pointed east.

"Toward Springfield?"

Jonathan grinned at her. "Never say never."

He put the car in gear.

As the Mustang pulled out of the motel parking lot, headed east, Tammy watched it from her perch. She didn't think it was possible to cry real tears, but she could feel them etching her face. She'd spent so much of her astral body's energy getting Jonathan to let go and move on that she hadn't realized she needed to let go of him, too.

It was time. He had been the love of her human life, but that was as much in the past for her as it was for Jonathan. She felt easy knowing that he would survive without her — in the early days, she hadn't been so sure. She felt at peace knowing that he could survive her. She couldn't bear to imagine him pining for her for the rest of his days, especially now that Sarah needed him as much as she did. And Aubrey.

Tammy smiled. She could let him go for Aubrey.

This was the last time she would see him, she realized. She would never appear to him again now that he had found a new light. But she would always watch over him and Sarah.

Always.

ABOUT THE AUTHORS

Julia London is the *New York Times* best-selling author of fifteen romantic novels, including *American Diva, The Perils of Pursuing a Prince,* and soon to be published, *The Danger of Deceiving a Viscount.* A finalist for the Romance Writers of America's RITA Award, she lives in Round Rock, Texas. Visit her website at www.julialondon.com.

Alina Adams is the *New York Times* best-selling author of *Oakdale Confidential* and Creative Content Producer for *Guiding Light* and *As The World Turns.* She lives in New York City with her husband and three children. Visit her website at www.alina adams.com.

The employees of Thorndike Press hope you have enjoyed this Large Print book. All our Thorndike and Wheeler Large Print titles are designed for easy reading, and all our books are made to last. Other Thorndike Press Large Print books are available at your library, through selected bookstores, or directly from us.

For information about titles, please call:
(800) 223-1244

or visit our Web site at:
www.gale.com/thorndike
www.gale.com/wheeler

To share your comments, please write:
Publisher
Thorndike Press
295 Kennedy Memorial Drive
Waterville, ME 04901